DARK HOLLOW

"Keene keeps getting better and better. Given how damn good he was to start with . . . soon, he will become a juggernaut."

—*The Horror Fiction Review*

DEAD SEA

"Delivering enough shudders and gore to satisfy any fan of the genre, Keene proves he's still a lead player in the zombie horror cavalcade."

—*Publishers Weekly*

GHOUL

"If Brian Keene's books were music, they would occupy a working class, hard-earned space between Bruce Springsteen, Eminem, and Johnny Cash."

—John Skipp, *New York Times* bestselling author

THE CONQUEROR WORMS

"Keene delivers [a] wild, gruesome page-turner . . . the enormity of Keene's pulp horror imagination, and his success in bringing the reader over the top with him, is both rare and wonderful."

—*Publishers Weekly*

CITY OF THE DEAD

"Brian Keene's name should be up there with King, Koontz and Barker. He's without a doubt one of the best horror writers ever."

—The Horror Review

THE RISING

". . . *The Rising*, is a postapocalyptic narrative that revels in its blunt and visceral descriptions of the undead."

—*The New York Times Book Review*

"Hoping for a good night's sleep? Stay away from *The Rising*. It'll keep you awake, then fill your dreams with lurching, hungry corpses wanting to eat you."

—Richard Laymon, author of *Flesh*

NO ORDINARY STRANGER

The man in black raised one hand and wiggled his fingers. As Stephen watched, the stranger's fingernails began to stretch and grow, turning into long black talons. Stephen blinked, and the man laughed hoarsely.

"Is that supposed to scare me?" In truth, it had, but Stephen wasn't about to let the guy know that.

"No," the man replied. "It's supposed to distract you."

"What do you—"

The man leaned forward and, with his other hand, punched Stephen just below his chest. Stephen grunted, more from surprise at the unexpected blow than from pain.

"Now *that*," the stranger said, "is supposed to scare you."

The man's arm was still extended. Stephen tried to pull away from him and found that he couldn't. Stephen coughed, and tasted blood in the back of his throat. Then the dark man pulled his arm back and held up his hand. There was something gray and pink clutched in the stranger's fist. His hand glistened wetly. . . .

Other *Leisure* books by Brian Keene:

DARKNESS ON THE EDGE OF TOWN
URBAN GOTHIC
CASTAWAYS
GHOST WALK
DARK HOLLOW
DEAD SEA
GHOUL
THE CONQUEROR WORMS
CITY OF THE DEAD
THE RISING

BRIAN KEENE

A GATHERING OF CROWS

LEISURE BOOKS NEW YORK CITY

For Skip Novak, Paul McCann and Grant Riffle

A LEISURE BOOK®

August 2010

Published by

Dorchester Publishing Co., Inc.
200 Madison Avenue
New York, NY 10016

ISBN 10: 0-8439-6092-2
ISBN 13: 978-0-8439-6092-1
E-ISBN: 978-1-4285-0908-5

The name "Leisure Books" and the stylized "L" with design are trademarks of Dorchester Publishing Co., Inc.

Printed in the United States of America.

10 9 8 7 6 5 4 3 2 1

Visit us online at www.dorchesterpub.com.

ACKNOWLEDGMENTS

This time around, thanks go to my family; Don D'Auria and everyone else at Leisure Books; my prereaders—Mark Sylva and Tod Clark; my assistants—Joe "Tomokato" Branson, "Big" Joe Maynard, and Dave "Meteornotes" Thomas; Tim and Brindi Anderson, who fed me during the last half of this book; Alethea Kontis, who let me use her bucket of snakes; Bob Freeman, who provided a luminol light when I really needed it; and the ubiquitous girl on the glider, whose name I now know. Thanks also go (for various and sundry reasons) to: C. Robert Cargill; Andrew Ramsey; Richard Gott and the entire staff of Antarctic Press; Keith Giffen; Mike Siglain; Ryan Penagos; Rich Ginter; Ed Gorman; Joe R. Lansdale; F. Paul Wilson; Thomas F. Monteleone; Chet Williamson; Jack Ketchum; Edward Lee; David J. Schow; Bryan Smith; J. F. Gonzalez and family; Wrath James White; Gene O'Neill; Stephen Poerink; Miss Muffintop and the boys in the warehouse; Richard Christy; Andy Deane and Bella Morte; Bill and Andrew at Moderncine; Paul and Elizabeth at Nimble Pictures; the MISFITS and the staff and volunteers of CONvergence; Mike Argento; Jim Lewin of The York Emporium; and as always, my loyal readers and booksellers, and the crazy bastards on the Brian Keene forum.

A GATHERING
OF CROWS

CHAPTER ONE

When the sun went down, and dusk gave way to
night, the mountain came alive. A chorus of insects
buzzed and hummed in the darkness. Birds chirped
from their treetop nests. Tiny frogs—called spring
peepers by the locals because of the peeping sounds
they made when they came out of hibernation each
spring—sang to one another from shallow, hidden
bogs and winding, narrow creeks. Nocturnal animals prowled the mountainside—coyotes and deer,
black bears and foxes, skunks and raccoons. Leaves
rustled, swaying in the light breeze. All of these
sounds and more combined to form a natural cacophony as loud as any city street. The mountain
thrummed with energy and life.

And then, all at once, sound and movement
abruptly ceased. The mountain fell silent. Animal and
insect, predator and prey—all were affected. Even the
breeze became still. The only remaining sound was
the low hum of the power lines, coming from the electrical tower on top of the mountain. The massive steel
structure loomed over the surrounding countryside
like a monolith, a modern-age Stonehenge, dour and
watchful. The ground around its base had been
cleared of trees and undergrowth and replaced with
gravel and cement. Beyond the concrete base was a

man-made clearing that cut through the forest like a scar. The clearing wound all the way down the mountainside, where further towers jutted up above the treetops. Nestled at the base of the mountain, far below the power lines, tucked safely between the river and the limestone foothills, was a small town. Its lights twinkled in the darkness like fireflies.

Mist rose from the ground around the tower's base and swirled slowly around the arches and girders. For a moment, the electrical hum grew louder. Then, one by one, five large crows with feathers as black as coal appeared, swooping down out of the moonlight and the darkness and the fog-enshrouded trees. They approached each other from different parts of the clearing and landed directly beneath the tower. Then, perched on the tower's lowest rung, they looked down upon the tiny town far below. The fog grew thicker.

A single black feather fell off one of the birds and drifted lazily to the ground, where it landed in a clump of ferns and weeds on the edge of the clearing. The feather lay there for a moment. Then the vegetation began to smoke, as if on fire, although no flames were visible. Within seconds, the vegetation had withered and turned brown. It crumbled and dissolved, leaving the feather to balance atop a small mound of ash.

The largest of the birds cried out. The caw echoed across the mountainside, seeming to gather strength in the darkness. One by one, the others joined in. The echoes boomed through the treetops. Soon, the birds' cries drowned out even the hum of the electrical transformers.

* * *

Nights in Brinkley Springs were usually quiet and serene. On most evenings, the loudest disturbance, if any, was Randy Cummings racing his four-wheel-drive truck up and down Main Street. Sometimes, if the wind was right, residents could hear the Ford's engine revving far up the mountain as he went off-roading with his friends. The truck's original paint job was hidden beneath a permanently caked layer of mud and dirt. Occasionally, Sam Harding would cruise by in his black Nissan; it had flames painted on the sides. He didn't drive fast, because he'd lowered the car to the point where hitting a pothole or a set of railroad tracks at any speed over twenty miles an hour would bottom it out, but he did like to turn the stereo up loud, and the bass would often rattle his tinted windows, as well as the windows of the houses he drove past. But most of the folks in Brinkley Springs agreed that since Randy and Sam would both be graduating in a few weeks, these were just temporary nuisances—at least until the next batch of kids got their driver's licenses.

The town was composed mostly of small, run-down, one- or two-story houses and a fragile smattering of battered mobile homes. Some of the dwellings had dirty and dented aluminum or vinyl siding. Most didn't even have that; instead, they showed bare, slowly rotting wood and peeling or faded paint. Shingles had been blown off roofs and never replaced. Porches sagged, waiting for a strong gust of wind to knock them over. For the most part, the homes in Brinkley Springs were built close enough together that you could see the next trash-strewn street or occasional outhouse peeking through behind them. The yards in front of the houses had more dirt than grass. Some held junk cars, engine blocks on cement blocks, tire swings, ceramic gnomes and cracked birdbaths, half-dead trees, stumps, weathered rabbit and chicken hutches, clothesline poles or tattered basketball nets. There was even a rusted, abandoned school bus on one weed-choked lawn. Other yards were completely vacant of even these trappings and contained only dead vegetation. Many of the houses had for-sale signs in front of them, and fully half of those were uninhabited, except by mice or the occasional snake.

No longer idyllic, Brinkley Springs barely warranted a glance from those who drove through it on their way to more exciting destinations. The town had two traffic lights and three four-way stop signs (all three bearing the rusty scars of having been peppered with shotgun pellets at some point in their existence). The town stretched twelve blocks in one direction and fifteen in the other, with a few small cattle, grain and horse farms on its borders. The black, potholed ribbon of U.S. 219 entered the town from the north, became Main Street for fifteen blocks and then transformed back into U.S. 219 again on the outskirts of town.

Most of the people in Brinkley Springs went to bed early, not out of boredom and not because of any quaint, old-fashioned ideas regarding propriety, but simply because they had to go to work the next morning, and that meant a long, arduous drive to other towns. Brinkley Springs had no industry— there were no factories or call centers or machine shops or office buildings. Nor were there any mining or timbering operations, as there were in other parts of the state. Indeed, other than Pheasant's

Garage, Barry's Market, Esther Laudry's bed-and-breakfast, the small post office, a scattering of threadbare antique shops and the few surrounding farms, Brinkley Springs had no jobs at all. The last business to start up there—a privately owned turkey processing plant—had shut down after five years of operation and moved to North Carolina in search of a cheaper tax rate. Soon after, the abandoned plant burned down. Some said the fire was suspicious—a chance for the owners to collect on insurance money. Others said it was an accident. More than a few just shrugged and said it was a sign of the times. Whatever the real culprit had been, the plant was never rebuilt. All that remained was a burned-out, weed-choked lot full of broken bottles, rats and copperhead snakes. No one expected new construction to change that anytime soon. Brinkley Springs didn't attract investors or businesses looking to expand. It was far off the major highways and interstates, wedged between the mountains and nestled deep in the heart of the Greenbrier River valley—a bedroom community for those who worked in Beckley, Lewisburg, Greenbank, Roncefort, Roanoke and the other bigger, more prosperous communities within the state or just across the border in Virginia.

Brinkley Springs had never been a big town, and with each passing year, its population shrank just a little bit more. Small businesses like the pizza shop or the movie-rental store closed and never reopened. Houses were abandoned when their owners passed away, and never resold. Potholes appeared in the streets and were never fixed. The town still had a V.F.W. post and a Ruritan Club, but their membership dropped with each passing year. The fire company still had quarterly bean suppers and their annual carnival, but each time, the attendance numbers dwindled. The tiny Methodist church had seating for two hundred people but had a weekly congregation of about fifteen. The Baptist church had been closed for two years, its doors and windows shuttered and boarded over. Brinkley Springs had no police force or school buildings. It was patrolled by the state police, who swung through once or twice a day just to make their presence known, and didn't show up otherwise unless somebody called 911. Its children were bussed to the bigger schools in Lewisburg. They left every morning and returned every evening, until they graduated. Then they went off to college or the military or a job somewhere else, and rarely returned again at all, except for holidays or a family occasion like a wedding or a funeral. And sometimes, not even then.

Still, despite all this, Brinkley Springs had its charms. The Greenbrier River ran along its eastern border and was a popular spot for both local and out-of-town fishermen, hikers and white-water rafters. The lack of posted property signs attracted hunters during deer, bear and turkey seasons, and a fair number of poachers even when those things weren't in season. The antique shops were an occasional draw for travelers and vacationers who liked to explore off the beaten path, as was Esther Laudry's bed-and-breakfast—a remodeled home built in the early 1900s—which catered to them as well as the occasional hiking or rafting enthusiast. But for the locals, Brinkley Springs was simply where they lived. Nothing more. Nothing less. A place to sleep, eat, shit and fuck. A place to play football with the kids on the weekends or watch TV at night. A place to store their cars and pets and clothing. A place to keep their stuff. Their real lives, the places where they spent most of their time, were at those jobs beyond the town limits.

Some people said that the town was dying.

They didn't know how right they were.

Concealed in shadow, five human figures sat perched upon the girders and steel crossbeams that the crows had occupied on the electrical tower earlier. They were dressed alike—black pants and shirts, black shoes, black hats, and long black coats that flowed to their heels. A passerby might have found their similar garb strangely reminiscent of America's Colonial period, except for its color and the way the fabric seemed to blend with the darkness. Even their facial features were similar; they each had pointed noses and chins, dark eyes and even darker hair. They only differed in size, but even that was slight. The largest stood well over six feet tall. The others were within a few inches of that. Each of them seemed to defer to the biggest, who sat idly, head bobbing back and forth strangely on his almost nonexistent neck as he stared at the town below. Finally, he spoke. His voice was like breaking glass.

"It is good to see you again, brothers."

"Indeed," the second one replied. "The years between each gathering seem to grow longer with time."

"Much has changed since we were last together in these forms," the third figure said, staring at the town and then up at the electrical lines.

"Not really," said the first. "Their technology has advanced since we were last all together like this, but they are still the same—ignorant, petty little beasts, for the most part oblivious to the larger universe around them. They do not change, even as their world changes around them. They are animated meat. Nothing more."

"So were we—once."

"But then we were freed. We were transformed by *his* grace. Glory be to Meeble."

The others nodded in agreement. Then the fourth figure raised one arm and pointed at the town.

"Is that it? This is why we were summoned tonight? This is where we will feed? This is where we will spread his work?"

"It is," the first answered. "Brinkley Springs, West Virginia."

"West Virginia?" The third figure arched an eyebrow. "Virginia? Are we close to Roanoke, then?"

"Yes," said the first, "but it is not the Roanoke you're thinking of. It is a different town. Named for that one, perhaps. And therein is a great example of irony. As I said, they are ignorant. They know not the importance of naming. They have forgotten it. The more they advance, the less they remember."

"Brinkley Springs." The second one frowned. "It seems . . . rustic."

"They always do," the first said. "They always have."

The second shrugged. "I do not doubt that, my brother. I just . . ."

"What?"

"I often wonder, with all of their advances, why we don't feed on a larger scale? Imagine how magnificent our night would be were we to focus our efforts on a major metropolitan area. Think of how much more we could do. To murder an entire city? That would be *glorious*!"

"Perhaps," said the first, "but then you are thinking of your own glory, rather than the glory of our master. Until the door is opened again and he walks this Earth once more, we must act only out of necessity, and then with utmost caution. Killing an entire city? To conduct our endeavors in such a grandiose manner would attract unwanted attention. Undoubtedly, there are still a few magi among them whose power matches our own. For all we know, they may have organized in the years since we last walked among them. We may be met with resistance."

"Yes, that is true. Perhaps we may find one who knows how to banish us from this realm."

The first one ignored the comment but the others murmured to each other. They fell silent when he spoke again.

"And," the first continued, "were we to focus our attention on an entire city, I daresay we would not finish before the dawn. It would be time to slumber again before we were done, and our efforts would remain incomplete. At the very least, we would certainly leave witnesses behind. They could tell others what had occurred, and when we awoke again, they might be prepared for our arrival. Our master, when he arrives—and he will arrive one day—would be . . . displeased."

A collective shudder ran through the group. They nodded silently.

"Sunrise comes early," sighed the third after a few minute's pause. "Would that we had more than one paltry night."

"We will," promised the first. "One day we will. He

has promised us it will be so. But for now, let us make the most of the time we *do* have. As you say, sunrise comes early. Until then, it is good to be with you all again, and it is good to be awake. I need to stretch my limbs after the long sleep."

"True," agreed the shortest. "And I am hungry. Nay—*famished*."

"As are we all. Let us begin. Let us feast. Let us murder. Let us glorify him from whom we have sprung."

And then they did.

The electrical tower was the first to fall. It crashed to the ground with a horrendous roar of twisting, shrieking metal and crackling sparks. Immediately, the twinkling lights disappeared in the valley below. The fallen cables hissed and spit, coiling and thrashing like wounded snakes. The leaves, weeds and other debris began to smolder. The figures seemed unconcerned at the prospect of a forest fire.

"Should we take down the others?" The shortest pointed at the other electrical towers looming above the treetops in the distance.

"Why bother?" The large one nodded toward Brinkley Springs. "That has achieved our first goal—to instill unease and seed their fear. The soul cage will do the rest, once we construct it from the five points. Don't waste time here. Why rend metal when we could be ripping flesh instead?"

Side by side, the five figures walked down the mountainside, laughing as they went. The grass in the clearing withered and died in their wake. The fog grew thicker. Trees groaned. A mother bear, crazed with fear, slaughtered her own cubs rather than letting them fall victim to the presence permeating the mountain. Then she repeatedly smashed her head into a gnarled, wide oak tree until brains and bark littered the ground. Deep inside its den, a rattlesnake swallowed its own tail, jaws opening wider to accommodate its length and girth. Driven by a nameless, unfathomable fear, a herd of deer flung themselves from a cliff and burst open on the jagged rocks below. A pack of coyotes that had been tracking the herd followed along a moment later, dashing themselves upon the deer's broken bodies. Bones splintered. Blood splattered.

Overhead, a thick bank of clouds drifted over the moon, slowly covering it until it was gone from sight.

Down in Brinkley Springs, the darkness grew deeper and the dogs began to howl.

CHAPTER TWO

When the power went out, Axel Perry was sitting in the wicker rocking chair on his sagging front porch, sipping a bottle of hard cider, listening to the spring peepers and thinking about his dead wife. For a few seconds, he didn't notice the electrical outage. After all, he had no radio or television playing in the background. The only time he watched television was when the West Virginia Mountaineers were playing, and he had no patience for the radio these days—the country stations all sounded like rock stations, and everything else was just the white noise of talk radio. Axel hated talk radio. Everybody was a conservative or a liberal these days, with no room for folks in the middle of the road. All of the good stuff had moved over to satellite radio. He'd thought about buying one, but money was tight and satellite coverage here in the valley was spotty at best. Most of the time, the signals were weak or constantly interrupted. The same thing happened with cell phones and wireless Internet service. Axel had dial-up Internet service that his son and daughter-in-law had bought him to go along with the computer they'd given him for his birthday. They'd come to visit for a week—driving all the way from Vermont to Brinkley

Springs—and had taken him to Wal-Mart and picked it out from the computers on display. Then they'd brought it home and made a big deal out of showing him how to work it. They said he'd be able to stay in touch more often, and that they could send him pictures of his grandkids instantly—he wouldn't have to wait on the mail. He'd tried it a few times, but his curiosity had soon waned. Looking at pictures of his grandchildren on a computer screen just wasn't the same as looking at them while paging through a photo album—and neither option compared to actually holding the kids in his arms or hearing them laugh and play in his backyard. Plus, staring at pictures of the grandkids just made his loneliness and sadness that much more complete.

At least once a day, Axel wished that he would die. If he'd had the nerve, he'd have killed himself. But he didn't have the nerve. What if he messed up? What if he made a mistake? What if he lay there in his home, paralyzed or wounded and unable to call for help? Who would find him? The answer was nobody, because no one ever checked in on him. He was an old man living alone in an old house, with only his old, waning memories to keep him company.

He missed his wife, Diane—gone ten years now, not from cancer or a heart attack or diabetes or any of the other plagues that came with old age, but from a drunk driver. They'd taken a bus trip together to Washington, D.C., to see the cherry blossoms for their fiftieth wedding anniversary. On the way back home, a drunken driver had drifted into their lane and sideswiped the bus. The bus driver then swerved off the road and hit a tree. A few folks were injured, but most escaped without a scratch. Except for Diane. She was thrown forward and banged her head against the seat in front of her—hard enough to cause her skull to separate from her spinal column. The doctor had called it internal decapitation. Axel had called it abandonment, and although he missed Diane every day and had been distraught over the loss, there were times when he grew angry with her for going off and leaving him behind to fend for himself. Learning to live on his own had been hard, and he still hadn't mastered it. Even now, with a decade to get used to the idea, he still found himself opening his mouth to tell her something throughout the day, maybe a passing comment regarding something he'd read in a magazine, or a bit of gossip he'd heard down at Barry's Market. Sometimes at night, he'd roll over and reach for her and wonder where she'd gone.

Still, he went on. He survived. What else was there to do?

Sitting on the porch at night, drinking a bottle of beer or hard cider (but never more than one; otherwise, he'd pay for it the next morning by spending an hour on the toilet) and listening to the spring peepers brought him peace and comfort—or at least as close to those things as he could get. The tiny frogs usually showed up in late March or early April. By the end of April, their nightly chorus was as ever present as the sky or the moon and stars. A million tiny chirplike croaks echoed from the riverbank and surrounding mountains. Sometimes, their song was muted, but it was never interrupted altogether. It would continue until fall, when the weather started to cool again.

A stray cat darted across the lawn. Axel called to it, but the wary animal kept running. He'd thought about getting a dog or a cat to help ease his loneliness, but had ultimately decided against it because he didn't know who would take care of it if he passed on.

The chair creaked as Axel leaned back and stretched. He raised the bottle to his lips, took another swig and closed his eyes, letting the sound of the peepers wash over him. Diane had always enjoyed listening to them, too. Unlike most of the other things they'd shared, he didn't get sad when listening to the frogs. Their sound seemed to buoy his spirits. Listening to them made him feel close to her.

"I miss you, darlin'. Wish you were here tonight."

Across the street, Bobby Sullivan sat on a pile of dirt in his front yard, playing with Matchbox cars. A plastic car carrier—one of the little ones that looked like a suitcase—was open before him, and more cars littered the ground around the six-year-old's feet. He made vroom-vroom sounds as he guided the cars through the dirt. His mother, Jean, hollered for him through the screen door, telling him it was time to come inside. Smiling, Axel watched the boy linger, slowly putting his cars away, trying to milk as much time as possible before his mother called for him again. Sure enough, she did, her voice more insistent this time. Bobby shuffled toward the house, shoulders slumped dejectedly. He paused to wave at Axel. Still smiling, Axel waved back. Bobby went inside. The screen door banged shut behind him. The Sullivan's porch light came on. The kitchen light glowed through the window. Inside, Jean and Bobby would be sitting down for supper. Occasionally, Jean brought a plate over to Axel. Most times, though, they ate as a family. Axel didn't know anything about Bobby's father, if he was alive or dead or if Jean even knew who he was. He guessed that didn't matter. The two of them—mother and son—made a fine family.

He glanced down the street. For-sale signs dotted many of the yards. The signs were as weathered and faded as the houses they advertised. Weeds grew up around them, the yards not mowed since the owners had left. Axel had known most of the people who lived in those homes at one time. They'd been his neighbors, and in many cases, his friends. Now they were gone, just like Diane—passed away or moved on, living in a retirement community or with their kids or, in the case of some of his younger neighbors, some place where the economy was better and taxes were lower and jobs still existed. He wondered what would happen to his house when he died. Would it sit here like all these others, dying slowly from wood rot and neglect?

These were supposed to be his golden years, but in Axel's experience, the only thing ever gold in color was piss. He thought about how excited folks had been at the prospect of a new president and a new beginning for the country. All that excitement had waned now. The nation was back to business as usual. Same old story. Same old song and dance. The media said things were getting better, that the economy was improving and folks were happier again. Axel thought that the media wouldn't know what things were like for the average American even if that average American were to walk up and bite them on the ass.

Sighing, Axel sat the bottle down and rubbed his arthritic hands. The spring peepers continued with their serenade, oblivious to his thoughts, concerns or mood.

Farther up the street, the porch light was on in front of Esther Laudry's bed-and-breakfast. Axel assumed that Esther must be happy tonight. She had a boarder, after all. That in itself was rare these days. And this wasn't just any boarder either. If the buggy parked outside was any indication, her overnight guest was Amish. Axel had run into Greg Pheasant earlier, and Greg had confirmed this. The Amish fella had come into town around four in the afternoon and had stopped at the garage that Greg ran with his brother Gus. He'd asked Greg if there was a hotel nearby. Greg had steered him toward Esther's, where he'd taken a room for the night. Greg said that the guy had seemed friendly enough. After parking his buggy along the street, he'd tied his horse down near the river. Axel didn't know much about the Amish, other than what he'd seen in that movie with Harrison Ford, but he supposed they must travel just like other folks. He'd heard tell that there was an Amish community up near Punkin Center. Perhaps this guy was on his way there to visit kin. If so, then good for him. Family was important.

For a moment, Axel's attention was distracted by another noise—a faint, far-away groan, the sound a tree might make as it fell over. There was a distant crash and then nothing, except for the sound of the peepers. He couldn't be sure if he'd imagined the sounds or not. His hearing wasn't as good as it had once been. He was just about to shrug it off when he noticed that Esther's lights had gone off. Across the street, he heard Jean Sullivan holler, "Oh, come on! I paid the bill." He glanced in that direction and saw that her lights were out, as well. Then Axel noticed something else.

The spring peepers had stopped singing.

He took a deep breath and counted, waiting for them to start again.

One . . . two . . . three . . . come on, you crazy little things. Sing for me.

He shivered. The air was growing chillier. His skin prickled and the hair on his arms felt charged.

The Sullivans' screen door banged open. Jean poked her head out.

"Axel," she called. "Is your electricity off?"

"I believe it may be out all over, Jean. Looks like Esther's is out, too. Reckon a line's down somewhere."

"Well, that's a relief. I thought they'd turned my power off."

Shaking her head, she went back inside. Axel strained his ears and heard her soothing Bobby. Then he went back to counting.

Four . . . five . . . six . . . come on, damn it. Peep!

Up the street, the Marshalls' mangy old beagle began to howl. The sudden noise startled Axel, and he jumped in his chair. The dog howled again. It was a lonely, mournful sound—not anything like the happy call a beagle made when it was chasing a rabbit. A moment later, it was joined by Paul Crowley's bear dogs in the kennel behind Paul's house. Then, one by one, all of the dogs in Brinkley Springs joined in. The sound was unsettling, to say the least.

"What the hell is going on?"

Then Axel remembered that there was nobody around to answer him.

He waited for the spring peepers to resume their chorus, but they didn't. Their silence was unsettlingly loud—much louder than the dogs were. Axel rubbed his hands some more and wondered what was happening. The aching grew more severe. He thought of Diane again, but this time, he wasn't sure why.

Jean Sullivan returned to the kitchen table, where her son, Bobby, sat in the dark. His eyes were big and round, and he had the tip of one index finger stuck in his mouth—something he'd done since he was a toddler whenever he was scared or nervous. She assured him that everything was okay, and then fumbled around in one of the drawers beside the sink until she found some half-burned candles and a box of wooden matches. She lit a candle, blew out the match and tossed the smoldering stick in the sink, and then walked around the first floor of their home, lighting all of the other candles she could find. Since she'd bought most of them at craft stores, the home soon smelled of competing fragrances—vanilla and strawberries and lavender and potpourri. The soft glow slowly filled the house, chasing away her discomfort. Jean wasn't sure why, but the sudden power outage had left her unsettled. The flickering candlelight made her feel better. She walked back into the kitchen and smiled at Bobby. He smiled back, clearly feeling better too, now that they had light again.

"What happened, Mommy?"

"I don't know, baby. Somebody probably crashed their car into a pole somewhere. Or maybe a tree limb fell down on one of the lines. I'm sure they'll have it up and running again soon."

"Can I watch a movie?"

"Not while the electricity is off. Maybe we can read a book tonight instead."

Bobby frowned. "But we never read books."

"Well, I've been meaning to fix that. Maybe this is a good time to start. Now finish eating. Mommy's got to call the power company and report the outage."

"Okay."

Bobby used his fork to move his meatloaf and peas around on his plate while Jean reached for the phone. Normally, she was resentful of the old rotary unit. She longed to have a cell phone, but simply couldn't afford it—not on welfare and WIC. Nor could she afford one of those digital electronic units she'd seen at Wal-Mart. For Jean, her old rotary phone with its antiquated dial had always been a reminder of all the things she couldn't give her son. Now, it was a lifeline. The folks with digital phones wouldn't be able to make calls because they had no power. She picked up the receiver, put it to her ear and then paused with her index finger hovering over the dial.

There was no dial tone.

"Shit."

Bobby gasped, then grinned. "You said a bad word, Mommy."

"Mommy's allowed to say a bad word when the phone lines are down."

"What does that mean?"

"It means the phone isn't working, just like the electricity."

"Does it mean I can say a bad word, too?"

"No. And eat your peas. I've told you before, moving your food around on the plate doesn't make it look like you've eaten any more. All it does is—"

A long, plaintive howl cut her off. Jean and Bobby glanced at the window and then at each other. Another howl joined the first, then several more.

"Why are all the dogs barking, Mommy?"

Jean shook her head. "I don't know, baby. I don't know."

"Maybe there's a bear outside. Can I go see?"

"No, Bobby. Now I'm not telling you again. Eat your dinner."

Jean moved to the kitchen window and peered outside. The barks and howls were louder now, seeming to fill the air. Outside, the street was dark, and she couldn't see much of anything. For a moment, Jean considered going over to Axel's house and checking on him, but then she decided against it. She didn't want to leave Bobby alone. Jean didn't know why, but her disquiet had returned, and this time no amount of candlelight would chase it away.

When Bobby began to playfully howl along with the dogs, she almost screamed.

Donny Osborne put the last box—marked on the side with black Magic Marker as PHOTO ALBUMS—in the back of his blue Ford pickup truck, grunting with the effort. Sighing, he slammed the tailgate shut. Both sounds, the sigh and the slam, had the tone of finality. He glanced down and noticed that one of his bootlaces was untied. Resting his foot on the rear bumper, he tied it again. The lace was damp from the dew on the grass. Despite the coolness in the air, Donny was sweating. After tying the lace and wiping his brow with the bottom of his T-shirt, Donny leaned back against the truck and sighed again. He tried not to look at the house because doing so filled him with sadness, but he couldn't help himself. As he stood there, catching his breath, his eyes were drawn back to it once more.

The house seemed smaller somehow. Maybe that was because he was an adult now. Everything seemed smaller these days. His childhood home. This street. Brinkley Springs. The mountains. Hell, even the whole damned state of West Virginia seemed to have shrunk. As he stood there, Donny wondered why this was so. Was it just a matter of perspective, that he remembered these things through a child's eyes but was looking at them now as a man? Or was it because he'd seen the rest of the world and understood now just how big it was, and how small this little section of the planet was? Was it because unlike 90 percent of his classmates and childhood friends, he'd gone beyond the state borders and discovered that there was a whole wide world out there, a world full of different cultures and people and outlooks and beliefs that were nothing like what they'd grown up knowing? That there were towns other than Brinkley Springs, populated with people totally unlike themselves—and yet sharing similar hopes and dreams and wants and needs?

Places like Iraq, for instance.

Donny snickered. It was a humorless, spiteful sound.

Maybe Iraq wasn't such a good example, although he had to admit, his second tour of duty in that godforsaken place had been much better than his first. By his second tour of duty, the much-maligned troop surge had worked, and as a result, he and the rest of

his platoon spent more time interacting with the civilians or watching movies and playing video games
back at Camp Basra than they did out on patrol.
That first tour had been hell—going from house to
house, searching for insurgents, never knowing when
you were going to get shot. And it was hard to tell
the insurgents from everyone else. They blended
with the populace. In Iraq, everyone looked like a
civilian, and all of them—friendly or otherwise—
had weapons. Just because a family had an old
Kalashnikov tucked away inside their cupboard, it
didn't mean they were the enemy. That would have
been like rounding up and arresting every hunter in
Brinkley Springs who owned a deer rifle. But even
the house-to-house searches weren't as bad as dealing with the suicide bombers and the IEDs. Many of
Donny's friends had lost their legs, arms or eyes to
roadside bombs. One minute, they'd been sitting in
a transport, and the next . . .

Well, what could you say about a country where
you could get your legs blown off while just driving
down the fucking road?

The thing that most amazed Donny now was how
much he actually missed the place sometimes. Oh,
not Iraq itself. Iraq was a cesspool. Iran could move
in overnight and nuke Iraq, reducing it to a radioactive crater, and Donny would be just fine with that.
But he missed his friends. His fellow soldiers. His
brothers. It was funny. Donny had spent six years in
the military just marking the days on his short-
timer's calendar, counting the minutes until he was
a civilian again. But now that he was out and back in
the world, all he could think about was the time he'd
served and the guys he'd served it with. Some of

them had never made it back home, like Tyler Henry
from York, Pennsylvania, killed when their convoy
hit an IED while crossing through the desert; Will
McCann from central Ohio, killed by a sniper inside
the Green Zone; or Don Bloom from Trenton, New
Jersey, who'd been captured by the renegade remnants of Saddam Hussein's fedayeen, tortured and
then, after being rescued, had gone AWOL somewhere inside the country. Nobody was sure why, or
where he'd gone, or what had happened to him. The
rumors ran the gamut, each one wilder than the
previous. Bloom had fallen in love with an Iraqi girl
and was hiding with her family. Bloom had crossed
the border into Jordan and became a smuggler.
Bloom had crossed the border into Syria or Iran
and was selling them military secrets. Bloom was
working for a private security contractor. Bloom had
joined up with Black Lodge, the paranormal para-
military group that didn't even exist but was the wet
dream of conspiracy theorists all across the Internet. All kinds of crazy theories, and Donny was
pretty sure that none of them were true.

Donny thought of Henry and McCann and
Bloom often, but he thought even more frequently
about his friends who *had* made it home—and the
few who were still there, counting the days on their
own short-timer calendars. He missed them terribly
and wondered if he'd ever see any of them again.
They'd promised to stay in touch. So had he. But
somehow, those promises had fallen by the wayside
when, one by one, they returned home to the real
world—a world of family and wives and kids and
taxes and jobs and college and mortgage payments.
Donny's real world was Brinkley Springs, and in

some ways, he hated the town more than he'd ever hated Iraq.

Donny Osborne was twenty-four going on eighty-four.

He glanced back at the house again, and his gaze lingered on the for-sale sign in the yard. The sign was new—less than a week old—but already looked weather-beaten and worn, just like the house itself. The realtor (a redheaded woman named Mallory Lau who, despite being twice his age, had mercilessly hit on Donny even though he kept declining her advances) had promised him she'd do her best, but Donny wasn't holding his breath. Brinkley Springs was full of similar signs, many of them from her real-estate office. With the economy still down, it was a buyer's market right now—except that there were no buyers. Each morning, new realtor signs seemed to have sprung up overnight. The houses weren't selling. New construction was nonexistent. In short, the town was old and sick and weary. The town was dying. No, not dying. Maybe the town didn't know it yet, but Brinkley Springs was dead.

Just like his mother.

Donny could have stayed in the military after his second tour of duty. He'd certainly wanted to stay in. He was decorated—including a Bronze Star— and he'd already made E-5. He'd been the type of soldier they needed more of, and the brass hadn't been shy about letting him know that the army offered him big bonuses and all sorts of extra benefits if he'd re-up again. He'd planned on doing it. It wasn't that he desired to make a career out of the army. He could do without combat, and the endless hours of monotony in between firefights—the "hurry up and wait" mentality so prevalent in the military. But he really didn't have any other options that appealed to him. He could have taken advantage of the G.I. Bill, of course, and let the government pay for his college education, but there was nothing in particular that Donny had wanted to study. He didn't know what he wanted to do with his life. All that he knew was that he didn't want to spend that life trapped in Brinkley Springs. The army provided him with a way to do that, a way to escape. Unfortunately, in the end, Brinkley Springs had sucked him back. A line of dialogue from the third *Godfather* movie ran through his head.

"Just when I thought I was out," Donny said, doing his best Al Pacino imitation, "they pull me back in."

He could have re-upped, could have gotten the big reenlistment bonus and the offer of full retirement at age forty, and never had to set foot in Brinkley Springs again, except for the occasional holiday when home on leave, had his mother not gotten sick.

The cancer had been slow but deadly, ravaging her body one cell at a time with unerring precision. The doctors down in Beckley had discovered it by accident. Mom had gone in for a checkup while Donny was still on his second tour in Iraq. They'd discovered a lump in her abdomen, but had assured her it was merely a lipoma, a benign tumor composed of nothing more than extra fatty tissue. And they'd been right. The lump they'd removed was benign, but the tumors they discovered beneath it during the operation were malignant. So were the ones that followed.

His father had died when Donny was ten years

old. He'd been coming home from work late one night after a full day of cutting timber on Bald Knob and had rolled his truck down a mountainside between Punkin Center and Renick. After plunging eighty feet, there wasn't much left of him or the truck. Investigators were never able to determine what had happened. Maybe a deer had run out in front of him. Maybe he'd fallen asleep. Maybe another car had run him off the narrow road. Or maybe it had just been one of those things—dumb luck, the kind that altered lives forever. In any case, no matter what the reason, his father had never come home that night.

His mother had never remarried. As far as Donny knew, she'd never even dated again. He had no siblings, so when his mother got sick, he'd returned home, come back to Brinkley Springs to take care of her. He slept in his old bedroom. At night, after his mother was asleep in a haze of painkillers and sedatives, Donny had lain in that old bedroom and stared at the ceiling. It felt like a prison, and with each passing night, the walls had seemed to draw closer.

Mom had lingered for just over a year. They'd tried various treatments, but none of them had worked, and some of them had made her sicker than the cancer itself. In the end, she'd succumbed. Donny had been by her side in the hospital when it happened.

Now she was gone, and in a minute, as soon as he climbed back in his pickup truck and started the engine, Donny would be gone, too. This time for good.

"I'm sorry, Mom."

The streetlights blinked out. Donny stared up at them, waiting for the illumination to return, but it didn't.

"Fucking town. Nothing works around here anymore. Even the lights are dead."

Something screamed in the night. Donny jumped, startled. It sounded like an injured woman or child. The cry came from the woods, shattering the stillness. After a moment, he realized what it was. The shrieks belonged to a screech owl. He'd been terrified of that sound as a young boy, but had forgotten all about it in adulthood—as adulthood had given him all new things to be afraid of.

"Damn it."

With a third sigh, Donny turned away from the house and clambered up into the cab of the truck. The seat springs groaned as he climbed inside. He slammed the door, rolled the window down and slipped his key into the ignition. He was about to start it when someone called his name.

"Donny? Donny, wait!"

Surprised, Donny leaned his head out the window and glanced behind him. The streetlights still hadn't returned, and at first, all he saw was a shadow. Then, as the figure drew closer, he recognized it. Marsha Cummings was hurrying down the street toward him. Her flip-flops beat a steady rhythm on the pavement.

I must be tired, he thought. *I didn't even hear her coming. How could I not have, with her wearing those flip-flops?*

Swallowing the sudden lump in his throat, Donny turned the key in the ignition. Nothing happened.

"Shit."

He tried it again, but the engine refused to turn over. When he tried the headlights, he found that they were dead, as well.

"Donny," Marsha called again. "Wait a minute, goddamn it!"

Sighing a fourth and final time, Donny let his fingers fall away from the keys. He waited for Marsha to reach him, and repeated the Pacino line under his breath.

"Just when I thought I was out, they pull me back in."

And that was when the dogs began to howl.

"Yo, turn this shit up," Sam said, reaching for the computer mouse. On the monitor, iTunes had just segued from Redman to Kanye West. The bass line thumped softly from two speakers and a subwoofer hooked into the back of the computer.

"Leave it alone," Randy warned, smacking his friend's hand away. "My parents are still awake. We don't need them coming up here. And besides, Kanye West is a bag of fuck."

"If you don't like him," Stephanie asked after sipping her beer, "then why is he on your iPod?"

"Because I used to like him. I just don't anymore. Dude be tripping all the time. Too much ego and not enough talent. And besides, his shit's outdated."

"Well," Stephanie persisted, "so are Redman and Ice-T, but you've got them on here. Hell, Ice-T was around when our parents were our age."

"Yeah, but that's classic shit. There's a difference between being a classic and just being outdated. Ice-T was an original gangster. Kanye ain't all that. He's a squirrel looking for a nut."

Randy turned his attention back to the video game he was playing with Sam. The two sat on the edge of his bed, controllers in hand, staring at the television. Stephanie sat in the chair in front of Randy's desk. Her gaze went from the television to the boys to the computer, and then back to the television again.

She sighed.

"What's wrong?" Randy asked her, his tone impatient.

"I'm bored. I mean, I didn't come over here to watch you two play video games all night."

Randy's attention didn't leave the television. "Then what the hell did you come over here for?"

"To spend time with you guys, asshole."

"I reckon we *are* spending time together."

"No, we're not. We're just hanging out in your bedroom."

Her cell phone beeped. Stephanie picked it up and smiled.

"It's Linda. Hang on, let me text her back."

She grew quiet for a few moments as she typed, and Randy tried to focus on the game. Then Stephanie's phone beeped again as Linda replied, and Stephanie squealed with laughter. Grunting, Randy dropped his game controller in frustration. On the screen, his character died a bloody death at the hands of Sam, who sat back and grinned.

"Now look what you did," Randy said to Stephanie. "You fucked with my concentration and I lost."

"It's not my fault!"

"Sure it is. You and Linda text like twenty-four/seven. Ya'll are lesbians or something."

"Asshole."

"Don't you get sick of each other?"

"Sounds to me like you're jealous."

Ignoring her, Randy turned to Sam. "I'm done, yo. This game sucks, anyway."

"Come on, Steph." Sam fished the controller out of Randy's lap and held it up. "Why don't you give it a try?"

"Okay."

She hopped out of the chair and took a seat between them on the bed. Smiling, she accepted the controller from Sam, whose hairless cheeks suddenly flushed red. He glanced away from her, shifting back and forth nervously when she giggled. The bed springs squeaked.

"Promise to be gentle?" Stephanie grinned.

"I reckon so," Sam murmured.

Randy stood up and crossed the room. Like Sam, his ears and cheeks were red, too, but unlike Sam, it wasn't from embarrassment. Sam was supposed to be his best friend. They'd known each other all their lives. They'd known Stephanie all their lives, too, and it wasn't until this year, when it suddenly became apparent that Stephanie wasn't just the little girl they'd always known anymore, that the relationship between the three of them had grown so complicated. Randy hated it when Stephanie tried to play him and Sam against each other. Worse, it bothered him even more that Sam was sucker enough to fall for it every time. Sometimes, she genuinely seemed to want to be with him. Other times, she seemed more interested in Sam. Randy hated how the whole situation made him feel.

Not for the first time, Randy wondered what would happen to them all after graduation. It was only a few months away. They'd have the summer together. He supposed that he and Sam would have to find jobs, although he didn't know how in the hell they'd do that when there weren't any jobs to be had. Stephanie would be going off to college in the fall. She'd gotten into Morgantown. What would happen then? Would she be like everybody else who left Brinkley Springs, and never come back?

"Where's your sister at tonight?" Sam asked.

Randy turned around to answer and noticed that Sam and Stephanie were sitting very close to each other on the edge of the mattress. So close, in fact, that their thighs and shoulders were touching. Neither seemed inclined to move. Randy wondered if they were even aware of it. A lump rose in his throat and something churned in his stomach.

"She went out," he said, trying to keep the edge out of his voice. "Donny's leaving tonight. She wanted to confront him before he goes."

"She ought to just let it drop," Sam said. "Hell, he's the one who left in the first place. Went off to Iraq and shit. Left your sis and his mother here. And what with his Mom being sick and your sister in love with him—that shit wasn't right, yo."

"She's in love with him," Stephanie declared. "It's easy to see why, too. Donny's . . ."

"What?" Randy and Sam asked at the same time.

"Never mind. All I'm saying is that it's easy to see why Marsha is still stuck on Donny. Love makes you do strange things."

"Randy?" The voice came from downstairs.

"Shit. It's my dad." He waved at Stephanie and Sam to be quiet. "What?"

"Turn that music down. The bass is coming through the ceiling."

"Okay," Randy yelled.

Muttering to himself, he walked toward the computer. As he did, the background music changed, switching from Kanye West to Foxy Brown and Kira singing "When the Lights Go Out."

"Oh," Stephanie said, "I love this song."

And then the lights went out, along with the computer, the television, the video game and all of the other electronics. Stephanie gasped. The bedroom grew dark. The windows were open, allowing the night air to come through the screens, and a slight breeze ruffled the curtains.

"Uh-oh," Sam said. "Must have blown a fuse."

"Listen," Randy said, holding a finger to his lips. "Ya'll hush up a minute."

Downstairs, Randy and Marsha's father was cursing, and their mother was asking him where the flashlight was. Outside, a dog howled. And then another. And then a dozen.

"Come on," Randy said. "Let's go see what's happening."

Sam and Stephanie stood up and followed him to the bedroom door. Randy reached for her hand and gave it a squeeze. She squeezed back, and her teeth flashed white in the gloom as she smiled at him.

"Besides," Randy whispered, "maybe it'll be more exciting than sitting here playing video games."

"Oh, I don't know," she said. "I was sort of having fun kicking Sam's butt."

Sam laughed behind them and Stephanie's smile grew wider. Randy let go of her hand and walked out into the hall, barely realizing that his hands had curled into fists.

Outside, the barking and howls grew louder.

* * *

Five black crows swooped in over the town and then split up, each heading to the outskirts. One glided to the town's northern point, another to the southern tip. One went east and another west. The fifth crow hovered over the center of town. When all were in position, each simultaneously shed a single black feather. The feathers floated slowly downward. As each one touched the ground, the birds croaked in unison. Their voices sounded human rather than crowlike—as if they were chanting.

The air around Brinkley Springs changed. A glow briefly surrounded the town, and then vanished.

When the lights went out, Esther Laudry had finished brewing hot water in her electric tea kettle. She'd just poured some into two dainty, porcelain tea cups decorated with red and pink roses when the power died.

"Oh, fiddlesticks . . ."

She tugged on the teabag strings and left the cups and saucers on the kitchen counter, allowing the tea to steep for a moment. Then she made her way to the laundry room, moving slowly—it wouldn't do to slip and break her hip in the darkness—and checked the fuse box by the light of a match. Everything seemed normal. None of the fuses were blown.

"Esther," Myrtle Danbury called from the sitting room, "do you need some help, dear? Is everything okay?"

"It's fine," Esther said, coming back into the kitchen. "The electricity is out."

"That's strange. It's not storming."

"No, it's not. Maybe somebody crashed into a pole. Or maybe a tree branch knocked down one of the wires. Just give me a moment to call the power company."

Esther reached for the phone, but when she tried dialing, she found that the phone lines were out, as well. She placed the phone back in its cradle, went to the kitchen drawer and pulled out a pink flashlight. When she thumbed the button, nothing happened. Either the batteries were dead or the flashlight was broken. Shaking her head, she picked up the teacups. They rattled softly against the saucers as she carefully carried them into the dark sitting room.

"It's chamomile," she said, sitting the cup and saucer down in front of her guest, "but I'm afraid we'll have to drink it in the dark."

"That's okay," Myrtle said, her voice cheery. "I like the ambience."

"You would. My flashlight isn't working."

"When was the last time you changed the batteries?"

"I don't know."

"I change mine twice a year, just to be sure. You can never be too cautious."

Esther frowned. "Just let me light a few candles."

She moved around the room, lighting a series of votive and decorative candles that were scattered among the knickknacks on various shelves and end tables. Soon the sitting room was filled with a soft glow and the competing scents of honeysuckle, strawberry, cinnamon, vanilla and peppermint. Sighing, Esther took her seat, and after an experimental sip, pronounced her tea too hot to drink.

"What did the power company say?" Myrtle asked. "Did they give you any idea how long it would be?"

"I couldn't get through. The phone lines are down, too."

"Well, that's odd."

"Yes, it is."

"Should we check on your boarder?" Myrtle asked.

Esther shook her head. "No, I'm sure he's fine. I imagine the poor man is asleep already. He said he'd ridden all day in that buggy. He was pretty tired when he checked in, and he asked not to be disturbed. You saw for yourself."

"I know. But still . . ."

"You just want to bother him with questions, Myrtle. Be honest."

"Well, don't you? You can't tell me you're not just as fascinated with him as I am."

"Sure, I'm interested, but I don't intend to bother him about it. Not tonight. He's worn out. And besides, it's not like he's the first Amish person we've seen. There's a whole colony of them up near Punkin Center."

"I thought those were Mennonites?"

"Aren't they the same thing?"

"I don't think so." Myrtle shrugged. "People from the Mennonite faith can drive cars and trucks. Only the Amish still insist on riding around in horse-drawn buggies. I think they are different facets of the same faith. Like Methodists and Lutherans."

Esther frowned again. She'd been a Presbyterian all of her life and had little interest in other denominations, especially when they were incorrect in regards to interpreting the Lord's word.

"But that's my point," Myrtle continued. "It would be fascinating to talk to him—to learn more about his faith. The Amish are a very spiritual people, you know."

Esther tried her tea again and found that it had cooled. She took a sip and sighed.

"You're forgetting," she said, "that when he checked in, and you asked him, he specifically stated he *wasn't* Amish."

Myrtle waved her hand in a dismissive gesture. "Then how do you explain his clothes and his beard? And why else would he show up in a horse and buggy? Mighty odd to be going around like that if he's not Amish."

"Lots of people have beards. And I daresay he's not the only person around here to use a horse."

"When he checked in, what did he list for his address?"

"That's personal information, Myrtle. I can't tell you that."

"Oh, nonsense. That's never stopped you from gossiping in the past."

Esther's frown deepened. Myrtle was her next-door neighbor and, she supposed, her best friend. Even so, she didn't appreciate being spoken to like this—even if Myrtle was right.

"Marietta, Pennsylvania."

"I know that area," Myrtle said. "I wrote about it in one of my books. Powwow magic was very big there at one time."

"Oh, here we go. You and your New Age books."

"Don't you scoff. I make a living from them."

Myrtle sounded slightly offended. Esther considered apologizing, but then decided against it. She knew all too well that Myrtle's self-published volumes barely made enough money to break even. In truth, Myrtle lived off the life-insurance policy left behind after her husband's death three years ago from the sudden and massive heart attack he'd suffered while turkey hunting. Esther suspected that the books were Myrtle's way of dealing with his death.

"And anyway," Myrtle continued, "powwow isn't New Age. It's sort of like what we call hoodoo around here, but based more in German occultism, Gypsy lore, Egyptology and Native American beliefs. It's uniquely American—a big old melting pot."

"Well, it doesn't sound very American to me. Germans and Gypsies and Egyptians and Indians? The only American part of that is the Indians, and Lord knows that didn't work out so well. Sounds occult to me."

"Oh, you'd like it. It's a mix of folklore and the Bible, with a little bit of white and black magic thrown in. Sort of like potluck supernaturalism."

"Hoodoo isn't magic."

"Well, sure it is!"

"My mother could work hoodoo," Esther said, "but she'd have struck you down if you'd called it magic. Her abilities were nothing more than the Lord working through her."

"You say tomato. I say—"

"Listen." Esther held up one hand and sat upright in her chair, head cocked to one side. "Do you hear that?"

Myrtle was quiet for a moment. "Dogs? It sounds like all the dogs in town just went crazy. Maybe there's a deer running through the streets or something?"

"Maybe."

"Anyway," Myrtle said, "we got off track. My point was that Marietta—where this man is supposedly from—is in Lancaster County, which is the heart and soul of Amish country."

"That doesn't prove anything. West Virginia is full of rednecks. Does that make us rednecks?"

"Of course not. But this is different. There's no doubt in my mind that the man upstairs is Amish, no matter what he says."

Esther murmured her consent, but in truth, she was barely listening to her friend. Her attention was focused on the howling outside and the darkness in the room. It suddenly felt to Esther as if her entire bed-and-breakfast was holding its breath. She shivered.

"Is it me," she whispered, "or has it gotten colder in here?"

"It has," Myrtle replied. "I didn't notice it until you mentioned it, but it definitely has. Do you want me to get you a shawl?"

"No, I'm okay. I hope the lights come back on soon."

"Me, too."

They sat in silence for a few moments, listening to the dogs and wondering what was going on. The temperature continued to drop—not enough that they could see their breath in the air, but enough to make them both uncomfortable. When Esther reached for her tea, hoping that it would warm her up, she noticed that the flames were dancing atop the candles, as if blown by a slight breeze.

"Did you see that?"

"The candles?" Now Myrtle was whispering, too.

"Yes. I reckon you must have left a door or window open."

"No," Esther insisted, "they're all closed. I closed them as soon as the cats came in for the evening."

Outside, the frenzied howls suddenly stopped as if someone had flicked a switch.

Levi Stoltzfus was asleep when the power went out. He lay on his back, legs straight, arms folded across his stomach, snoring softly. He dreamed of a girl in a cornfield. Her light, melodic laughter drifted to him as she danced through the rustling, upright rows, always staying two steps ahead of him. He wanted to catch her. Wanted to hold her to him, out here in the middle of the field where nobody could see them. He wanted to smell her scent and feel her skin. He wanted to run his hands through the long, blonde hair she kept hidden beneath the mesh-knit bun on her head.

She danced out of sight again, and Levi called her name. Her laughter came to him once more, borne on the summer breeze. The cornstalks swayed around him. Grinning, Levi continued the chase.

But when he finally caught up with her, he saw that something else had found her first. She lay on the ground, eyes open but unseeing, legs splayed, dress torn, skin the color of cream, and there was blood. So much blood. Too much . . .

Levi's eyes snapped open just as the electricity died. He did not scream or shout. In fact, he made no sound at all. But the girl's name was on his lips and her memory left him shaken and drenched in sweat.

He sat up, semi-alert, and rubbed the sleep from

his eyes. Until the dream, his rest had been a good one, but not nearly long enough. He'd been on the road all day, riding along eight hours' worth of West Virginia back roads. (There was no way he could take the buggy onto a major highway or Interstate.) He was sore and tired. More importantly, his horse, Dee, had also been sore and tired. Levi had been grateful when he came across the bed-and-breakfast in Brinkley Springs, and he was certain that Dee had been grateful, too.

He became aware that there were dogs howling outside. Yawning, Levi glanced around the unfamiliar room and tried to get his bearings in the dark. Mrs. Laudry, who had insisted that he call her Esther, had pointed out the digital alarm clock on the nightstand when she'd shown him the room earlier. When he looked for it now, he saw that it was dead. There had been a light on out in the hallway. He remembered the soft glow creeping under his door before he'd gone to sleep. Now, the light was extinguished.

Downstairs, he heard the murmur of voices. Both were female. After a moment, he recognized one as Mrs. Laudry. He assumed the other must be her friend Mrs. Danbury. He decided that it would be better not to let them know he was awake. Levi had no doubt that Mrs. Danbury would jump at the chance to pepper him with questions about his supposed faith. Like most, she'd automatically assumed that he was Amish, even after he'd denied it. Levi had always found such assumptions mildly irritating. He'd tried explaining to people over and over again that he was no longer Amish, but after all this time, they still insisted on referring to him as such. They never understood that he simply preferred the long beard of his former people and enjoyed adhering still to their plain dress code—black pants and shoes, a white button-down shirt, suspenders and a black dress coat, topped off with a wide-brimmed straw hat. Why should his mode of dress and method of transport matter to people? Why should they find it so odd? He drove a horse and buggy because it was more economical than a gas-guzzling SUV. And because Dee was one of his closest constant companions (along with his faithful dog, Crowley, who was back home).

Yes, he had been Amish at one time, but that was long ago. Levi didn't like to dwell on it. In truth, his excommunication from the church and his professed faith still chafed at Levi's pride, even after all this time. When he was cast out, it had cost him everything—his love, his friends, his community. Still, he'd had no choice. He did what the Lord expected of him, using the talents the Lord had given him. If the church didn't see that, then so be it. He just wished it didn't hurt so bad.

He'd tried to fit in among the "civilian world" (as he often thought of it), but soon discovered that he was an outsider there, as well. Away from the Amish, he was nothing more than a curiosity. An oddity. He was pointed at and discussed behind his back. He didn't fit in among the English (the term his fellow Amish used to describe people not of their faith). Levi didn't like being an outsider. He didn't like being alone. But like everything else in life, it was God's will, and Levi's cross to bare. Sometimes, the weight grew so heavy . . .

He was no longer Amish. Now, he was something

else, and it was that something else that he didn't need Myrtle Danbury discovering. She'd introduced herself as an author, and the foyer of Mrs. Laudry's bed-and-breakfast had featured several of the woman's books on display—slim, cheaply produced trade paperbacks with garish lettering on the covers. A quick glance had told Levi everything he needed to know. The subjects ranged from healing crystals to channeling ancient Lemurian deities. Mrs. Danbury was a New Ager, the bane of Levi's existence. Nothing annoyed Levi more than New Age amateur mystics, except for maybe Evangelical Christians. In his experience, the majority of both were hypocrites and con artists, wolves dressed in sheep's clothing, preying on those who refused to think for themselves and discern God's truths from mankind's lies. In Levi's opinion, that was the problem with religion in general. The Christians, Muslims, Jews, Buddhists, Sikhs, Satanists, pagans, Hindus, Cthulhu cultists, Scientologists and every other religious group or cult, no matter how big or how small, thought that their way was the right way. In reality, none of them had it completely right, for it was not meant for them to know all of the universe's secrets. They fought each other, killed each other, committed atrocities against each other, all in the name of their particular god or gods, without any understanding of just how wrong—how completely off base—they really were.

New Agers were the worst. At times in life's journey, when the Lord gave him a task to complete, Levi had needed the assistance of other occultists and magicians, those not given to practicing the same disciplines that he followed. Levi had always seen this as a necessary evil. The old adage, "The enemy of my enemy is my friend," quite often applied. But no matter how dire the situation or its consequences, he had never sought help from the crystal-worshipping, herbal-supplementing, Atlantean-spirit-channeling crowd. And deep down inside, Levi knew that even if he had, they wouldn't have welcomed him. Even the New Agers would have turned their backs on him.

In the end, Levi always walked his road alone, even among the splintered ranks of occultism's lunatic fringe. He was a stranger to everyone but himself . . . and God.

Outside, the howling increased, disturbing his maudlin ruminations. Their cries grew more frenzied. Levi wondered what was going on. He reached out to the nightstand and fumbled for his cell phone, which he'd plugged in to charge before he went to sleep. Like everything else in his life, the cell phone was often a point of confusion among those who assumed he was still Amish. He wondered what they expected him to use instead. A carrier pigeon? Two paper cups tied together with string? Telepathy? Actually, he had used telepathy a handful of times in his life. He tried to avoid it as much as possible, however, because he didn't like the nosebleeds that came with it.

All at once, the dogs stopped howling. Somehow, the silence seemed worse than the noise had been.

Levi flipped open the cell phone and was surprised to see that it was dead. If there had just been no service, he could have understood. His service had been spotty for the last three days, ever since entering the mountains. But there was no power whatsoever—no backlight, no time, not even a tone when he experimentally pushed the buttons. He wondered if a power surge could have done it, and glanced at the electrical outlet in the wall. He could barely make it out in the gloom, but from what he could tell, there was no cause for alarm. The outlet wasn't smoking or sparking.

Levi slid out of bed and shivered as his bare feet hit the floor. Was it his imagination, or had it grown noticeably colder in the room? Gooseflesh prickled his arms and the back of his neck. He stood up, walked quickly to the small, plain dresser and opened the top drawer. He quickly pulled on his clothes and shoes. He patted the pocket over his left breast and felt a reassuring bulge where his dog-eared and battered copy of *The Long Lost Friend* was. The book was a family heirloom. It had been his father's, and his father's before him. Levi never went anywhere without it. The front page of the book held the following inscription:

> *Whoever carries this book with him is safe from all his enemies, visible or invisible; and whoever has this book with him cannot die without the holy corpse of Jesus Christ, nor be drowned in any water, nor burn up in any fire, nor can any unjust sentence be passed upon him.*

Levi had never had any reason to doubt the inscription's truth, except for maybe the last part, the bit about unjust sentences. He knew about those all too well. Sometimes it seemed to him that life was nothing but a series of unjust sentences.

Once he'd gotten dressed, Levi dropped his hands to his sides, closed his eyes and waited. His breathing slowed. The world seemed to pause as he concentrated.

After a moment, he felt it. His eyes opened again. Something was coming.

No, not coming. Something was already *here*.

"Oh, Lord . . ."

Pulse racing, Levi ran to the window, no longer caring if his host and her annoying friend knew he was awake or not. He looked out the second-story window and surveyed the scene below. Then, as his heart began to beat even faster, Levi crossed the room and yanked open the door. He dashed for the stairwell, reciting a benediction against evil as he took the stairs two at a time and plunged toward the first floor.

"Ut nemo in sense tentat, descendere nemo. At precedenti spectaur mantica tergo. Hecate. Hecate. Hecate."

He leaped the last four stairs; his boot heels landed on the floor with a loud thump and his teeth slammed together. Picture frames and other fixtures shook on the wall. A ceiling fan swayed back and forth, sending flecks of dust drifting to the floor. Mrs. Laudry and Mrs. Danbury bustled into the room as Levi headed for the exit.

"Mr. Stoltzfus," Esther gasped. "What is it? What's wrong?"

Levi turned to them, and the fear and uncertainty he saw in their faces mirrored what he felt in his heart. He tried to project a calm demeanor.

"I'm sorry to alarm you, ladies, but I'd like to ask you both to stay here."

"Why?" Esther's eyes shone in the darkness. "Does this have something to do with the power outage?"

He nodded. "Perhaps."

"The phones are out, too. What's going on?"

"I'm sure it's nothing, but I thought I'd check around your property and make sure everything is okay."

"Did you hear something?" Myrtle asked. "Is there somebody outside?"

"Not at all. At least, I don't believe there is. It's just a precaution. Nothing more. But I'll take care of it. The two of you shouldn't be out on a night like tonight. It's the least I can do to repay your generous hospitality. Plus, it will give me an opportunity to make sure my buggy is secure. I don't have much, but I wouldn't want my belongings getting looted during the blackout."

"Oh," Esther said, "that would never happen here. Nothing ever happens in Brinkley Springs. Especially bad things like that."

Levi wanted to tell her that she was wrong, that something bad was indeed happening in Brinkley Springs right now, but he didn't. Instead, he forced a smile. A sour taste rose in his mouth.

"I'm sure you're right, of course. But still, better safe than sorry. You ladies stay here. I'll be right back."

He reached for the doorknob and hoped they couldn't see how badly his hand was shaking. Then he stepped out into the night, shivering as the darkness embraced him in ways the girl in the cornfield from so long ago never could.

CHAPTER THREE

Stephen Poernik had just passed the green and white sign on U.S. 219 South that said WELCOME TO BRINKLEY SPRINGS, AN INCORPORATED TOWN, when his faithful Mazda pickup truck suddenly died. There was no advance warning. One moment, he'd been doing a steady forty-five miles an hour and scanning the radio, searching for some heavy driving music, or anything other than bluegrass, preaching and talk radio, which seemed to be the only three programming choices this part of West Virginia had to offer. The next instant, the engine, lights and radio all went dead. The truck didn't stall. It simply shut off. The headlights and the rest of the electrical equipment shut off with it. Cursing, Stephen coasted to a stop in the middle of the road, just past the welcome sign.

"Well, shit."

He glanced down at the dashboard gauges, but had trouble reading them in the dark. Stephen reached above him and flicked the switch for the dome light, but it was dead, as well. He leaned over the steering wheel, squinting at the gauges. They seemed fine. As far as he could tell, there wasn't a problem with the engine temperature. He put the truck in park and then turned the key. His attempts were fruitless. Nothing happened. He didn't even hear the starter clicking. Apparently, he'd lost all power.

Stephen didn't know much about fixing vehicles. He knew that he'd be up Shit Creek under the hood, but decided to give it a try anyway. Maybe it was something simple like a loose battery cable. He hoped so. Otherwise, he was screwed.

He reached down beneath the heater vent and tugged the hood release. Then he opened the door and hopped out of the truck. Stephen was immediately struck by the silence. He'd spent enough time on these rural back roads to become familiar with the sounds of the night—crickets and other insect songs, the chirping of spring peepers, the occasional call of an owl or whippoorwill, the barking of a dog or even just the sound of another car approaching on the road. He heard none of these things. It was almost as if Brinkley Springs existed in some sort of noiseless vacuum. Even the wind seemed nonexistent. Standing on the road next to the truck, with one hand on the open door, Stephen felt uneasy. For a moment, he considered reaching into the glove box and grabbing his SIG Sauer P225. He never left home without it. (Stephen's thoughts on handguns were that he wasn't on parole and didn't live in New York, so fuck the permit.) He paused, and then decided against it. For one thing, he might need both hands to look at the engine. For another, if a cop or somebody pulled up, they'd be a lot less sympathetic to his plight if they saw him brandishing a weapon. Besides, he was just being silly. His unease was just a bad case of nerves. Nothing more. He'd been driving all day and needed some sleep.

Sleep. Not that he slept all that well anymore. Not since losing his job as a cabinetmaker, thanks to the disastrous economic policies of the last two presidents. He'd been suffering from bouts of insomnia and depression ever since. He was trying to be patient, of course. Trying to give this new presidential administration more time to fix things. After all, they'd been handed a shit sandwich. It was hard not to become disillusioned with something as inherently fucked-up from top to bottom as the American political system, but he'd given them a chance, hoping they could turn things around, hoping for the change that had been promised over and over again during the campaign. And he had to admit, things were starting to look and sound better. But at the end of the day, he was still unemployed. These days, there just weren't many job openings for cabinetmakers and glassblowers. The only other thing Stephen had ever worked as was a blackjack and roulette dealer. At age fifty-five, with both his beard and his long black hair that hung to the middle of his back now shot with gray, he was too old to get back into that game. That's why he was out here on the road. He'd been driving around with a book of sample pictures, trying to find craft markets and antique stores that would sell his woodworking and stained-glass wares. Stephen wasn't much of a people person, and he disliked going from business to business, but he had no choice. His hope was that he could find enough outlets and sell enough goods to support his family full-time. If not, at least it would supplement his meager unemployment checks.

He'd been fortunate, and with his third marriage lasting twenty-three years now, Stephen considered himself a lucky guy. Things would turn around. Things would get better again.

They *had* to.

"Look on the bright side," he whispered. "At least you've still got your health." And he did, too. Standing at a few inches over six feet tall and weighing about one hundred ninety-five pounds, Stephen was in remarkably good shape, especially considering the life he'd led. Granted, he wasn't in prime workout shape. He didn't have the physique of a bodybuilder, but he was still healthier than he'd ever thought he'd be at this age.

He walked around to the front of the truck and placed his palms on the hood. The metal was warm, but not hot. He didn't see any steam or smoke drifting out from underneath. He felt around beneath the hood, found the latch and released it. Then he raised the hood and stared at the engine. Even if he'd known what to look for, it was hard for him to see anything clearly in the dark. He turned around and glanced at the welcome sign, and noticed that someone had peppered it with buckshot at some point. Shaking his head, he let his gaze wander toward town, and then it struck him that there were no lights on. Sure, it was nighttime, and most of the townspeople were probably asleep, but even so, there should have been some illumination. The streetlights weren't functioning. There were no nightlights glowing in the windows of any of the houses. The entire town was dark. Maybe the power was out?

A flutter of motion caught his attention. A large black crow swung down out of the coal-colored sky and landed on one of the dead streetlights. It tilted its head and stared at him. Then it opened its beak and croaked. The sound reminded Stephen of rusty hinges. It didn't sound like a normal birdcall. It sounded almost like some garbled, guttural language. The sound seemed very loud in the stillness.

"Hey buddy," he said to the bird, "any chance you could call Triple A for me?"

The crow continued staring at him. It croaked again.

"No? I didn't think so."

The crow cawed a third time. If he hadn't known better, Stephen would have thought he heard distinct syllables in the cry.

"Get the fuck out of here, you weird bird."

Stephen turned his attention back to the motor. He leaned down and sniffed, but the engine didn't smell hot. He smelled antifreeze and oil, but neither seemed to be overpowering, as they would be if he had a leak. Clueless as to what else to do, he slammed the hood and moved back around the side of the truck again. He climbed into the cab and reached for his cell phone. Then he glanced at his watch and checked the time. His wife, Noralyn, was probably still awake, curled up on the couch with their two Siamese cats, Princess and Eddie (short for Edgar Allan Poernik). He'd call her, let her know what had happened, and then he'd call for a tow truck.

Except that when he flipped the cell phone open, it, like the Mazda and the lights in town, was dead. Stephen pressed the button twice, just to make sure, but there was no power. That didn't make sense. He'd given it a full charge the night before, plugging it into a wall socket at a Motel 6 he'd stayed at in Walden, Virginia. He'd used it only a few times today—

once to call Noralyn and tell her good morning, and twice to check his voice mail, to see if one of the antique stores or craft markets he'd stopped at had called him back. Both messages had been from automated telemarketing machines—one offering him an extended warranty on a car that he and Noralyn no longer owned and the other for some kind of ringtone service for his cell phone. He'd quickly hung up on both of them. Other than those three calls, he hadn't used the phone all day. There was no way the battery should have been run down already. As if trying to prove this, he thumbed the power button again. The cell phone remained dead.

"Goddamn it!"

The crow squawked again, almost as if it were laughing at him. Stephen whirled around and raised his middle finger. The bird seemed nonplussed. It stepped off its perch and glided down to the ground, where it stood in the middle of the street, head cocked to one side, and continued to stare at him. Stephen stomped his foot at it.

"Go on. Get the hell out of here. Scat!"

The crow remained where it was. Defiant and aloof. Almost dismissive of him. It croaked again. He could have sworn it was laughing.

"Suit yourself, you stupid fucking bird."

Stephen decided to walk into town and find some help. Even though the lights were out, there had to be somebody awake. A twenty-four-hour convenience store or a gas station. A cop making the rounds. The local insomniac, up late and listening to *Coast to Coast AM* or maybe watching infomercials on the tube. Kids out partying. Someone. Anyone. He'd find out if there was a mechanic or towing service who could help him tonight. If not, he'd find a place to sleep—hopefully a hotel room or a bed-and-breakfast—call Noralyn from their phone and let her know what had happened and then take care of the truck first thing in the morning.

He leaned into the cab and grabbed his large duffel bag off the floor. Inside the bag were his clean clothes, toiletries, iPod, the sample book, which displayed pictures of his handiwork, and other assorted items he'd carried with him on this road trip. Next to the duffel bag was a black plastic garbage bag that held his dirty laundry. He decided to leave that in the truck but bring everything else along. If someone wanted to break into the Mazda and steal his dirty skivvies, then let them. Obviously, if they were that desperate, they needed underwear more than he did. He opened the glove compartment and pulled out the handgun. Then he grabbed the box of bullets. Stephen knew better than to drive around with the pistol loaded. If he ever *did* get caught with it, that would just make matters worse—the difference between a small fine and a possible felony charge, depending on which state he was driving through and who was in office at the time. He also tossed the useless cell phone into the bag.

Stephen was suddenly overcome with an immense feeling of homesickness. He missed Noralyn and the cats. He wished he were there with them now instead of stranded along the side of the road in Bumfuck, West Virginia. Stephen had a fairly large personal library, well over two thousand books, most of which were horror, suspense or mystery fiction. What he wouldn't give right now to be curled up and reading one of those, rather than here.

Before zipping the duffel bag shut, Stephen pulled out his iPod and inserted the headphones. He used it quite a bit back home, whenever he was watering or mowing the yard. The only reason he hadn't been using it tonight was because he'd lost the cigarette-lighter adapter that powered it, and he hadn't wanted to run the battery down before he could recharge it again. Now, he didn't care. He felt sad and dejected and more than a little angry at his current situation, and he needed some music to cheer him up. He didn't care what kind. Stephen's musical tastes had always been eclectic. As he went for help, he'd put the iPod on randomize and let the music carry him away—ride a wave of Fred Astaire, White Zombie, Steve Howe, Black Sabbath, Yes, King Crimson, Judas Priest, Blue Öyster Cult, Robert Fripp, AC/DC, Guns N' Roses, Robin Trower, Jimi Hendrix or whatever else the iPod decided to surprise him with. Sometimes, Stephen forgot that he owned certain songs or albums until he heard them played back to him while the iPod was on randomize.

Stephen smiled. He felt better already. He stuck the tiny headphones into his ears, pressed play, and nothing happened.

"Oh, goddamn it! Not the iPod, too."

He glanced down at the piece of equipment. Like the truck and the lights and the cell phone, it was powerless.

"What happened in this place? Did somebody set off an EMP or something?"

He stuffed the useless iPod and headphones back

in the duffel bag, locked the truck, climbed down out of the cab and shut the door. Then he turned toward town and jumped, startled. The crow was gone. Standing in its place was a tall, thin man dressed entirely in black.

Or is he? Stephen thought. *What kind of material are his clothes made out of? It looks almost like he's wearing the night itself—like the darkness is reflecting off him. That can't be right. I must be more tired than I thought.*

Slowly, the man in black began walking toward him. The figure kept his head lowered, and Stephen had trouble making out any distinguishing characteristics. He wore a large, floppy-brimmed black hat, and it concealed his features. All that Stephen could see was a shock of jet-black hair sticking out beneath the brim of the hat, a long, pointed chin with a cleft in the center and a cruel, thin-lipped mouth.

"Excuse me," Stephen called. "Any chance you have a cell phone on you? I broke down, and mine's not working. Hell, nothing's working."

The man didn't respond.

Stephen tried to meet his eyes as he drew closer, but the stranger's face remained hidden in shadow.

"Or maybe you could tell me where the closest gas station is?"

Still the man didn't respond. He moved in silence, swiftly closing the distance between them. Stephen's heart began to beat faster. There was something wrong with this guy. Stephen had seen some odd things in his life. He wasn't necessarily a believer in the supernatural, but he'd experienced enough not to discount it either. He didn't count anything out—including this dark man. Maybe the guy was a serial killer. Or maybe he was possessed.

Oh, stop being stupid, he thought. *You're freaked out and now you're putting it on this guy. He's probably just deaf. Or has special needs. Or doesn't speak English.*

"Hey, friend," he tried again, trying to keep the uncertainty out of his voice. "You're kind of creeping me out here. How about we try this again?"

The man did not respond.

"Do you speak English? *Habla español?*"

The man shrugged.

"Okay, so you *can* hear me. What's with the attitude, man? I just want some help. I broke down."

The stranger stopped in front of him, only a few feet away, and raised his head. Despite his proximity, Stephen still couldn't get a good look at his face. He did see the man's eyes, however. They were set deep in his face and glinted in the dark like embers on coal.

But there's no light, Stephen thought. *That's weird. What am I seeing reflected in them if there's no light?*

The man smiled, revealing white, even teeth. Stephen couldn't be sure, but he thought they might be pointed. He took a half step backward.

"What do you want?"

"To kill you," the man said simply.

"W-what? Hey, what are you . . . ? Shit."

Stephen wasn't much of a survivalist. He'd just lucked out in the lottery drawing for the Vietnam fiasco and had always considered himself fortunate that he didn't have to face that horror. He'd known people that had served, of course. Guys who'd been less fortunate, and even a few who'd volunteered. Some of them had talked about their experiences in Vietnam. Most hadn't. While Stephen knew full well that he'd never truly understand what it had been like, he knew himself well enough to understand that if he had gone to Vietnam, he'd have been one of those guys who came home irreparably damaged—if he survived at all. But he was no coward either. He might not have been a badass, but he could handle himself just fine. He didn't know any martial arts, but that didn't matter. In Stephen's opinion, fights by definition weren't fair. Plus, he had another advantage. Stephen's father had been a cop, and as a result, though he wasn't much of a hunter, he could shoot the shit out of a handgun.

"Seriously," Stephen said, "quit fucking around. I'm not in the mood, buddy. Not tonight."

The man stepped closer. Stephen caught a whiff of him, and winced at the stench. The smell was bad enough to make his eyes water. The stranger reeked of roadkill, like he'd just rolled around in a five-day-dead possum or something.

"Jesus Christ—"

"Is not here right now," the man in black replied. "And even if he were, he could not save you."

Stephen stopped, setting his feet shoulder width apart and facing his opponent. He held his breath so he wouldn't get nauseous from the stranger's awful stench. The man hadn't displayed a weapon. He didn't seem to be carrying a knife or a handgun. Still, there was no telling what he might have hidden beneath the folds of that long coat. The man was only an arm's length away now, and Stephen decided that there was no time to open the bag and pull out the SIG Sauer P225. He had three choices—try to talk the guy down, run away or rely on his fists. Stephen decided to go with the first and follow with the last. Running away wasn't an option. This stranger was obviously mentally ill, and if he abandoned the truck, the guy might vandalize it instead.

"That's far enough," he said, fighting to keep his tone firm but even. "I'm warning you, freak."

The man in black ignored him and continued to draw closer.

Stephen decided that, if forced, he'd lead with an elbow to the nose and then follow it up with a quick kick to the outside of his opponent's knee. That should make the guy think twice about continuing to fuck with him.

And then, before Stephen could do any of these things, the man in black raised one hand and wiggled his fingers. As Stephen watched, the stranger's fingernails began to stretch and grow, turning into long black talons. Stephen blinked, and the man laughed hoarsely. The sound was like dry leaves rustling in the wind.

"Is that supposed to scare me?" In truth, it had, but Stephen wasn't about to let the guy know that.

"No," the man replied. "It's not supposed to scare you. It's supposed to distract you."

"What do you—?"

The man leaned forward and, with his other hand, punched Stephen just below his chest. Stephen grunted, more from surprise at the unexpected blow than from pain. In truth, there wasn't much pain. Instead, there was just a cold sensation that spread rapidly across his chest and abdomen. His eyes filled up with water.

"Now *that*," the stranger said, "is supposed to scare you."

The man's arm was still extended. Stephen tried

to pull away from him and found that he couldn't. Startled, he tried again. As he did, Stephen coughed, and tasted blood in the back of his throat. Then the dark man pulled his arm back and held up his hand. There was something gray and pink clutched in the stranger's fist. His hand glistened wetly.

That looks like . . . raw meat? Where did he get that?

Stephen became aware that something warm and wet was running down the side of his chin. He smacked his lips together. They felt dry all of a sudden, and the coldness was spreading to his arms and legs.

"I'm not sure what this is," the man in black said, frowning as he glanced at the grisly trophy in his hand. Shrugging, he tossed it to the side of the road. It landed in the grass and gravel with a squelch. "You people have too many useless things inside of you. It's a wonder you ever made it out of the oceans. As a species, you're so inferiorly designed. Then again, you were made in *His* image. And our kind has the unfortunate luck of manifesting in your image, rather than our own. We were once you, you see? Now we are something better. But never mind that."

He punched Stephen again. Blood flew from Stephen's mouth, splattering the stranger's coat. This time, there was pain—a sharp, overpowering agony that seemed to jolt through him as if he'd been shocked. It blazed, and then, as suddenly as it had begun, the pain faded again, replaced by the coldness. Stephen choked as the man held up his hand again, revealing a new item.

"This is your heart, of course. A bit easier to recognize than that last piece."

Stephen toppled backward, barely feeling it as his

head cracked on the blacktop. He heard the sound it made, but he couldn't be bothered to wonder what it was. Dimly, he thought that perhaps someone was cracking eggs on a stove.

"And these are your intestines. I can divine your future just by looking at them. Hmm. Your future does not look bright. Here, hold this."

The attacker slipped something warm and slimy into Stephen's hand, but he couldn't see what it was. The last thing Stephen was aware of was the man in black crouching low and leaning over his face. Then the stranger's terrible, cruel mouth opened wide, and Stephen Poernik died before he could scream.

CHAPTER FOUR

"You fucking asshole!"

Marsha raised her hand to smack Donny, but he grabbed her wrist and squeezed—light enough not to hurt her, but firm enough to make her stop. Her anger was evident in both her expression and tone, loud enough to be heard over the howling dogs.

"Calm down," he said, trying to soothe her.

Marsha stomped her heel down on the arch of his foot. It hurt, even through the thick leather of his boots. Yelping, Donny let go of her wrist and Marsha pulled away. Before he could react, she punched his chest. Donny shook his head, confused, and seized both of her wrists.

"Stop it, Marsha. What the hell is wrong with you?"

"Me?" Her tone changed from angry to flustered. "What's wrong with *you*? Were you really going to just leave again without saying anything? Just like before?"

Donny opened his mouth to respond, but all he could muster was a choked sigh. He released Marsha's wrists and let his arms hang limp at his sides. Then he stared down at the pavement, unable to meet her wounded, accusatory glare.

"You're right," he muttered. "I'm an asshole, and I'm sorry. I just figured that—"

"That what? You'd take off again, just like you did after graduation? That you'd mess with my head some more? Is this how it's going to be from now on, Donny? Just when I get over you and start to move on, you'll come waltzing back into town again, play me and then leave?"

"No. I told you, it's not like that."

"Well then, explain it to me."

The dogs quit howling, but neither of them noticed.

"I didn't mean to hurt you the first time. But this town, Marsha . . . I just couldn't take it. When we were growing up, I always hated it here. You know that. And you were going away to college, and I couldn't handle the idea of you going away and leaving me stuck here."

"So you decided to do it to me first? You ran off and joined the army and I'm the one who got left behind instead."

"That wasn't supposed to happen. You wanted to be a veterinarian. You were supposed to be going to Morgantown in the fall."

"And I was, until you left. And then, instead of college, I got months of therapy and shrinks and drugs. I got Prozac instead of a degree."

"I didn't mean for you to—"

"To try to kill myself? You can't even say it, can you?"

His silence was answer enough.

"Well, that's what happened, Donny. Whether you want to acknowledge it or not. I tried to kill myself."

"And I've told you before that I'm sorry about that, Marsha." He raised his head and met her eyes. "You don't know how sorry I am. I loved you."

"I loved you, too, asshole. And if you'd really fucking loved me, you'd have said good-bye. That's the worst part. Remember when we were kids, and you and Ricky Gebhart spent all day one summer gathering garter snakes and putting them in a five-gallon bucket?"

"Yeah, I remember."

"And then you assholes dumped the bucket over my head. I was so mad at you, and you followed me around for the rest of the summer, apologizing every single day. Because you cared. But after all those years growing up together—not to mention that we were supposed to be in love—you didn't care enough to say good-bye when you left."

"I wrote you letters."

Marsha paused. "When?"

"Once in boot camp. And a couple of times in Iraq. Once while we were on leave in Kuwait. And I tried calling you from Italy, but I wasn't used to the time-zone change and it was the middle of the night here. I woke your dad up."

"He never told me."

"That's because he didn't know it was me. When he answered, I couldn't say anything, so I just hung up."

"Bullshit. I don't believe you. And I definitely never got any letters."

"That's because I never mailed them."

"Why not?"

Donny shook his head. "I don't . . . It's hard to explain. I know why, but I don't know how to put it into words. It . . . things were different over there. I mean, we grew up here, and all we knew was Brinkley Springs. That was our whole world."

"You make it sound like we never went anywhere else. What about Myrtle Beach and the state fair and that class trip we took to New York City when we were juniors?"

"Yeah, but that's still America. The world is more than just America. You see that when you get out there. We're just a small part of things, and Brinkley Springs . . . hell, it ain't even on the map. All the stuff that happens here, all the trivial bullshit and drama and gossip in people's lives? That doesn't mean shit out there." He swept his hand toward the horizon.

"I don't understand," Marsha said. "What does any of this have to do with why you never mailed me the letters?"

Donny took a deep breath and leaned back against the side of his truck. "Like I said, it's hard to explain. I changed. I saw some shit that . . . well, it wasn't very pretty. I did things that I ain't proud of. We all did. It was war, you know? Everything was different, and Brinkley Springs just seemed so far away. It was like you were part of another life. You were somebody that another version of me had known—and that other me was dead. He didn't exist anymore. He was back here in Brinkley Springs, and that was a million miles away."

"You could have told me."

"I tried. I told you in every letter. But I never sent them because I figured you'd already moved on, and I didn't want to make things worse. I didn't know about the suicide attempt or any of that. Believe me, if I had, things would be different. I just figured you'd gotten over me and gone to college and met somebody and forgotten all about me. It wasn't until I came back home, after Mom got sick, that I found out the truth."

"You must have heard from other people. You must have known."

Donny shook his head. "Not really. Mom sent me e-mails and letters, but she didn't tell me what was going on with you. She never even mentioned you. I reckon she thought it would have upset me. And she'd have been right about that. And I never heard from anyone else. The church sent me Christmas cards, but that's about it."

"And now you're leaving again."

"Yeah."

Marsha wiped her eyes, smudging her mascara. Donny reached for her, but she pushed him away.

"Leave me alone. You've done enough damage already."

"Marsha . . . I didn't mean to hurt you. I loved you. Hell, I still love you."

"Well, you've got a funny way of showing it! If you love me, then why are you running away again?"

"I'm not running away. It's just this town. This place. I don't like it here. I never have. Growing up, I couldn't wait to leave. The only things that ever tied me to this place were my mom and you. And now Mom is gone."

"And I'm not enough to keep you here." Her tone was flat and resigned. "I never was."

"That's not true."

"Of course it is."

"You could come with me."

"I told you before, Donny. I can't do that. My family is here."

"You were gonna leave them for college."

"That was then. This is now. They've been here for me. You haven't. I can't just leave them now."

"Well," Donny sighed, "then I guess that's—"

Somebody screamed, a high, warbling shriek that echoed down the street and was then abruptly terminated. Both Donny and Marsha jumped, startled by the sound. They glanced around, peering into the darkness.

"What was that?" Marsha reached out and clutched his hand, squeezing hard. "*Who* was that?"

"I don't know. Stay here."

Marsha squeezed his hand tighter. "What? Where are you going?"

"To check it out. Somebody is—"

Another scream ripped through the night. This one came from a different direction. It was joined seconds later by more shrieks. A dog yelped in pain or fright. Then the streets fell silent again. Donny was reminded of the uncanny quiet that often followed a firefight.

"Jesus Christ," he whispered. "What the hell is going on? The power, the dogs and now this . . ."

"I'll call 911." Marsha pulled her cell phone out of her pocket, flipped it open and then frowned. "My battery can't be dead. I just recharged it."

Donny reached for his and shook his head. "Mine's dead, too."

"What would make that happen? The lights are out, but what would kill our cell phones?"

"An EMP."

"What's that?"

"Electromagnetic pulse. I mean, the cell-phone towers could be down, but even then, the phones would still have power. Only thing I know of that would knock them out completely is an EMP. But that's—"

A woman's voice interrupted, hollering for someone named Brandon. She sounded distraught and panicked.

"That's Mrs. Lange," Marsha whimpered. "Brandon is her little boy."

She raised one trembling hand and pointed at their house. Donny glanced in that direction just as the front door banged open. A little boy dashed outside and ran down the porch, followed by a woman.

"That's them," Marsha gasped. "What's happened?"

Donny and Marsha started toward the fleeing figures, but skidded to a halt as another figure emerged from the dark house. Neither of them recognized the man. He was tall and thin, and hidden beneath a long, dark coat and a wide-brimmed black hat. They only caught glimpses of his shadowed face as he raced after the fleeing mother and son. The man moved quickly, seeming to almost glide across the porch and down the steps. He caught up to Mrs. Lange and slashed at her legs with one hand. Donny and Marsha noticed that his fingernails were like talons. Mrs. Lange belly flopped onto the lawn. Her son paused and turned around, screaming when he saw what was happening.

"Run, Brandon," she hollered as the black figure loomed over her.

"Stay here," Donny told Marsha, and then charged across the street.

The attacker straddled Mrs. Lange's prone form and grasped her ponytail. Then he placed one foot on her back, right between her shoulder blades, and yanked up her head. Mrs. Lange wailed as her entire scalp was torn away. Brandon, Donny and Marsha howled along with her. As Donny reached the screaming boy, the dark figure grabbed Mrs. Lange's bare head with both hands and slammed it repeatedly against the ground. She jittered and shook, and then lay still. The man knelt over her body, rolled her over and then placed his mouth over hers.

"Mommy!"

Donny grasped the boy's shoulders, and Brandon screamed.

"Let me go! My mommy . . ."

"I'll help her," Donny said. "You run over there to my friend Marsha."

Brandon stared at his mother's still form with wide, terrified eyes. Mucous and tears coated his upper lip. He whispered her name one more time and then turned and fled toward Marsha.

"Hey," Donny shouted at the killer. "Don't you fucking move, motherfucker!"

The man in black raised his hand and waved, beckoning Donny forward. His lips were still pressed to Mrs. Lange's mouth. Gritting his teeth, Donny ran toward him. As he approached, the killer raised his head. Donny caught a glimpse of something white and glowing—like cigarette smoke with a light inside of it—drifting from Mrs. Lange's gaping mouth. The man seemed to suck it into himself. Then he stood up and laughed.

"Donny," Marsha screamed.

Donny halted in his tracks and risked a glance over his shoulder. Another similarly dressed figure was racing down the street toward them. The odds were no longer in his favor—especially against an opponent who could rip a woman's scalp off with his bare hands.

"Fuck this," Donny whispered. "I need a gun."

He turned and ran back to Marsha and Brandon. Behind him, he heard footsteps racing after him. He glanced to his right and was alarmed to see that the second arrival was also closing the distance between them.

"Run," Donny hollered.

Marsha grabbed Brandon's hand and they ran down the street, but then Brandon twisted out of her grip, turned and ran back toward Donny. Ducking as he fled, Donny reached out to grab the boy, but Brandon darted past him, screaming for his mother.

"Hey," Donny yelled. "Get back here!"

He spun around, pausing long enough to see that their second attacker had been distracted by a man who had emerged from his home, apparently to investigate all of the commotion. Donny knew the man's face, but not his name. The guy stood on his front lawn, dressed only in a ratty pair of boxer shorts and a white T-shirt. He clutched a shotgun in his trembling hands, but instead of raising it, he simply stood gaping as the black-clad figure bore down on him.

Marsha shrieked. Donny's attention went back to Brandon, and he cried out in despair when he saw that it was too late. The boy dangled in the air, his feet kicking ineffectively at the killer's stomach and crotch. One of the man's hands encircled the boy's throat. The other hand was buried deep in Brandon's guts. The dark man chuckled as he withdrew his fist and pulled out the child's intestines like a magician producing a stream of scarves. As the glistening strands looped around his feet, he pulled Brandon close and kissed him. Next door, the second killer had taken the shotgun from its owner and was repeatedly skewering him with the barrel.

Donny struggled with his instincts. Part of him wanted to rush to Brandon and aid the boy, even though he knew it was probably too late. Another part of him wanted to charge the boy's killer and beat him to a pulp. He knew how unrealistic this was. Both men had displayed uncanny—if not inhuman—strength and speed. He doubted his fists would do much good against such a foe. It would be smarter to take advantage of this momentary distraction and get Marsha out of here before the strangers turned their combined attention back to them. Weeping, he turned and ran.

Even after all Donny had seen and experienced overseas, abandoning Brandon and the next-door neighbor was one of the hardest things he'd ever done.

Marsha was behind the wheel of his truck. The driver's-side door hung open, and Donny saw that she was repeatedly turning the key with one hand and smacking the steering wheel with the other.

"It won't start," she cried.

"Come on. Move, damn it."

Taking her hand, he pulled her from the cab and led her across a front yard and between two houses. He heard somebody shout inside one of the homes, but he didn't stop. He guided Marsha through a backyard and onto the next street, and tried to figure out what to do next.

All around them, Brinkley Springs continued to scream.

* * *

Levi heard the first scream as he darted out the front door. He ignored it, focusing instead on the task at hand. Whatever was happening, whoever was screaming, he wouldn't be able to help them without first obtaining his tools. The Lord had put him here. That much was certain. Earlier, Brinkley Springs had seemed like nothing more than a good place to stop for the night. He had planned on leaving early the next morning, just after breakfast. Levi had been traveling to the Edgar Cayce Association for Research and Enlightenment headquarters in Virginia Beach. While their library was renowned as one of the largest collections of metaphysical studies and occult reference works in the world, there was a second collection—one not open to the general public—that Levi needed access to. Among the library's invaluable tomes was an eighteenth-century German copy of King Solomon's *Clavicula Salomonis*, which Levi needed to make a copy of for himself. His stop in Brinkley Springs had been intended as nothing more than a brief respite from the long and arduous journey. Both he and Dee had needed the rest. But there would be no rest tonight. No rest for the wicked, and no rest for God's warriors either. He'd been placed here on purpose, because only he could combat the threat that the town now faced. This was what he did. This was his calling, his birthright and, quite often, his curse.

Back home in Marietta, Levi's neighbors thought that the nice Amish man who lived in the small one-story house next door was a woodworker—and they were partially right. Half of the two-car garage at the rear of his property had been converted into a wood shop (the other half was a stable for Dee). During the week, he spent his time in the wood shop making various goods—coat and spoon racks, chairs, tables, dressers, plaques, lawn ornaments and other knick-knacks. Each Saturday, he'd load the items into the back of his buggy and haul them to the local antiques market. It was an honest, decent living and paid for his rent, groceries, utilities and feed for Dee and his dog, Crowley.

But what his neighbors didn't know was that Levi also had another, more secret vocation. He worked powwow, as had his father and his father before him. Usually, he was sought out for medical treatments. His patients were mostly drawn from three groups: the elderly (who remembered the old ways), the poor (who didn't have health insurance or couldn't afford to see a doctor or go to the hospital), and people who'd forsaken the mainstream medical establishment in search of a more holistic approach. Patients came to Levi seeking treatments for a wide variety of ailments and maladies. He dealt with everything from the common cold to arthritis. Occasionally, he was called upon for more serious matters—stopping bleeding or mending a broken bone.

But powwow went beyond medicine. It was a magical discipline just like any other, and once in a while, Levi was charged with doing more than helping the sick or curing livestock. Once in a while, the threats he faced were supernatural, rather than biological, in origin. Levi knew that tonight would be one of those times.

More screams rang out as Levi reached the buggy and climbed up into the back. His weight made the buggy shift, rocking the suspension. Even though the wheels were chocked, the axles groaned slightly. The buggy's floor was as messy as that of any automobile. Road maps, emergency flares, a flashlight, assorted wrenches and screwdrivers, a pack of tissues and empty fast-food cartons were strewn about haphazardly. He'd meant to clean it out in the morning. Now he had more pressing concerns.

Levi crawled forward through the debris on his hands and knees, careful to keep his head down and out of sight as much as possible. The night had grown dangerous. As if to punctuate this, a gunshot echoed through the night. Judging by the sound, the shooter was only a few blocks away. If the echo was any indication, the weapon was a large-caliber rifle rather than a handgun. He listened carefully, but heard no police sirens—just more screams and shrieks.

A man peeked out of a house across the street and then ducked back inside, slamming the door behind him. As Levi reached the rear of the buggy, he heard footsteps coming toward him. He turned around and saw two men, each carrying a hunting rifle, running his way. They appeared nervous and unsure of where to go. He raised a hand in greeting and they stopped.

"You know what's going on?" one demanded.

Levi shook his head. "No, but it sounds bad, whatever it is. Perhaps you gentlemen would be safer inside, with your families."

The second man scoffed, looking at Levi as if he'd just offered them a rabid dog.

"Screw that noise," he said. "I reckon the best thing we can do for our families is to find out what the hell's going on. First the power goes out. Then all the damn dogs start acting crazy. Making a fuss. Now everybody's screaming and shooting."

"I bet it's the Al-Qaeda," muttered the first. "Reckon they could be going after Herb Causlin's beef farm."

"You think so, Marlon?"

"Yeah. I figure they're hitting America's food supply. Herb's cattle would be a good place to start."

"That's true." The second man adjusted his grip on the rifle. "Reckon you could be right."

"I really don't think it's Al-Qaeda," Levi said. "And if it was, why would they go after a small beef farm in West Virginia?"

The men stared at him, frowning. One spat a brown stream of tobacco juice onto the street. The other let his eyes travel up and down, taking in Levi's garb.

"You're a weird fucker, aren't you?"

Levi smiled. "You have no idea."

"Haven't seen you around town before, come to think of it. What's your name, fella?"

"You may call me Levi Stoltzfus. And you're right, I'm not from around here. I was passing through on my way to Virginia Beach. You should be glad that providence brought me here."

"Provi-what? That place in Rhode Island?"

The second man nudged his friend in the ribs as another, more distant gunshot echoed through the streets. "Come on, Marlon. Let's see what's doing."

The two ran off without another word. Levi watched them go. When they were out of sight and the street was empty again, he pulled a dirty canvas tarp off a long wooden box at the back of the buggy. He laid the tarp aside and wiped his hands on his pants. The box was padlocked and covered with powwow charms to protect its contents from thieves, witchcraft and the elements. The sigils were painted onto the wood, and in some cases, carved deep into the surface. There were holy symbols and complex hex signs, as well as words of power. Levi ran his fingers over the two most dominant etchings.

I.
N. I. R.
I.
SANCTUS SPIRITUS
I.
N. I. R.
I.

SATOR
AREPO
TENET
OPERA
ROTAS

He'd carved them himself, just as his father had taught him, carefully inscribing the words from *The Long Lost Friend*—the main powwow grimoire—as well as words, charms and sigils from other occult tomes he owned that dealt with other magical disciplines. Most of the books had been passed down to him from his father, but since then, Levi had gained access to books that his father would have frowned upon. As he often did during times like this, Levi wondered what his father thought of him now, as he looked down on Levi from the other side. Was he proud of his son? Did he approve? Did he understand that sometimes you had to use the enemy's methods and learn the enemy's ways if you were to defeat them? Or like the rest of Levi's people, did his father disapprove even in death of how Levi used his talents?

There was no way of knowing, of course. It would remain a mystery until the day when Levi saw him again. The day when the Lord called him home. Sometimes, Levi prayed for that moment. Yearned for it. But he feared it, too. Feared what the Lord's answer might be when he finally stood before Him in judgment.

"Your will be done," he whispered. "That's what it's all about, right, Lord? Your will?"

Another scream pulled him from his thoughts. Levi shivered. The night air was growing chilly and damp. He reached into his pocket, produced a key ring and removed the padlock. Then he opened the box and, despite the growing chaos around him, sighed in a brief moment of contentment. The interior of the box smelled of kerosene and sawdust and dirt. They were comforting smells. They spoke to Levi of hard work and effort and honesty. Many people had boxes like this on the backs of their buggies or in the beds of their pickup trucks. Usually, they held tools of some kind. Chainsaws, shovels, screwdrivers, wrenches, hammers, spare engine parts, oil or gasoline cans. Levi's box held tools, as well, but they were different tools, the ones of *his* trade.

A rapid volley of gunshots erupted. Levi could tell from the sound that it was two different weapons—a rifle and a handgun. They were far enough away to not immediately concern him, but close enough to tell him that whatever was happening was coming closer.

He reached into the box and sifted through the contents. Normally, a duct-tape-wrapped bundle containing a dried mixture of wormwood, salt, gith, five-finger weed and asafedita—a charm against livestock theft—was at the top of the box, to protect Dee during those times when Levi left the buggy unattended. He'd had her since she was a foal, and the horse—along with his dog—was Levi's closest companion. She was descended from an old line, and her family had aided his family for a very long time. Her safety was of paramount importance to him. Since she was stabled beyond the town's outskirts, he'd tied the bundle around her bridle. No harm could befall the horse as long as the bundle remained with her. He felt satisfied that Dee would be safe. He wished that he could say the same for the people of Brinkley Springs.

He reached into his pocket and pulled out his slim, battered copy of *The Long Lost Friend*. Written on the cover in tiny, faded gold lettering was the following:

The Long Lost Friend
A Collection
of
Mysterious & Invaluable
Arts & Remedies
For
Man As Well As Animals

With Many Proofs
Of their virtue and efficacy in healing diseases and
defeating spirits, the greater part of which was never
published until they appeared in print for the first
time in the U.S. in the Year of Our Lord 1820.
By
John George Hohman
I N R I

Just holding the volume in his hand made him
feel better. This was his primary weapon—an unabridged edition, unlike the public-domain versions
one could find online. Those were watered down
and edited. This was the real thing.

Smiling, Levi returned the book to his pocket and
then focused his attention on the box. He sorted
through the books and trinkets. It was an odd assort-
ment. The first item was an e-book reader loaded
with the unabridged versions of Frazer's *The Golden
Bough*, Francis Barrett's *The Magus* and Parkes's
Fourth Book of Agrippa, as well as the collected works
of John Dee and Aleister Crowley and a scattering of
scanned pages from the dreaded *Necronomicon* and
other esoteric tomes. Also in the box were a knife,
wooden matches, a cigarette lighter with a cross em-
blazoned on its side, a small copper bowl, plastic
freezer bags filled with various dried plants and
roots, a peanut-butter jar filled with desiccated locust
shells, a black leather bag filled with different stones
and gems, a vial of dirt, a second vial filled with water, a third filled with oil, a small compass, a mummified hand wrapped in cloth, pendants and other
assorted jewelry, a lock of hair tied together with red

string, fingernail clippings held together with a strip of masking tape, flint arrowheads, baby-food jars filled with various powders and debris, his Rods of Transvection and Divining and many other items. There was also a black cloth vest with many deep pockets.

He put on the vest. The garment was snug around his middle, but it would suffice. He selected the compass, a small bundle of dried sage, another of dried rose petals, a canister of paprika, a second filled with salt, the vials of oil and water, the cigarette lighter and the knife, and stuffed them into his vest and pants pockets. His pants bulged around his thighs when he was finished, and he had to tighten his belt in order to keep his pants from falling down around his ankles. Satisfied, Levi quickly shut and sealed the box. The padlock snapped into place with a sound of finality.

The buggy's axle groaned again as he hopped back down. Levi stood in the street and glanced up at the moon. It was bright and full and cold. The breeze brushed his face and ruffled his hair. Bowing his head, Levi murmured a prayer.

"The cross of Christ be with me. The cross of Christ overcomes all water and every fire. The cross of Christ overcomes all weapons. The cross of Christ is a perfect sign and blessing to my soul. Now I pray that the holy corpse of Christ bless me against all evil things, words and works."

He hoped that the prayer and the items in his pockets would be enough to face whatever evil had been visited upon the town. Ideally, he would have fasted for several days before undertaking this task, but these were far from the ideal circumstances. The screams grew louder and more numerous. Armed against whatever might be causing them, Levi waded into the night, ready to do battle.

A ᴄᴇᴍᴇᴛᴇʀʏ ᴏꜰ ᴄʀᴏᴡꜱ   81

lay down on the floor, then the light continued. The creature grew bolder, and came ____ closer. A squeak or two over ____ her feet in ____ fur, over the little

CHAPTER FIVE

Trish Chambers danced around in her darkened living room, singing ELO's "Shine a Little Love" in a breathless falsetto. Her treadmill had died when the power went out, and her iPod had stopped working, too, but she wasn't going to let that stop her from getting into shape. She was dressed in a faded gray T-shirt and a pair of black loose-fitting sweatpants. The sweats hadn't always been so baggy, and it was their distinct lack of snugness that kept her going, no matter how exhausted from her exercise routine or disillusioned with her diet she became. Two months of working out every night—of running on the treadmill or dancing along with Richard Simmons and sweating to the oldies—had delivered results. All she had to do was keep going, and she did. Electrical outage be damned. She was divorced, thirty-two and desperate to find someone again.

Not that Brinkley Springs offered her many choices when it came to finding someone to date. Trish worked at the bank in Lewisburg, and the choices there weren't much better. All of the male employees were either married or gay. A friend of hers had suggested she try one of the online dating Web sites, but Trish hadn't quite worked up the nerve yet. She decided to wait until she was happy with her body. After all, she'd spent the last twelve years of her life trying to make someone else happy—her ex-husband, Darryl. Now it was time to focus on herself. If she was happy with who she was, then it would be easier to find someone else who'd be happy with her. A man like she'd always dreamed of. Someone who would take her breath away.

She switched from ELO to Garth Brooks's "Friends in Low Places," singing out the vocals with an exaggerated drawl, and did a series of jumping jacks. The knickknacks on the shelves trembled and the ceiling fan swayed back and forth, but Trish didn't care. She pressed herself for another three minutes and didn't stop until she heard the gunshot.

Gunfire was a normal sound in Brinkley Springs. Lots of people hunted in the mountains around town, or engaged in a little backyard target shooting from time to time. On the Fourth of July, many residents often celebrated by firing their guns into the air. Normally, the sound of gunshots was nothing to be concerned about. Trish was just about to start exercising again when she realized that the gunfire was accompanied by multiple screams.

"What in the world?"

Breathing hard from the past half hour's exertion, she padded to the front door and looked out the window. The streets were dark, and she couldn't see anything. More shots echoed down the streets, followed by more cries of alarm. Trish was just about to open the door and peek outside when she heard glass breaking in her bedroom. Her hand fluttered to her chest and her breath caught in her throat.

More glass tinkled, as if falling to the floor. Then she felt a slight breeze drift through the house. Someone had broken in.

She reached for the phone, picked it up and dialed 911. Then she brought the receiver to her ear. There was only silence. No emergency operator. No ringing. Not even a dial tone. Whimpering softly, she placed the phone back in its cradle and tiptoed toward the kitchen. Her cell phone was lying on the counter. If she could reach it in time . . .

Laughter drifted from her bedroom, cold and malicious and definitely male. Her heart rate, already rapid from her exercise routine, increased.

Trish kept a pistol in the house, a Ruger .22 semiauto. She'd bought it at the gun store on Chestnut Avenue after she and Darryl split up because she'd been nervous being alone in the house at night. She kept it loaded. ("No sense having an unloaded gun in the house," her daddy had always said.) The weapon was in the top drawer of her bedroom nightstand— right next to the window the intruder had gained entry through, judging by the sound.

Fat lot of good that does me.

She wondered if the intruder could be Darryl. She wouldn't have thought so. He'd been pretty satisfied with the divorce, because it meant he could cat around at the bars and elsewhere without fear of getting caught. But if he'd been drinking, she wouldn't put it past him. Maybe her lawyer had been right. Maybe she should have gotten a restraining order.

Trish reached the end of the living room and was just about to step into the kitchen, when her bedroom door banged open at the far end of the hall and a figure dressed entirely in black leaped out into the hallway and rushed toward her. Trish backed away, screaming, aware that other people were shrieking right outside her house. She collided with an end table, sending a lamp her aunt had bought her as a wedding present crashing to the floor. Then the dark figure was upon her. He stank like something dead. The last thing Trish noticed was how big the man's mouth was. Darkness engulfed her. She opened her mouth to scream again, and her attacker stifled her cries with a savage, forceful kiss that suffocated her. She was aware that he was laughing as he did it. His body shook and jiggled against hers as he wrapped both arms around her and squeezed.

Trish heard her spine snap as he took her breath away.

Clutching a 12-gauge shotgun, Paul Crowley stood in his backyard and squinted, peering into the darkness. The air was chilly, and Paul shivered as the breeze rushed over him. He was clad in a dirty pair of jeans and a loose-fitting, faded John Deere T-shirt with mustard stains on it. The stains were fresh—leftovers from his dinner, which he'd eaten in front of the television again, sitting in the recliner and watching a nature program on PBS.

Paul didn't care much for PBS's liberal bias, but he enjoyed shows about wildlife and nature, and since he didn't have cable or satellite, PBS was his only option. Tonight's program had been about crows. Paul didn't have much use for the damned things. Nasty little creatures. They carried the West Nile virus and other diseases. In the spring, they rooted through his garden and ate up all the seeds he'd planted. In the fall and winter, they fluttered around in the woods, making a fuss and alerting wild game to his presence. Paul had missed shots at plenty of deer and wild turkeys over the years thanks to motor-mouthed, obnoxious crows. When he'd been a boy, Paul's daddy had told him that a group of crows could kill and eat a newborn lamb. Maybe that was why a group of crows was called a murder. He'd been surprised to learn from the program that crows could imitate a human's voice. Apparently, they were highly intelligent and cunning. Paul didn't care. Just because they were smart didn't mean they were any less of a nuisance.

He'd fallen asleep in the recliner during a segment about scientists training crows to pick up trash, and had slept until the sound of his dogs' barking woke him, causing Paul to jerk upright and almost tumble out of the chair. That might have been bad. He certainly wasn't old yet—at least, not what he considered old—but living alone, had he broken a leg or hip or knocked himself out, there'd have been no one to find him.

Since his retirement seven years earlier, Paul had spent every day out in the woods with his six bear dogs. They were mutts—crossbreed mixes of black and tans, beagles, German shepherds and Karelians, mostly. He loved the dogs and they loved and respected him. Each day, except on Christmas, Thanksgiving and Sundays, Paul got up at the crack of dawn, loaded the dogs into his pickup truck and headed up into the mountains. During bear season, he hunted. When black bears weren't in season, he allowed the dogs to track and run them. They did this all day long, usually returning home just before sundown. Paul enjoyed it, and all of the walking across ridges and hills kept him in great shape. It kept the dogs healthy, too. Each one was equipped with a radio collar and GPS device so he could track them if they got lost in the mountains—which they often did, especially if a mother bear or her cubs gave them a long chase.

He knew the dogs better than he knew most people. He'd come to recognize the subtle changes in their barks and what the differences in tone meant, and that was how he knew upon waking that the dogs were upset by something. He'd stood there in the living room, yawning and blinking and wondering how long the power had been out, and realized that the dogs weren't just distressed. They were absolutely terrified.

Wondering what had gotten them so riled up, Paul had hurried through his darkened home, grabbed the 12-gauge and rushed outside just as the dogs fell quiet. He checked the pen and found them huddling together at the back, trembling and frightened, their pink tongues lolling as they panted. He whispered soothing words to them and then crept around the property. He couldn't find anything amiss. There were no signs of a trespasser—no footprints in the wet grass or evidence indicating someone had tried to break into the house. He was just about to go inside when the disturbance erupted again. This time, instead of the dogs howling in fright, it was his fellow townspeople. The cries and screams seemed to be coming from all four directions at once. An occasional gunshot peppered the commotion. Curiously, there were no sounds of car engines or screeching tires or sirens.

"I don't like this," Paul told the cowering dogs. "I don't like this one bit. Sounds like somebody's done snapped and gone on a killing spree, like you see on the news. You boys stay here. I'll go have a look."

He tiptoed around to the front of the house and glanced both ways. As far as he could tell, the electrical outage wasn't confined to his street or block. It seemed to have affected the entire town. The yells and other noises seemed distant, but as he stood there listening, they slowly began to draw closer.

Paul ran back into the house, found his cell phone and started to dial 911, only to discover that the phone wasn't working. He stared at the blank, lifeless screen and then tossed it onto the counter in frustration. He hurried into the living room and went to the floor-to-ceiling bookshelves he'd built into one wall. They were lined with paperback and hardcover books—western novels by Ray Slater, Ed Gorman, Al Sarrantonio, Zane Grey and Louis L'Amour, history books about Vietnam, World Wars I and II, and the Korean Conflict, and nature books, including a massive, two-volume field guide to North American fish and game. In between the books were framed pictures of his wife (taken away from him by pancreatic cancer two months before his retirement) and their son and daughter-in-law (all grown now and living on the West Coast). A few dusty knickknacks occupied other empty spaces. On top of the shelf was a radio that played extreme weather alerts for Brinkley Springs from the National Weather Service, bulletins from the Department of Homeland Security and FEMA and announcements from local law-enforcement and emergency-response crews. He'd bought it on sale at the Radio Shack in Beckley several years before, and it had proven invaluable time and time again, especially during the winter months. One of Paul's favorite features was the battery backup, which kept the radio functioning during a power outage.

Except it wasn't working now. Like the cell phone, the emergency radio sat lifeless.

"Well, if that don't beat all. Cheap piece of Chinese junk. Don't nothing work anymore the way things used to."

Muttering to himself, Paul stalked back out of the house as the noises outside grew louder. Someone ran down the sidewalk as the screen door slammed shut behind him, but Paul couldn't see who it was. He wondered if they were running to something or away from something. He noticed that the dogs were still cowering in their kennel. Hefting the shotgun, he approached it again. Being in their proximity made him feel more assured.

"That you, Paul?"

Startled, he jumped at the voice, nearly dropping the 12-gauge before he recognized the speaker as Gus Pheasant, who lived next door. Gus owned the local garage, along with his brother, Greg. Although both men were twenty years younger than Paul, he liked them very much and often got together with them in the evenings. Greg was divorced and Gus had never married, so they had their bachelorhood in common. They'd often invited Axel Perry—another widower—to join them, but the old man never did. Paul got the impression that Axel liked to be alone. It was a shame. He didn't know what he was missing. Although he would have never said it aloud, Paul found that spending time with them made his own evenings a little less lonely. He liked the gruff companionship, liked playing cards and drinking a few beers and arguing sports and politics and women.

"Yeah," he called, "it's me, Gus. What in the hell is going on?"

"I don't rightly know. Sounds like World War Three's done started though, don't it?"

Gus stepped out of the shadows. He looked shaken. His complexion was pale and his eyes were wide and frightened. His hair stuck up askew, and his pajamas were soaked with sweat and stuck to his body, including his prodigious beer gut. Paul's gaze settled on Gus's feet. The man wore a pair of fuzzy Spider-Man slippers. The costumed character's big red head adorned the toe of each and seemed to stare up at Paul.

"Gus, what in the world are you wearing?"

The mechanic glanced down at his feet and then shrugged, clearly embarrassed.

"Oh, shoot. Forgot I had those on. I rushed out of the house so quick . . ."

"What are they?"

"Bedroom slippers."

"I can see that. But they seem a little—"

"I didn't buy them," Gus interrupted. "Lacey Rogers bought them for me."

"Lacey Rogers is eight years old, Gus."

"I know that. Do you really think these are the type of slippers an adult would buy for me?"

"Well, what's Lacey Rogers doing buying you a present, anyway? That don't seem right."

"Remember last year when they did the Secret Santa thing at church?"

Paul nodded. Each member of the congregation had pulled a slip of paper out of the offering plate. Written on the slip was the name of a fellow parishioner. They then purchased a gift—under twenty dollars—for that person. Paul's Secret Santa had been Jean Sullivan, who'd bought him two pairs of wool socks for hunting.

"Lacey pulled my name," Gus explained. "Her parents said she picked these out herself down at the Wal-Mart. I couldn't very well return them, now could I?"

"No, I don't guess so. That would have broke her little heart."

"Exactly. And I have to say, they do keep my feet warm at night."

"Well, you look like a damned fool." Paul's voice was gruff, but his grin nearly split his face in half.

"Your phone working?" Gus asked, clearly anxious to change the subject.

Paul shook his head. "Nope. Ain't nothing working. My cell phone and emergency radio are dead, too. The cell I can understand. Service ain't never been that reliable around here. But the radio should still be working. It's got a battery backup. I don't understand why it would quit like that."

"Same here," Gus confirmed. "It ain't just your radio. Everything in my place is dead. It's like something fried all of the electronics. Hell, I couldn't even get my damned flashlight to work. How's that for weird?"

"It's something, alright."

"What do you suppose it means?"

"I don't rightly know," Paul said, "but whatever it is, it ain't good."

Another gunshot echoed across town, followed by an explosion.

"Holy mother of God," Paul said, jumping. "What was that?"

"I don't know. All I know is it's been a weird day and it just keeps getting stranger."

"How do you mean?"

Gus paused. "Well, first there was this Amish fella come riding into town on a horse and buggy. Real pretty horse. Very gentle, but very big. She'd be a prize mare. He's got her tied up down by the river tonight. He asked me and Greg if there was a hotel in town and we sent him over to Esther's place."

"Amish?" Paul grunted. He'd known a few Brethren in his life—Amish, Mennonites and Moldavians. All of them had been good people. Hard workers. Very handy with a hammer and a saw. "I don't see how that would be connected to what's happing now, though."

"I don't reckon it is, but you never know. Maybe it's—"

Paul paused as a man ran by them, weaving around parked cars on the street and tottering back and forth. Paul recognized him as one of the cashiers at the local convenience store, but he didn't know the man's name. At first, Paul assumed the guy must be drunk, but then he noticed the man's torn trouser leg and the blood on his calf, and realized he was injured.

"Hey," Gus called, apparently not knowing the cashier's name either. "You okay, fella? What's going on?"

The fleeing man didn't stop. He shuffled past them, not even bothering to look in their direction as he answered. "Dark men . . . they're going house to house . . . killing folks. Killing everybody. Even the pets."

Paul took a step forward. "What do you mean?"

"No time! If you're smart, you'll run now. I mean it. They're killing everyone."

"Who?"

"The dark men. Run!"

"What was that explosion?" Paul asked.

"Someone shot the propane tank behind the fire hall. Now get going, if you know what's good for you. I ain't waiting around for the dark men."

"Hey! Just wait a goddamn minute, fella. We don't understand what you're talking about."

Without another word, the man fled on, trailing dark spots of blood on the asphalt. Gus and Paul looked at each other.

"Dark men?" Gus arched one eyebrow. "What do you suppose he meant by that?"

"I don't know. Black folks, maybe?"

Gus shook his head. "No. I've talked to him plenty of times down at the shop. He's brought his car in to be serviced, though I can't remember his name. He seemed like a nice enough guy. Never struck me as a racist."

"Just because a fella ain't telling nigger jokes or wearing a Klan robe don't mean they're not racist. You can never tell."

"I still don't buy it," Gus said. "And besides, even if he was racist, it still doesn't make any sense. Why would a bunch of black folks want to shoot up Brinkley Springs?"

"Not saying they are. I'm just trying to figure out what he meant. He said dark men."

"Well, if we stand out here long enough, I reckon we're liable to find out the hard way what he meant."

Paul nodded. "I suspect you're right. Not sure what to do, though. Don't hear any sirens or anything. Just screaming."

They paused, listening. Gus shuddered.

"I hope my brother is okay."

"Where is Greg, anyway?" Paul asked him.

"At home sleeping, I guess. Wish I could call him and find out."

Paul glanced at his cowering dogs and then out into the street. The breeze shifted, bringing with it the unmistakable smell of smoke. It made his eyes water. He hesitated, weighing his options. On the one hand, he should stay here and look after the dogs and his belongings. The fleeing cashier had mentioned that pets were being killed. But on the other hand, it sounded like there were a lot of people out there who needed help. People that he knew. Some that he'd known his whole life. It didn't seem right to hunker down here while they were in trouble. He turned back to Gus.

"Want to go check on your brother?"

"I'd like to. Do you think it's safe?"

"No. But it beats standing around here waiting for whatever is happening to find its way to us. We'll make sure he's okay. Then I'll come back here and watch over my dogs."

Nodding, Gus squared his shoulder and straightened up. "Sure. Just let me change my shoes."

"Yeah," Paul replied, glancing back down at the bedroom slippers. "I reckon you might want to do that first. Might want to put some clothes on over those pajamas, too. And Gus?"

"What?"

"Might be best if you bring along a gun."

"I reckon you're right."

Artie Prater slept, which was exactly what he'd been afraid of. His wife of five years, Laura, was out of town. She worked for the bank in Roncefort, and once a year, all of the bank's employees went on a mandatory weeklong retreat. This year, they were in Utah, enjoying steak dinners and attending seminars about things like team-building and synergy. Artie liked to tease Laura about these things, but only because he was secretly jealous. He'd been unable to find work for over a year, and it bothered him that he couldn't provide for his wife or their new son, Artie Junior. The upside was that while she was at work every day, he'd been able to stay home and take care of Little Artie. Laura reciprocated by getting up with the baby at night, which relieved Artie to no end.

Artie had always been a deep sleeper. His mother had once said that he could sleep through a nuclear war, and that wasn't far from the truth. He'd slept through 9/11, waking up in his college dorm room later that night and wondering why everyone was staring at the television and crying. Since becoming a father, Artie's biggest fear was that the baby would wake up crying, perhaps hungry or in need of a diaper change or shaking from a nightmare, and he'd sleep through it. That's why he was grateful when Laura was there to get up with Artie Junior at night, and that's why he dreaded these rare times when she wasn't home.

They had a baby monitor in the house. A small

camera was mounted above Little Artie's crib. It broadcast a signal to the monitor, which was plugged into the bedroom's television. With Laura out of town, Artie had turned the volume on the television all the way up, filling the room with white noise and the soft sounds of his son's breathing. Then, bathed in the glow from the screen, he'd sat back in bed with his laptop and played a video game. It was early—too early to sleep—but Little Artie had been tired and cranky, and Artie knew from experience that he should rest when the baby rested. He promised himself that if and when he got tired of the game, he'd sleep lightly.

Except that he hadn't. He'd fallen asleep playing the game, barely having the presence of mind to sit the laptop aside before passing out. He slept through the power outage, and did not wake when both the laptop and the television shut off, as well as the baby monitor. He slept through the howling dogs and the terrified screams and the numerous gunshots. He slept through the explosion. He slept as his neighbors were murdered in their homes and out on the street. He slept, drooling on his pillow and snoring softly as two shadowy figures entered his home. He slept, unaware that in Artie Junior's nursery, a large black crow had perched on the edge of his son's crib. He slept as the crow changed shape. He remained asleep as the bedroom door opened and a shadow fell across him, as well.

He didn't wake up until the baby screamed, and by then it was too late.

The last thing he saw was the figure in the room with him. The baby's screams turned to high-pitched, terrified shrieks. Artie bolted upright and flung the sheets off his legs, but before he could get out of bed, the intruder rushed to the bedside and loomed over him. The man's face was concealed in darkness. It shoved his chest with one cold hand and forced him back down on the bed. In the nursery, the baby's screams abruptly ceased.

"W-who . . . ?"

"Scream," the shadow told Artie. "It's better when you scream."

The pounding on Axel's door grew louder and more insistent. The chain lock rattled and the door shook in its frame. Candlelight flickered, casting strange shapes on the walls. The pounding came again. Gripping his walking stick like a club, Axel tiptoed into the living room and peeked through the curtains. Jean Sullivan stood on his porch, holding Bobby in one arm and beating on the door with her fist. Breathing a sigh of relief, Axel lowered the stick and hurried to the door. He fumbled with the locks as Jean hammered again.

"Mr. Perry? Axel? It's Jean from next door. Please let us in!"

She sounded frantic. Releasing the chain from its hasp, Axel turned the knob and yanked the door open.

"What's wrong?" he asked. "What is it?"

Jean stumbled into the house and slammed the door shut behind her. Bobby held tight, his arms and legs wrapped around his mother. The boy looked terrified. Axel stared at them both in concern.

"What is it?" he asked again.

"Didn't you hear me knocking? Or all the noise outside?"

"No," he admitted. "I don't hear so good these days. I came inside after the dogs started barking. Was going to fix myself a bite to eat, but with the power out, I decided to just go to sleep instead. I was laying down when I finally heard you. I'm sorry."

"It's okay." Jean turned around and locked the door behind her.

"Did you say there's trouble? What kind of trouble?"

"I don't know." She turned back to him. "People screaming and shouting. Gunshots. Something exploded on the other side of town. I think there are a couple of fires, too."

Axel gaped. "Good Lord . . ."

"Bobby, I need to put you down, sweetie. Mommy's arms need a break."

Shaking his head, the boy buried his face in her hair and clung tighter.

"Bobby . . ."

"No, Mommy. Bad things are out there."

"We're safe now. Mr. Perry won't let anything happen to us."

"Your mother's right," Axel said, not understanding any of this, but trying to sound brave for the boy. "Whatever's going on, it can't get you in here."

Bobby peered doubtfully at the old man from between his mother's hair.

Grinning, Axel raised the walking stick. "If it does, I'll whack it with this."

"That's just an old stick."

"Oh no, it's much more than an old stick. You see, this walking stick has magic."

"No it doesn't."

"Bobby," Jean chided, "be polite."

"But, Mommy, there's no such thing as magic. It's

just make-believe, like in the cartoons and Harry Potter."

Axel winked at the boy. "Magic is more than just stories, Bobby. Where do you think the lady who made up those Harry Potter books got the idea from? I reckon magic has been around as long as human beings have, and that's a long, long time."

He paused. Axel couldn't be sure, but he thought he heard somebody screaming outside. He wondered if he should go out and check, but then decided that Jean and Bobby were his primary responsibility now.

"So what can it do?" Bobby asked, pointing at the walking stick.

"I cut this branch off a magic tree a long, long time ago when I was just a little older than you. We lived way down in a hollow on the other side of Frankford, back near where the quarry is today. There was a cave at the far end of the hollow—more of a sinkhole, really. My daddy filled it up over the years because our cows kept falling into it. But next to the hole was a big old willow tree, just as gnarled and ugly as I am now. The tree's name—"

"Trees don't have names, Mr. Perry."

Jean frowned. "Bobby, manners!"

The boy stuck his bottom lip out and pouted. "But I called him mister."

"It's okay," Axel soothed. "Everything has a name, Bobby. Not just people, but animals and trees and even rocks. God gives everything a secret name. This old willow tree's name was Mrs. Chickbaum."

"That's a funny name."

"Aye, I reckon it is. But that was what my mother said its name was, and she knew about these things."

"Was your mommy magic?"

Axel was surprised to find himself tearing up as he answered. "Yeah, she was. My mommy was magic. And so was old Mrs. Chickbaum. Not in a way that you'd probably understand. The tree couldn't fly or turn people into salamanders. But you felt better in its shade. You rested easy underneath its branches. There was a little spring to the left of her trunk, and that water was just about the best I've ever tasted—clear and fresh and ice cold."

"So Mrs. Chickenbaum made things better?"

"That's right. Nothing bad happened around her. And this walking stick came from Mrs. Chickbaum and I've had it ever since, and it's always brought me nothing but good luck, for the most part. So I reckon we'll be safe enough here. Okay?"

Bobby smiled, and then slowly relaxed. "Okay, Mr. Perry."

Jean lowered him to the floor and sighed. Axel heard her back crack and her joints pop as she straightened up again.

"He's not as light as he used to be," she said, stretching.

"No," Axel agreed. "He's growing quick. Gonna be a fine boy, Jean. You do good with him."

"Thank you, Axel. You're good with kids."

He shrugged, blushing. She smiled then, and Axel saw some of the fear ease from her face. He motioned toward the couch.

"Why don't you two sit down?"

"We'd better not," Jean said, glancing back to the door. "It's really bad out there."

"And you don't know any more than what you told me?"

She shook her head. "Not really. But with the

power and the phones out, and the dogs, and now all this screaming and such—I'm scared."

"Well, I don't suppose we should be standing around here talking about it in the living room. I reckon we're sort of exposed up here. Maybe we should head down into my basement for a while? I hunker down there when there's a tornado warning or a really bad storm. We'll be safe enough. It's not finished—not much on the eyes. Just a concrete floor and cement block walls, but it's dry. I've got a kerosene heater I can turn on to keep us warm. And the stairs are the only way in or out, so we'll have plenty of warning if somebody breaks in or anything."

"That's a good idea."

"I'll get a few bottles of water and such from the kitchen. Can you help me carry it? This danged arthritis makes it harder for me to do things like that these days."

"Sure," Jean said, and then turned to her son. "Bobby, come on. We're going downstairs with Mr. Perry."

The boy was standing in front of the mantel, staring up at a picture of Axel and Diane in happier days.

"Who is that?" he asked, pointing at the picture.

"That's my wife," Axel explained. "Mrs. Perry."

"How come she doesn't live here with you?"

Jean hissed. Her hand fluttered to her mouth. "Bobby . . ."

"It's okay," Axel said. He knelt in front of the boy. His knees groaned at the effort. "Mrs. Perry passed on some time ago."

"Do you miss her?"

"Oh, yes. Not a day goes by that I don't. She was magic, too, you know. A different kind of magic, maybe. Not the type like that old willow tree, but magic all the same."

"How?"

"She made my life better just for being in it."

He made his way to the kitchen and opened the refrigerator. Jean and Bobby followed along behind him. Axel was dismayed to notice that the appliance was already warming inside. He pulled out a few bottles of water and three apples, and then quickly shut the door again. Jean took some of the items from him and handed one of each to her son.

"I'm not so scared anymore," Bobby said.

Jean patted his head with one free hand and ruffled his hair. "Good. See? I told you Mr. Perry would know what to do."

"Yeah."

Somebody screamed in Axel's front yard. Jean heard it first, then Axel. It was a woman, judging by the sound, though they couldn't be sure. The sound warbled without pause and then ceased abruptly.

"I reckon we'd better head downstairs," Axel whispered. "And we should probably be quiet from this point on. I'll snuff the candles out up here and re-light them once we're in the basement."

He beckoned for them to follow him and then tiptoed to the basement door. He juggled his walking stick and the items in his hand, and finally managed to open the door. The staircase and the handrail both disappeared into blackness halfway down. Cold air drifted up from below. Axel wondered if he'd left one of the cellar windows open.

"Careful now." He said it so quietly that Jean and

Bobby both had to lean forward to hear him. Then he started forward, using his walking stick to guide him in the dark. Bobby followed along close behind him, timidly holding onto Axel's pants leg with one hand. Jean brought up the rear and shut the door behind them.

The darkness became absolute.

Ron Branson and Joe Dickie hid behind the post office, wondering what to do. The evening had started out like normal. The two of them had been polishing off a case of Golden Monkey Ale, playing cards and talking about various women in town who they'd never have a chance to sleep with. Then the power had gone out and the shouts and screams had started, followed by gunfire and explosions. They'd gone outside to see what all the fuss was about and had ended up walking through the neighborhood in dazed, abject horror. Their pleasant, warming buzzes had evaporated, leaving them cold and sweaty. Both men shivered, more from fear than the night air. They clung to one another and listened to the town dying.

"Wish I owned a gun," Joe whispered. "I'm not allowed to on account of my prick parole officer. He comes around and checks my place like clockwork."

Ron nodded. "We should get some. One for each of us. Who do we know that owns a gun?"

"Are you serious? This is America. Ninety percent of the fucking town has a gun. Listen. That ain't firecrackers we're hearing."

"But what are they shooting at? I don't see anything except dead folks."

"Maybe they're shooting each other," Joe suggested.

"Maybe somebody put something in the water that made everyone go crazy."

"That don't make sense. Half the people in town are on well water. And did you see Vern Southard lying back there? He wasn't shot. It looked like something had tore him apart. His face and arms were ripped plumb off."

Joe was about to respond when something large and black swooped down out of the night sky and collided with his face. With some disbelief, he saw that it was a crow. He caught a whiff of a bad odor, like spoiled milk. He had time to utter a surprised, muffled squeal, and then pain lanced through him as sharp talons slashed his bulbous nose and a razor beak plucked his eyes from his head with two quick pecks. Ron reached out to help him, but when he wrapped both hands around the frenzied bird, the crow changed shape, shifting in his hands like water. He let go and stared as it turned into a man.

The fuck is he dressed up like a pilgrim for? Ron thought, dimly registering his best friend's screams. *It ain't Halloween.*

The dark man punched Ron in the throat, decapitating him with one powerful blow. Then he stood over Ron and fed as his soul departed. Finished, the killer turned his attention back to the dying blind man.

Joe heard its laughter and screamed louder in an attempt to drown out the sound.

Randy, Sam and Stephanie sat huddled together on the couch. Randy's mother sat next to them. A single candle lit the living room. Stephanie wept softly, her face buried against Sam's chest. Randy felt pangs of

guilt and regret each time he looked at them—
regret that it wasn't him who was consoling her, and
guilt that he felt that way. Randy's father paced nervously, going from window to window and peeking
outside. Each time he parted the blinds with his fingers, Randy's mother begged her husband to stop.

"Jerry," she whispered, "somebody will see you!"

"We need to know what's happening. It sounds
like World War Three out there."

"All the more reason to sit down over here and
stay out of sight."

Sighing with frustration, Jerry Cummings let the
blinds slide shut again. Then he turned and faced
his wife.

"Marsha is out there."

"I *know* that . . ." Cindy Cumming's eyes were
wide. Mascara ran down her cheeks. "What are we
going to do?"

"She's with Donny," Randy said. "She'll be okay,
Mom."

"Yeah, but what about us?" Sam's voice sounded
hollow.

Jerry crossed the living room to the front door
and peered through the window.

"You're going to attract attention," his wife said.
"Whatever is—"

A long, agonized wail cut her off. They couldn't
tell from which direction it had originated, but it
sounded nearby.

"It's getting closer," Jerry said. "I think that was
next door."

"I want to go home," Stephanie sobbed. "My parents
and my little brother are at home. I need to be there
with them."

Randy glanced at Sam, annoyed that he wasn't doing more to comfort Stephanie. If it had been Randy, he'd have stroked her hair and whispered soothing words and promised her that everything would be okay. Sam did none of these things. He merely sat there, mute and dumbstruck. He looked uncomfortable, and when he glanced up and saw Randy glaring at him, he shifted uneasily. The couch cushions groaned beneath him.

"You can't go home right now, sweetheart." Cindy reached over and patted Stephanie's knee. "But I'm sure your family is fine."

Stephanie didn't look up from Sam's chest. Her voice was muffled. "How do you know?"

Cindy opened her mouth to respond, paused, looked at the others and then closed her mouth again. She removed her hand from Stephanie's knee and wiped her eyes. Randy noticed that his mother's hand was shaking.

"We don't know," Jerry said, and Randy got the impression that his father was talking to himself rather than to the rest of them. "That's the problem."

"Let's try calling them again," Sam suggested. "Maybe try calling Marsha's cell phone again, too, while we're at it."

Jerry shook his head doubtfully, but before he could speak, another volley of gunfire echoed down the street. He flinched.

"It sounds to me like somebody is going door-to-door, shooting folks."

"Maybe we're just hearing people fighting back," Randy suggested, trying to sound brave for both his mother's and Stephanie's sakes. "Could be that—"

Something thudded against the back of the house.

Slowly, all of them turned to face the kitchen and the sliding glass doors that led out onto the patio and the Cummingses' backyard. Even Stephanie looked up. Randy's breath caught in his throat when he caught sight of her tear-streaked cheeks. They glistened in the dim candlelight. A lump formed in his throat. Then his attention was drawn to the flame atop the candle. It flickered and danced as if blown by a slight breeze, but the air inside the house was still. He looked up to see if anyone else had noticed it, but they were all focused on the patio doors. The thudding sound returned, followed a second later by something scuffing across the patio's cement foundation.

"What was that?" Cindy mouthed.

"Stay here," Jerry whispered. "I'm going upstairs to get the gun."

Unlike most of the men (and many of the women) in Brinkley Springs, Jerry Cummings wasn't much of a hunter. As a result, Randy hadn't spent much time hunting either. He'd gone out a few times with Sam and Sam's father and uncle, but he'd found it didn't interest him. Randy didn't like the cold or the tedium. Despite his lack of enthusiasm for hunting, he did enjoy target shooting, and his father had taken him out to the woods many times and let him shoot the family's Kimber .45, which Jerry kept secured in a lockbox on the dresser. They'd killed many empty soda cans and plastic water bottles.

His father motioned at all of them. "Don't move. Don't make a sound. I'll be right back."

As he started for the stairs, something brushed against the glass on the other side of the patio doors. Cindy gasped and Stephanie whimpered. Sam moaned, his eyes wide. He hugged Stephanie tightly, and Randy wondered if it was to comfort her or himself. The sound came again, more forceful this time. The doors rattled in their frame. Then something tapped the glass.

Jerry ran for the stairs and took them two at a time. They heard his footsteps above them as he hurried toward the bedroom. The tapping sound continued, slow and rhythmic. Clenching his fists, Randy stood. It seemed to him that it took a very long time to do so. His heart pounded and his ears felt like they were on fire. Unable to see past the curtains that covered the sliding glass doors, he slowly crossed the living-room floor. Sam, Stephanie and his mother watched in horror.

"Randy!" Cindy reached for him. "Get back here."

Tap . . . tap . . . tap . . .

He shook his head, not bothering to turn around. His mother called for him again, louder this time. Still not looking back, Randy waved his hand impatiently and continued toward the kitchen.

"Dude . . ." Sam made a choking noise. "You heard what your dad said."

Randy ignored them both. The only words of concern he wanted to hear were from Stephanie, but fear seemed to have rendered her mute. He stared at the doors, wondering what was out there.

Tap-tap . . . tap-tap . . . tap-tap . . .

Swallowing hard, Randy strode forward, his mind made up. Whatever was out there, he wasn't going to let it fuck with his friends and his family any longer. He kept his gaze focused on the doors and felt the living-room carpet give way to linoleum floor beneath his feet. He skirted the kitchen table and drew closer. It was darker in the kitchen than in the living room, and Randy wished for a moment that he'd brought the candle with him.

The tapping became more insistent, changing to a rapid-fire staccato. Randy stopped in front of the sliding glass doors and realized that whatever was making the sound was doing it from near ground level. He reached for the curtains and hoped that Stephanie couldn't see his hand shaking.

"Randy Elmore Cummings . . ."

Randy cringed, his hand pausing in midair. Frightened or not, his mother clearly meant business. She only used his middle name when she was seriously pissed off at him. Worse, that middle name had now been revealed to his best friends—both of whom he'd managed to keep it secret from for the past eighteen years. Shaking his head, he reached again for the curtains. The tapping grew louder, as if whatever was on the other side of the patio doors was agitated at the delay. His fingers brushed against the coarse fabric.

Tap-tap-tap-tap-tap-tap . . .

A hand slammed down on his shoulder and squeezed hard. Randy yelped, both in pain and surprise. He looked up, and his father was beside him, clutching the handgun in one fist. Even though he'd fired it many times in the past, the weapon looked bigger than Randy remembered.

"Dad—"

Removing his hand from his son's shoulders, Jerry raised one finger to his lips. Randy fell silent. The tapping on the glass resumed, frantic and angry.

With it came a dry, rustling sound. Randy held his breath. Jerry grasped the curtain and pulled it aside.

A large black crow stood on the other side of the glass, tapping at the doors with its beak. It stopped, tilted its head up and stared at them. Both Randy and his father exhaled at the same time. Then Jerry laughed.

"What is it?" Sam called. "What's out there?"

Jerry turned around to face them. "It's just a bird. That's all. Just an ugly old crow. Big sucker, too."

The others murmured among themselves, and Randy, whose attention was still focused on the bird, heard the relief in their voices. He tried to speak, tried to get their attention, but suddenly he had no breath. The bird was changing. As he watched, it turned shadowy, blurred. And then it *changed*.

A tall man, dressed all in black, stood on the patio where only a second before there had been a crow. He grinned at Randy, revealing rows of white teeth. Too many teeth. Randy didn't think human beings were supposed to have that many in their mouths.

The man in black raised a fist.

Randy whined softly. "Dad . . ."

Still grinning, his father started to turn toward him. The stranger's fist smashed through the glass doors, and he grasped Jerry Cummings by the ear.

"Come here." The man's voice reminded Randy of fingernails on a chalkboard.

Jerry had time to utter a startled yelp, and then his attacker yanked him forward, pulling his head through the shattered hole. Glass fragments fell to the kitchen floor. The gun slipped from Jerry's hand and spun like a top on the linoleum. Randy screamed, dimly aware that his mother, Sam and Stephanie were doing the same behind him.

Laughing, the man on the patio jerked Jerry's head down. Long, jagged shards of glass slashed his face and throat. Blood spurted, running down the doors on both sides. Jerry wailed and thrashed, arms flailing, legs kicking wildly as the stranger pushed his head even lower. Another shard speared his eye, and Randy heard a small pop, like air rushing from a sealed plastic bag. His father's cries ceased. Jerry jittered once more and then lay still. His body went limp and the glass slipped even farther into his eye socket.

Randy gaped, crying as the killer grasped his father's hair with both hands and tugged him through the opening. The remaining glass shattered as Jerry's corpse was pulled through. Randy flinched as the stranger lifted his father's head and kissed him on the mouth. The murderer's cheeks seemed to balloon for a moment, as if he'd swallowed a mouthful of something. Then he casually tossed Jerry's lifeless form aside and stepped through the hole.

"Didn't you hear me knocking? I was gently tapping, tapping at your chamber door."

Randy scrambled backward, tripped and fell. He sprawled across the kitchen floor and spotted his father's gun. He reached for it, but the invader moved quicker, kicking it away. The weapon slid across the floor and slammed against the kitchen cabinets.

"It wouldn't have done you any good," the man said, looking down at him. The tip of the killer's black hat brushed against the ceiling fan. "But if you don't believe me, go ahead and try. I'll wait."

Randy skittered backward, sobbing. The man

followed along, clearly enjoying the sport. His laughter echoed through the kitchen.

"What do you want?" Randy shrieked.

"Your soul. They taste better if you're scared."

The man leaned over him and Randy closed his eyes.

"Youuuu get away from my son!"

Footsteps pounded across the floor. Randy's eyes snapped open in time to see his mother leaping over him, flinging herself at her husband's killer. She beat the intruder with her fists, but the man in black swatted her aside. She crashed into the refrigerator and then stumbled to her feet. Groaning, Cindy grabbed the salt and pepper shakers from the countertop and flung them. Both bounced off the figure's shoulders and smashed on the floor, spilling their contents all over the linoleum. A thrown coffee mug suffered the same fate. Then Cindy seized a steak knife from the dish drainer.

"Get away from us," she screamed. "Jerry! What did you do to my Jerry?"

"Mom."

"Randy," Sam shouted. "Come on!"

Randy clambered to his hands and knees and crawled toward the handgun. Grains of salt from the spilled dispenser stuck to his palms. The intruder's attention was focused on his mother. The killer taunted her, leaning in close and then darting out of the way as she repeatedly slashed at him with the steak knife. They repeated this dance again, the killer giggling as Cindy shrieked.

"Run, Randy." Her eyes didn't leave her tormentor. "Get out of here."

"Leave her alone," Randy shouted as his fingers

curled around the pistol. He jumped to his feet and pointed the weapon at the man in black, holding the .45 with both hands and spacing his feet apart at shoulder width, just as his father had taught him. "I mean it, you son of a bitch. Get the fuck away from her."

The dark figure didn't even turn around. "Go ahead. Take your best shot."

"I'll do it," Randy warned. He hoped his voice didn't sound as terrified as he felt.

"Then do it already, boy, and be done with it. My brothers and I have many more to deal with tonight. You make such small morsels."

"Randy," Cindy said, "go find your sister. Make sure she's safe. Get out of here."

"I'm not leaving you, Mom. That fucker killed Dad."

"Sam," she cried. "Stephanie. Get him out of here."

"Come on, Randy," Sam urged again. "Let's go get help."

"I'm not leaving my mother here, so fuck off!"

The man in black turned around to face him. His smile was terrible to behold.

"I'm going to turn your mother inside out now. Would you like to watch?"

Cindy lunged forward and drove the steak knife into his back with both hands. At the same time, Randy pulled the trigger. The .45 jerked in his hands, and he felt the reverberation run all the way up his arms. The blast drowned out all other sound, and Randy's ears rang in the aftermath.

Grunting, Cindy stumbled backward and slipped again to the floor. Randy noticed that there was blood spattered across the white refrigerator door. It hadn't been there a moment before. He wondered where it had come from. Then he saw more of it on the front of his mother's sweatshirt.

"Oh my God."

The killer, his expression impassive, calmly reached for the knife jutting from his back. He pulled it out and dropped it to the floor. Then he smiled again.

"But I shot you." Randy tossed the gun away in frustration. "I shot *you*, not my mom."

"Indeed. The bullet passed through me and into her. And for that, I thank you, boy. You helped expedite things for me. As a reward, I shall make your death quick and painless. Just give me one moment."

He turned back to Randy's mother and knelt beside her. Cindy struggled to sit up, but slumped back down again.

"M-Mom . . . I'm sorry."

Her eyes flicked toward him. Randy noticed a thin line of blood dribbling from one corner of her mouth.

"Marsha," she wheezed. "Go find your sister. It's okay, baby. I love you."

"Mom . . ."

"Dude." Sam had opened the front door. A gust of wind blew into the house, and the screams of the neighbors grew louder. "Come on, man, before he kills you, too."

Randy glanced at Sam and Stephanie, then back to his mother and the stranger, and then down to the discarded gun.

"Forget it," Sam shouted. "You already shot the fucker once, and it didn't faze him. Come on!"

"Oh, Jesus." Stephanie stared at something across

the street. "There's another one. What's it doing to the Garnett's dog?"

Randy turned back to his mother again, intent on rushing forward and pushing the intruder away from her. The man was kissing her, just as he had kissed Randy's father. Cindy's eyes were closed. Balling his fists, Randy opened his mouth and—

"Randy?" Stephanie's voice cut through his rage and distress. "We have to go. We have to go *now*. Please?"

He glanced from her to his mother, and then back again. The man in black stood up and sighed.

"Ah, that was tasty. Now come here, boy. I promised I'd make it quick, and I keep my word."

Randy took a faltering step backward. The killer moved forward and then stopped, recoiling as if he'd been shocked. He glanced down at the floor and hissed. Randy looked down and saw that the intruder's toe was at the line of spilled salt.

"You little bastard. Come here."

"F-fuck you. You killed my parents."

"And now I'm going to kill you. Come here. I won't ask again."

Randy noticed that the man still hadn't moved. He seemed unable or unwilling to come any closer.

It's the salt, he thought. *I don't know why, but he doesn't like the salt.*

"Fuck you." This time, his voice didn't waver.

The killer's eyes widened. "You have the touch, don't you, boy?"

"I don't know what you're talking about. Touch this, you son of a bitch." Randy grabbed his crotch.

"Amazing," the intruder whispered. "You don't know."

"Randy?" Stephanie's voice was pleading. She sounded near tears again.

With one last glance at his parents' bodies, Randy turned and fled. Tears streamed down his face as he followed Sam and Stephanie through the open door. He noticed that they were hand in hand, but at that moment, he didn't care.

"Run," the man in black called after them. "Flee, if you wish. There is nowhere for you to go, little bugs. One of my brothers will see to you in due time."

The street and yards were chaos, but none of it registered with Randy. He only caught fleeting glimpses as he ran across the grass toward his truck. Homes were burning. Bodies lay in the street. Another dark figure, almost identical to the one they had just faced, strode across the roof of the house next door, menacing two people who had crawled to the edge.

Sam unlocked the doors. Randy watched in despair as he guided Stephanie to the Nissan and yanked the passenger door open. She hurried inside and he slammed the door behind her. Then he looked up and noticed Randy.

"What are you doing?"

"Truck . . ." It was all Randy could manage to say. He pointed at the 4×4.

"Follow us," Sam said, and quickly climbed behind the wheel. Then, a second later, he swore.

Stephanie glanced around, frantic. "What's wrong?"

"It won't start!"

Randy stumbled toward them. Sam sat behind the wheel, frantically turning the key back and forth in the ignition. Randy placed his hand on the Nissan's hood and was just about to tell them to get in his truck when Sam's engine suddenly roared to life.

"Got it," Sam shouted. "You coming?"

"I'll be right behind you."

Randy ran over to his truck and fumbled for the keys. They jingled in his trembling hand as he unlocked the door. The people next door screamed as they plummeted to the ground. The man in black on the roof turned in Randy's direction and waved. Randy gave him the finger and then slipped into the cab. He started the truck and the engine roared to life. The man on the roof seemed startled by this. He leaped to the ground as Randy raced away, pressing the accelerator all the way to the floor and struggling to keep sight of Sam's brake lights as the black Nissan lowrider with flames painted on the sides raced into the darkness. The CD player beeped and then began playing the Geto Boys' "Still," which Randy had been listening to the last time he was in the truck. Now, he barely heard the music.

"I'm sorry," Randy sobbed as he whipped around the turn and followed Sam. "I'm so sorry."

The truck's massive tires crunched over a corpse lying in the middle of the street, but Randy didn't even notice.

CHAPTER SIX

Most of the people Levi met as he waded through the chaos were either in shock or half-crazed with fright. A few ran away from him as if he were the Devil incarnate, stalking the streets of Brinkley Springs. A few more people shot at him, not bothering to ask questions or give warning first. One particularly terrified old man had thrown a bottle of whiskey at him and then followed it up with a lit wooden match. As a result of these confrontations, Levi had a hard time gaining a coherent understanding of what was occurring. Many of the townspeople were as clueless as Levi himself. They'd heard the screams and gunshots and explosions, but had no idea what was happening. Others mentioned men in black and crows. Neither image was particularly useful.

Men in black was too vague of a term. It could mean anything. A group of gunmen dressed in dark clothing. Agents from some government agency or perhaps Black Lodge. It could even be one of the many different manifestations of Nyarlathotep—a supernatural who some mistakenly believed to be a demonic servant of Cthulhu but who, in reality, was simply the messenger of God. Somehow, Levi doubted it was any of these things. Human gunmen wouldn't have explained the feeling that had come over him earlier. No, whatever forces were at work here in Brinkley Springs, they were almost certainly of supernatural origin. And Nyarlathotep, on the rare occasions that he manifested himself on Earth, wasn't known for massacring people—which was what was happening here, if the reports Levi was hearing from the panicked survivors was correct. God's messenger did occasionally appear as a man in black, but he also manifested as a worm, a hummingbird, a pillar of fire, a burning bush, a giant hand or one of a hundred other forms. He did no harm, other than imparting a message to whomever was chosen to hear it. Then he disappeared again.

So forget the men in black, Levi thought as he snuck through a small cemetery behind a tiny Baptist church that—judging from the moldering plywood nailed over the doors and windows—had been abandoned by its congregation long before tonight. *Focus on the crows. People keep mentioning they saw big black crows. What does that tell me?*

He tried to remember everything he knew about crows, as they related to occult lore. If he'd been back home, if he'd had access to his library, the task would be a snap. But between the adrenaline coursing through his body and his own fear, amplified as it was by the town's collective horror, he'd have to trust his memory, instinct and years of experience.

So, what do I know?

The first thing that came to Levi's mind was Raven, a deity of the Native American tribes who had once inhabited the Pacific Northwest. According to their beliefs, Raven was sometimes a generous benefactor and, at other times, a mischievous trickster, credited with doing everything from creating the Earth to stealing the sun. But since Brinkley Springs, West Virginia, was on the other side of the country, and since there were a number of other tribes who had worshipped other deities between here and there, he doubted this had anything to do with Raven. The Hindu god Shani was usually depicted as being not only dressed in black, but dark in color, as well. Shani also traveled around the world on the back of a giant crow. That seemed to fit, but as far as Levi knew, Shani was a god of justice who would have abhorred the atrocities taking place. What else was there? There was Odin, of course, with his two pet ravens, Hugin and Munin. Celtic mythology told of Morrigan, also known as Badb, Fea, Anann, Macha and others. One of the goddess's forms was that of a crow. The Welsh had the giant king of the Britons known as Bran the Blessed, whose name meant "crow." Levi wondered for a moment if Brinkley Springs' residents were primarily of Germanic, Irish or Welsh descent. Probably so, but even then, none of those possibilities felt right.

Crows were present in Ovid's *Metamorphoses*, as well as in Chaldean, Chinese and Hindu mythology, and they were mentioned quite often in Buddhism, especially the Tibetan disciplines. One physical form of Dharmapala Mahakala was a crow. Crows had watched over the first Dalai Lama and had supposedly heralded the births of the first, seventh, eighth, twelfth and fourteenth Lamas. Levi was certain, however, that he could rule the Dalai Lama out as a suspect.

He stuck close to the church walls, remaining in

the shadows. Lost in thought, he didn't notice the dead dog until he was almost upon it. The poor creature had been impaled on the black wrought-iron fence that surrounded the churchyard. One end of the iron rod jutted from the dog's anus. The other end stuck out of its mouth. Judging by the expression in the dogs face, it had been alive when the act was perpetrated. Without even really thinking about it, Levi reached out with two fingers and closed the poor dog's eyes. Then an idea occurred to him. If he could find a dead human—one whose death was connected to these mysterious crow figures or the men in black—he could summon their spirit and get the answers from the departed. It stood to reason that a murder victim, especially one killed in so gruesome a fashion, would be able to answer questions about the person or persons who had killed them.

All he had to do was find a corpse, and given the current situation, that should be an easy task.

Levi grasped the iron bars and vaulted over the fence. His hands came away sticky with blood and fur. Frowning, he knelt and wiped them on the grass. Then he stood up again and walked around the side of the church, sticking once more to the shadows to avoid being seen. A black car with flames painted on the side raced past, followed closely by a revving pickup truck. That struck Levi as odd. He hadn't heard or seen any other running vehicles this evening.

Flames flickered in the night, casting the side streets and alleys with an orange glow. Though none of the buildings in his proximity were ablaze, the fires were close enough that Levi could smell the smoke. His eyes watered. The curtains in a few houses fluttered as he sneaked past them. When he reached an open space and ran out of cover, he darted down the sidewalk. Broken glass crunched beneath his feet. An obese woman, sobbing uncontrollably, stood on the corner, leaning against a mailbox.

"Excuse me," Levi called. "Are you okay? Have you been injured?"

She glanced in his direction and then her sobs turned to screams. She ran away, her speed belying her size. Shaking his head, Levi continued onward.

He found a dead body at the next intersection. The victim was a middle-aged white male. His head and limbs were still intact, but his genitals had been torn off, leaving a ragged, gaping hole in his crotch. Blood shone black on the asphalt beneath him, and his shirt and the tattered remains of his pants were crimson. Levi knelt next to the corpse and stuck the tip of his right index finger into the gore. The blood was sticky but not yet congealed. He placed his palm against the corpse and found that the flesh was cool, but still pliant. Whoever the man was, he hadn't been dead long. Levi glanced around for the missing penis and testicles and spotted them lying on the curb—which meant that whatever had murdered this man hadn't consumed the grisly prize. Nor had it eaten or mangled the rest of him. The killing had been quick, almost perfunctory, if not for the brutality of it. This hadn't been about torture or revenge. This killing had served a purpose, albeit a quick one. But what? His blood hadn't been drained. His flesh hadn't been consumed. So why kill him in this fashion?

There was only one way to find out. Only one person who would have the answers—the dead man himself.

Lord, he prayed silently, *as always, I am your humble servant and your mighty sword. Guide my hand tonight as if it were your own. Let our victory be swift and just, and though my methods might not all be yours, let their purpose be to thy everlasting glory.*

Levi stretched the corpse out, making sure the head was pointing north and then extending the arms and legs straight out from the torso. He noticed purple splotches on the underside of the limbs. The remaining blood in the man's body was beginning to settle. He stood up then and wiped his hands on his pants. He grimaced at the stickiness on his palms, and was reminded of the dog that had been impaled on the church fence. There was starting to be a lot of blood on his hands tonight, and the symbolism was not lost on Levi. He wondered if it was the Lord trying to send him a message, or if this was simple synchronicity. It didn't matter, either way. If he didn't stop this slaughter, and soon, all of the blood in Brinkley Springs would be on his hands.

He reached into his pocket and pulled out a stick of chalk with his red right hand. Then he knelt again and drew a pattern around the corpse. He followed this with several arcane symbols, drawing each one quickly but carefully. He could afford no mistakes. Something as simple as one line or dot out of place could have unexpected—if not disastrous—consequences. Despite the chill in the air, sweat dripped from his forehead and the tip of his nose. Levi was careful not to let any of it fall inside the pattern. He worked in silence, except for the screams and occasional gunfire that still echoed across the town.

When he was finished, Levi stood up and surveyed his handiwork, ignoring the aches and pains in his joints and back. Satisfied that he'd done it correctly, he stood over the body, careful not to let his shoes touch the chalk lines.

"I'm deeply sorry about this," he whispered. Then he raised his voice and chanted in a guttural combination of ancient Sumerian and a language not normally spoken by human tongues.

A black crow hovered above the carnage while two of its brothers, both still in human form, eviscerated a family of four—father, mother and their children, a boy and a girl. Insatiable, they feasted greedily on the departing souls of the parents and the boy, pausing only to engage in a tug-of-war game with the little girl, using her arms as a rope. The limbs popped from their sockets. Sinew and muscle twisted and tore. The girl's shrieks reached a fevered pitch. The crow swooped downward, resuming its human guise.

"Don't play with your food."

Its brothers laughed. They pulled harder and the limbs came free. The girl toppled to the ground, unconscious yet writhing. They jostled one another for the departing soul, but stopped suddenly.

"Do you feel that?"

"Yes. What is it?"

"Someone in this town still knows the ways of old. He or she seeks congress with the realms beyond."

"If they can do that, then perhaps they are skilled in other works. Perhaps they can defeat us?"

"Reach out. Do you feel their power? This one is dangerous."

"Indeed."

"Find them immediately. But be careful. This one isn't like the others. This one is like those we faced of old."

Without another word, all three reverted to crow form and flew into the night, leaving the mangled bodies where they'd fallen. The birds soared in different directions, searching the darkness for the source of the disturbance, and their cries were terrible to all who heard them.

At eighty-nine, Jack McCutchon was the oldest man in Brinkley Springs. He lived by himself and fended for himself, something which he took great pride in. He still exercised every day, walking from his front door to the end of the driveway and back again, and still had most of his teeth. Sure, he had to wear hearing aids, but other than that, he thought he was in pretty good shape.

Jack wasn't afraid of being old, and he wasn't afraid of dying. He wasn't afraid of much, in fact. As a radioman in the air force, Jack had flown bombing missions over Japan during World War II. One night, they'd been only eight thousand feet over a Japanese village. At that height, they'd been able to smell burning flesh even inside the plane's hull. The heat and thermals from the explosions had buffeted the aircraft, tossing it about like a child's toy glider. One moment, they were cruising along at eight thousand feet. The next, they were shooting straight up to ten or fifteen thousand. Some of the other planes in the bomber group had actually flipped over from the turbulence. Jack's crew had made it safely back to base, but he'd never forgotten that night. It was the most frightening experience of his life.

Until the man dressed in dark clothing broke into his house and confronted Jack in his chair, where he'd been doing a crossword puzzle. His hearing aids sat on the end table next to him.

"What are you supposed to be?" Jack wheezed, his hand going to his chest. Suddenly it was very hard to breathe. "A pilgrim or something?"

Jack died of fear before the intruder even touched him.

Hand in hand and gasping for breath, Donny and Marsha ran, turning down one street and then another, darting through backyards and alleys and glancing over their shoulders as they fled. Marsha stumbled, but Donny pulled her upright and urged her onward. Panting, she resisted and tugged her arm away.

"I've got to rest. Please? Just for a minute."

Nodding, he guided her to a row of shrubbery in front of an abandoned house. They ducked down behind the untrimmed bushes and caught their breath. Their stifled gasps were punctuated by screams and cries from nearby streets.

Marsha shivered.

"Are you cold?" Donny asked.

"No," she whispered. "I'm scared."

"Me, too."

"Even after . . . what you saw over there?"

"Sure. Iraq was Iraq. This is different. I lived here."

Despite their situation, Marsha noticed that he referred to Brinkley Springs in the past tense rather than the present. She decided not to mention it. Now wasn't the time.

Donny reached out and took her hand again. "What are you thinking about?"

"I don't know. Everything. Brandon . . . He was just a kid. We shouldn't have just left him like that."

"No," Donny agreed. "We shouldn't have. It wasn't right. But if we hadn't, then we'd both be dead right now. I don't give a shit about me, but I couldn't let anything happen to you."

Marsha stared at him, unable to speak. She squeezed his hand and he squeezed back. Then Donny cleared his throat and peered through the branches, watching the street.

"I hope my parents and my brother are okay," Marsha said. "They have to be, right?"

"Where were they tonight?"

"At home. Mom and Dad were watching TV and Randy had friends over—Sam and Stephanie."

"You mean little Stephanie Hall?"

"I sure do. Except she's not that little anymore."

Donny grinned. "No kidding? Is he going out with her?"

"Who knows? I think she likes playing him and Sam against each other."

"Well, that's not right. I always liked your little brother. He's a good kid. Little weird, what with all the hip-hop stuff, but still a good kid."

"You don't have to live with him. He's a pain in the ass." Her voice softened. "But he likes you, too. He was excited when he heard you were back. I think he hoped you'd stick around. He missed you, Donny. We all did."

Donny didn't reply. Instead he focused on the street again. Marsha sensed that she'd struck a nerve and decided it might be best to change the subject.

"Where are we going, anyway?"

"I don't know," he said. "We should hide somewhere. I don't reckon it makes sense to go back to my mom's place. No way of knowing if those fuckers are still around there or not. If they are, they've got us outnumbered."

"Who were they?"

"Something . . . not normal. Did you see how fast they moved? Nothing normal moves like that."

"What are you saying, Donny? That they were demons or something?"

"Hell, I don't *know* what I'm saying. I mean, I didn't used to believe in that stuff. But I heard things. Over in Iraq. Guys talked, you know? I reckon you see enough of the worst shit imaginable, then you start to believe in evil. Real evil, like what they taught us in Sunday school when we were little. There's so much more to our planet, Marsha. It's a big world out there beyond these mountains, and we don't know as much about it as we think we do."

Marsha opened her mouth to respond, but he cut her off.

"Look, forget it. All I'm saying is that we need to be careful. We got lucky back there, and if we come across those fuckers again, I don't think we'd get that lucky a second time. I need to make sure you're safe. I don't know what I'd do if one of them got you."

"Donny . . ."

He turned toward her, and Marsha saw the tears in his eyes. She reached for him, cradled his face in her hands and then pulled him toward her. He didn't resist. Their lips met, and when Marsha closed her eyes, the darkness seemed to fade a bit.

Somewhere overhead, a bird cried out.

* * *

Levi stopped chanting and frowned in concern. There had been no reaction to his summons. By this point in the ritual, the departed soul should have returned to the body, regardless of which plane of existence it now inhabited. He checked the symbols and incantations and reconfirmed that all were in place and correct. Then he addressed the corpse.

"Can you hear me? If so, then I command you to tell me who did this to you."

The dead man didn't answer. Levi watched the corpse's face, looking for some sign of movement or awareness, no matter how slight, but nothing changed. The body was as soulless and empty as when he'd first found it. But why? What had gone wrong? This was simple necromancy, after all. Not a discipline to be trifled with or taken lightly, of course, but not nearly as hard as many other occult tasks. Even if the man had been dead for hours, Levi should still have been able to pull the soul back. It wasn't until decay set in that such a summoning became useless. After all, how could a dead man be expected to answer questions with a decomposing tongue?

"Are you there? Please, I only want to help. Perhaps you are confused by your situation? Can you tell me your name? Can you tell me who did this to you?"

Silence. Levi's frown deepened. There should have been some spark, some indication that the soul had temporarily returned to its former home. For whatever reason, he had failed. He was no closer to knowing what he was dealing with, and while his questions remained unanswered, the situation in Brinkley Springs grew more desperate by the minute. Even now, the screams drew closer. He needed to face this—whatever it was. He had to save these people. Had to defeat it. But to do that, he needed the name of the entities. He needed to know whom or what he was fighting. All power stemmed from naming. Without a name, the situation was hopeless.

Desperate, Levi racked his brain for an alternative. His hands curled into fists and his fingernails dug into the skin of his palms. He didn't notice the pain. For a brief moment, he found himself wishing that the Siqqusim—a race of incorporeal beings used as soothsayers by the ancient Sumerians—weren't sealed away in the void. He could have done as the Sumerian priests used to do and cast one of the entities into the body of this dead man, thus giving it a voice. But to do so—to breach the veil—was beyond his abilities. Indeed, he didn't know anyone on Earth who could achieve that.

So what's the point of standing around here and mulling it over? What's wrong with me? I'm better than this. I bested Nodens two years ago. I should be able to do this. Think, man. Think!

"Crows," he whispered, staring up into the sky. "Dark men dressed in black. The systematic slaughter of innocents. But why? For what purpose? Simple cruelty? What am I dealing with here, Lord? Any help you can give me would be greatly appreciated."

The heavens were as silent as the corpse. Levi had expected as much.

"God helps those who help themselves," he muttered. "But He sure doesn't make it easy for them."

Hurrying footsteps caught his attention. Levi glanced up in time to see two young people—a man and a woman—step out of the shadows. The man appeared to be in his midtwenties. He wore blue jeans and a flannel shirt, both of which hugged the contours of his body. He was in good physical shape. His brown hair was cropped close to his head and shaved down to stubble on the sides. Levi recognized the haircut. It was what members of the military called a "high and tight." He assumed that this young man was either a soldier or a marine—or had been until recently. The woman he was with appeared to be about the same age. She was slim and pretty, with mournful brown eyes that matched her long hair, and a fair complexion.

Spotting him, they halted. The girl gasped. Both of them were obviously terrified. They glanced down at the body and then up at Levi. He held up his hands and smiled to show that he meant them no harm.

"Hmmm," Levi murmured. "Maybe the Lord is answering prayers tonight after all."

As Randy roared along behind Sam and Stephanie, he felt a sick mixture of fear, revulsion and shock. He'd turned the CD player off because it was too much of a distraction. His eyes were wide as he gaped at the destruction. He didn't see the man who had killed his parents, nor the man's compatriots, but the signs of their passage were visible on every street corner. Racing through downtown and struggling to keep up with Sam's faster car, it was impossible for Randy to avoid the killers' handiwork. Brinkley Springs was no longer recognizable as the place he'd grown up in. Fires burned unchecked in a dozen homes and businesses. Cars and trucks sat vacant along the streets and in driveways, some with their doors hanging open or hoods up, as if their owners had experienced car trouble. He thought again of when they'd first fled. Sam's Nissan hadn't started at first—not until Randy had leaned against it.

Corpses, both human and animal, lay sprawled in the streets, yards and sidewalks. Randy knew most of them—if not their names, then at least their faces—but he forced himself not to think about it. If he pretended that he didn't know them, that their deaths had no more meaning than some random NPC in a video game, then maybe it wouldn't hurt as bad. Some of the corpses showed no obvious signs of trauma. Others had been mauled and mangled—eviscerated, torn apart, heads and limbs tossed aside with careless abandon. And a few had suffered even worse fates. A man jutted halfway through the pawn shop's plate-glass window. Shards of glass had severed his head from the nose up. A small child lay sprawled in a plastic wading pool. The pool was filled with blood. A man had been impaled with his own arms and legs. The grisly appendages stuck out the front of his torso as if they'd grown from it. Several people had been burned alive. Their charred remains still smoked on their lawns. A red and brown and pink pile of slop next to a woodpile and a chopping block with a bloodied ax embedded in it defied description, but Randy was pretty sure he knew what it was. Bile rose in his throat as he looked away. Across the street, a woman hung from a tree limb, dangling at the end of an extension-cord noose. Her breasts had been torn off and her stomach ripped open. Her innards lay on the ground at her feet. Carved into the bark of the tree was a single word in big block letters.

CROATOAN

As he sped by, Randy wondered what it meant. It was a strange word. Certainly not one he'd ever heard before. He wasn't even sure it was English. And who had carved it? The men in black, maybe, but how? Randy had some experience carving his initials into trees. When he was fourteen, Randy and Cathy Wilson had gone together for a whole summer. They'd had a favorite spot down along the Greenbrier River—a secluded section along the riverbank, hidden by a stand of tall birch trees. They'd gone there nearly every day and spent the afternoons swimming and talking and making out. Randy had convinced her to go skinny-dipping, but despite his best efforts, he'd never made it past third base. Near the end of the summer, he'd used the lock-blade hunting knife his grandfather had given him for his birthday to carve his and Cathy's initials— along with a big, if somewhat lopsided, heart—into the trunk of one of the old birch trees. Despite the soft bark, it had taken him all afternoon, and that was just four small letters and a crude heart. The strange word on the hanging tree was eight letters long, and each of the letters was a good ten inches high.

He promptly forgot about it as they hit a straight-away near the outskirts of town. Sam accelerated and Randy had no choice but to do the same. He glanced down at the speedometer. The needle was edging toward seventy-five miles per hour.

"Slow the hell down, Sam. It ain't gonna do us any good if you and Stephanie end up wrapped around a motherfucking telephone pole."

He knew, of course, that his friend couldn't hear him, but Randy didn't care. Hollering at Sam made him feel better. It took his mind off the horrors around them. It helped him forget about what had happened to his parents. Randy bit his lip and gripped the steering wheel hard. He moaned, long and low, and then the tears started again. He blinked his eyes, trying to clear his blurry vision, but every time he did, he saw the grotesque images. His father, bleeding from dozens of lacerations, shaking and jittering as the glass shard speared his eye. His mother, bravely holding the steak knife and trying to defend him. The way the killer's voice had sounded when he promised to turn Randy's mother inside out. How his ears rang and his hands grew numb when he pulled the trigger. Worst of all, Randy remembered the look on his mother's face when the bullet passed through the intruder and slammed into her instead.

"I'm sorry, Mommy." He wiped his eyes and nose with the back of his hand. "I didn't mean to leave you there. I just didn't know what else to do. And there was Steph . . ."

What would Marsha say when she found out? What would she think of him? She'd probably hate him, and she had every right to. He'd abandoned their mother. He'd *shot* her. It was bad enough that he couldn't save his father, but he should at least have been able to defend his mother. Instead, he'd killed her.

Randy hoped that his sister was okay, hoped that she was with Donny. If anybody could kick these weird fuckers' asses, it was Donny Osborne. If Marsha was with him, she'd be in good hands. She had to be. Marsha was all that Randy had left. Marsha and Stephanie . . .

They blew past Pheasant's Garage. It was dark, just like the rest of the town. As Randy caught up to Sam, something occurred to him. They hadn't encountered any other cars or trucks since escaping his house. Oh, they'd seen plenty parked along the street or in driveways, and they'd seen some wrecked. But nobody had driven past them. Not even a motorcycle. He wondered why? What did it mean? Surely, they couldn't be the only ones trying to get out of town.

His thoughts returned to Stephanie. He studied her silhouette through Sam's rear window. When this was over, he was going to tell her how he felt. Enough was enough. Life was too short. He'd never really thought about that before. Sure, he'd known people who died—his grandparents, and a friend of his had died of leukemia in the fourth grade. But those deaths were different than tonight. He needed Steph to know how he felt about her, no matter what the consequences. Hopefully, Sam would understand and be okay with it.

Just beyond the garage, they passed a Mazda pickup truck with out-of-state tags parked along the side of the road. In front of the truck was a small pile of ashes that stirred as they sped by. Randy glanced in the rearview mirror and saw the ashes swirling in his wake. He glanced forward again, practicing what he'd say to Steph—

—and then Sam's car imploded.

It happened so fast that Randy couldn't be sure of what he saw. One second, they were zooming toward the sign that told folks they were leaving

Brinkley Springs. The next, it was as if Sam's Nissan had slammed into an invisible brick wall. There was a shockingly loud sound of a collision, and then the car crumpled, accompanied by the tortured shrieks of metal and fiberglass—and of Sam and Stephanie. The sounds lasted only a second. By then, the engine block was shoved through the rear bumper.

Randy slammed the brakes and spun the steering wheel. He felt the truck almost tip over as it slid sharply to the side, stopping only inches from the wreckage. He flung the door open and leaped out. The car was no longer recognizable. Neither were his friends. Earlier tonight, they'd sat in his bedroom, listening to music and playing video games and laughing and talking and breathing. They'd had arms and legs and heads and hair. He refused to believe that the scraps of raw, dripping hamburger that were strewn through the wreckage was all that remained of them. He inched forward, screaming Stephanie's name, and something crunched beneath his heel. Randy lifted his foot and glanced down. He'd stepped on someone's finger. He couldn't tell if it was Steph's or Sam's.

Randy bent over and wretched. Vomit splashed his shoes and steamed on the road. He took a deep breath, screamed and then threw up again. His stomach cramped and spasms shook his body. He vomited a third time and then gasped, trying to catch his breath. He smelled gasoline and motor oil and blood. He staggered backward, moving away from the wreckage. Wisps of white smoke rose from it . . . but then he realized that it wasn't smoke. The shredded metal and fiberglass and rubber wasn't on fire. These wisps were something else. There were two of them—small, ethereal puffs of white. They reminded him of the way his breath looked when he exhaled on a cold day. They drifted above the accident scene like cigarette smoke, slowly gliding upward. Suddenly, there was a flash of light that made Randy think of the bug-zapper light in his parents' backyard. The two white clouds flattened out and then disappeared. The entire sky flashed blue, and then the darkness returned.

"What the fuck? *What the fuck?*"

With his throat raw and his eyes nearly swollen shut, Randy charged forward, wanting only to escape this new horror. He paused after taking a few steps. What if he slammed headfirst into the same unseen barrier that had stopped his friends?

He glanced back at the wreckage. His vision blurred and the world began to spin. Randy's sobs finally ceased as he toppled backward, hit his head on the ground and lost consciousness.

Donny was thinking about the kiss. About how warm Marsha's lips had been. How she'd tasted. How her tongue had felt sliding across his. How her breath had caressed his face. He didn't want to; he'd been trying instead to focus on keeping them both alive, but he just couldn't help himself. It had brought back all kinds of memories that he'd thought he buried once and for all. He was disappointed and angry with himself. As wonderful as it had been, the kiss would just make things more difficult. Marsha was already having a hard time with him leaving. He still planned on doing so, just as soon as this crisis was over.

Marsha gasped, and squeezed his hand hard. Donny glanced at her, and then in the direction she was staring.

The first thing he noticed was the dead body lying in the middle of the street. Despite the horrific groin injury, it wasn't as grisly as some of the corpses they'd seen tonight—but it was certainly the strangest. The body had been positioned like da Vinci's *Vitruvian Man* drawing (which one of Donny's fellow soldiers had sported as a tattoo on his bicep). Some sort of weird circle had been drawn around the corpse with chalk. The circle had four points and was decorated with bizarre symbols. Donny didn't recognize any of them.

The second thing Donny noticed was the dark-haired man standing over the body. Donny didn't know him, and he could tell by the look on Marsha's face that she didn't know him either. His manner of dress and his long, unruly beard identified him as Amish, which was strange. To the best of Donny's knowledge, the closest Amish enclave was over near Renick. The man appeared to be in his midthirties, although Donny couldn't be sure. His complexion and build seemed youthful, but his eyes were older. Judging by his expression, the stranger was just as startled as they were. Then Donny noticed the blood. It was all over him, smeared on his clothes and face. His hands, especially his right hand, were stained crimson.

"Despite how this may look, I didn't kill him, if that's what you're thinking."

The accent confirmed what Donny already suspected. The man wasn't from Brinkley Springs, nor even from West Virginia. He was certainly a Yankee.

Donny detected what sounded like a Pennsylvanian accent.

"I'm inclined to believe you," Donny said. "But there's blood all over your hands."

The Amish man looked at his palms and then back up at them. His expression turned sad.

"Yes, there is. Too much blood, I'm afraid. You have no idea."

Donny nodded at the corpse. "Looks like that guy had his pecker torn off, roots and all. I don't reckon you could have done that."

"No, of course not. But I guess you've no reason to believe me."

"I didn't say you did it. No offense, but you don't look strong enough to do something like that. But no, to answer your question. I don't think you did it. We've seen the ones who could."

The stranger flinched. He took a step toward them, and Marsha slid closer to Donny's side. Her grip on his hand tightened. He slid one arm around her for comfort.

"You saw who did this?" The stranger's tone was excited.

"I'm guessing it was the same people."

"Where? How long ago?"

Donny shrugged. "Ten minutes ago, maybe. Back that way. That's why we're going this way."

"Show me."

"Hell, no. Trust me, mister. The last thing you want to do is tangle with those guys."

"There's more than one?"

Donny nodded.

"How many?"

"We saw two of them," Marsha said. "Dressed all in black. They're wearing old-time clothes, like they're Pilgrims or something."

The stranger frowned, as if puzzled.

"Why do you care?" Donny asked.

"Because somebody has to. Because it's my job to care about things like this."

"What are you, some kind of cop? Because, to be honest, you sure don't look like one."

The Amish man smiled. "I'm not a police officer. I guess you could say that I'm more of a private detective. I specialize in what you'd probably call 'weird' occurrences."

"You're certainly in the right place tonight," Marsha muttered.

The stranger smiled and nodded, and then wiped his bloody hands on his pants. Donny noted that the effort didn't do much good. All the stranger succeeded in doing was making more smears.

Something flashed overhead. All three of them glanced upward, but the sky was dark again.

"Heat lightning," Marsha said.

"Maybe," the stranger agreed. "Or maybe it was something else."

"What's your name?" Donny asked.

"You can call me Levi Stoltzfus."

That struck Donny as odd. The stranger hadn't said *my name is*. Instead, he'd said *you can call me*. He chalked it up to just a quirky speech mannerism— perhaps something from the Amish or Pennsylvania Dutch.

"I'm Donny Osborne and this is my girlf . . . my . . . This is Marsha Cummings."

He felt Marsha stiffen slightly next to him. She'd noticed his near slip of the tongue.

Levi tipped his hat to them. "It is very nice to meet you both. Now please, I hope you don't think me rude, but I must know more about what you encountered. Tell me everything. Every detail, no matter how trivial or unimportant it might seem to you."

"We stick around here any longer," Donny said, "and I reckon they'll find us. Trust me, you don't want that to happen. Come on, Mr. Stoltzfus. You can hide with us."

They started to move past him, but Levi stepped in their way.

"Do you both live around here? Are you locals?"

Donny nodded. Marsha said nothing.

"Well, then," Levi continued, "if you care about your town—if you care at all about your family and friends and loved ones—then tell me, quickly, whom you saw and how I can find them. I'm not asking you to come with me. I just want information."

Donny sighed. "Can we at least get under cover? I don't like standing out here in the open."

"Of course," Levi said. "I think that would be best."

They hurried into the nearest yard and hid in the shadows alongside a house. When they were settled, Levi nodded at Donny in encouragement.

"We were standing out in the street," Donny began. "The power went out all across town and then all of the dogs started barking and howling at the same time. Then my cell phone wouldn't work and my truck wouldn't start."

"My cell phone didn't work either," Marsha said.

"Does that happen often? Power outages and your cellular network going down?"

"Not that often," Marsha replied. "I mean, our coverage isn't the best, on account of the mountains and everything, but it's never been like this. And I don't just mean that the network is down. My cell phone is dead. It won't even power up."

"Same with everything else," Donny added. "Flashlights—anything electronic or battery operated seems to be out. It's like somebody set off an EMP inside Brinkley Springs. My truck was just serviced. There's no reason it would have been fucking dead like that."

"I saw two vehicles race by earlier," Levi said. "A car and a truck. But otherwise, the streets have been empty of vehicular traffic."

"But why?"

"I don't know yet. What happened after you lost power?"

"We were . . . talking." Donny glanced at Marsha as he explained. She lowered her gaze. "The dogs stopped howling and then everybody started screaming. We heard it coming from all over town. Gunshots, too. It sounded like there was a house-to-house battle going on. Then this weird guy appeared."

Marsha shuddered, and Donny was surprised to find himself shivering, as well.

"Go on," Levi urged softly. "Tell me about him."

Donny did, recounting their escape in short, halting sentences. He fought back tears as he told of the slaughter, and the fear and despair they'd both felt in running away and leaving Brandon and the neighbor behind. When he mentioned the strange abilities that the men in black had possessed, he assumed

Levi would make fun of him, but the Amish man merely stroked his beard and listened intently, his expression showing no disbelief. When he was finished, Donny felt physically exhausted and emotionally drained. He noticed that Marsha was crying, and he slid his arm around her shoulder to comfort her. The memory of their kiss came to him again. He leaned down and kissed the top of her head. Her hair smelled like honeysuckle shampoo just as it had when they were in high school. Something stirred inside of him.

"None of this makes any sense," Levi muttered. Donny got the impression that the Amish man was talking to himself rather than to them. When Levi looked up again, he almost seemed surprised that they were still there. "Are you sure you've told me everything?"

"The kiss," Marsha said.

For a moment, Donny thought she was talking about the kiss they'd shared in the bushes, and then he realized what she meant.

"They leaned over each person as they killed them," Donny said. "And then they kissed them."

"Kissed them? How do you mean? A gentle kiss on the forehead to honor their victims in some way?"

"No. This was . . . obscene. It's like they were sucking the air from their lungs or something."

Levi became alert. His eyes blazed. Donny thought at first that he'd said or done something to anger the man.

"What is it?" he asked.

"Sucking the air from their lungs . . . or the souls from their bodies?"

Donny shrugged. "I don't know about that."

"It's okay. I do. This still doesn't make sense, but at least now I know what they might possibly be after."

Levi placed a hand on Donny's shoulder, and Donny was surprised at the man's strength. He felt it radiating through him.

"Tell me how to get there," Levi said. "The street where you first encountered them."

"You don't need directions. If you want to find them, just follow the closest scream."

Something fluttered softly in the darkness. All three glanced upward and saw a large black crow perched directly above them atop the eaves of the house. It tilted its head and croaked, almost as if mocking them.

"I don't think that will be necessary," Levi whispered. "It appears that they've found us instead."

CHAPTER SEVEN

The crow cawed again. The sound echoed through the night, loud and obnoxious. Then the bird spread its massive wings and swooped toward them. Donny and Marsha stood transfixed, gaping as it approached. Levi stepped in front of them.

"Stay behind me."

"It's just a bird," Donny said.

"No, it isn't. This is something else."

The crow landed in the yard and then seemed to blur. It grew, changing shape, transforming into a tall man. The entire process took only seconds. Behind him, Levi heard Donny and Marsha gasp. He knew how they felt. The transformation was simultaneously incredible and terrifying. He'd certainly never seen anything like it before, and he'd seen a lot in his travels. Encountering it like this left him momentarily stunned. He knew of therianthropy and zoanthropy, of course. They were two terms that described the same thing—the metamorphosis of human beings into animals, and vice versa. His library back home was full of examples, and although he had never witnessed it personally, Levi knew associates and peers who had, and he'd heard their stories. Werewolves were the most obvious example, but the phenomena extended far beyond mere lycanthropy. In many Native American, Chinese, West African, Central American and Pacific Island cultures, there were incidents of people turning into dogs, cats, bears, boars, owls, leopards, cheetahs, hyenas, lions, lizards and even sharks. Some scholars believed that this was where stories of centaurs and mermaids had originally come from, as well as human-animal hybrid deities like Ra and Anubis, but Levi knew better. Indeed, most of what passed for mankind's collective knowledge regarding religion, the paranormal and their own human history was incorrect. Man's understanding of shape-shifting was no different.

"Holy shit," Donny said.

Marsha whimpered in agreement.

The figure took form, rising to its full height. It was a man, dressed in black, archaic clothes that made Levi's outfit seem positively risqué. Looking at the Puritan-style hat, cloak and garments, Levi was reminded of the "Terror of Salem"—the Reverend Cotton Mather, scientist, theologian and witch hunter. The man's face seemed hidden in perpetual shadow. Only his cruel eyes and crueler mouth were clearly visible. The sight filled Levi with dread.

So fast, Levi thought. *It changed so quickly . . . What am I facing here? What* are *these things, Lord?*

Whatever its identity, this was no mere shape-shifter. If a human being turned into a wolf or bird or anything else and then transformed back to their human form again, they'd have an aura. All living human beings had auras. Levi had been able to see auras since birth, and his father and grandfather had taught him how to read them when he was just a child. Just like snowflakes, no two auras were alike.

Their colors varied, encompassing the entire spectrum. A trained eye could tell if a person was healthy or sick, happy or sad, just by noting the color of their aura. Different colors meant different things. Levi learned a lot about the man standing before them by reading his aura. It was black, just like the shadows concealing his face and the strange garb covering his body. Human auras were never black. That meant the man was something else.

Something inhuman.

That alone didn't frighten Levi. He'd dealt with more than his fair share of supernatural entities over the years. Indeed, just two years before, he'd defeated Nodens, most powerful of the Thirteen, and stopped the beings' attempt to breach the walls of this Earth and drown it in eternal darkness, snuffing out all life. Their battle had started with a confrontation much like this. Levi had encountered a seemingly human woman whose aura was black. While investigating, Levi had soon learned that the woman was nothing more than an empty shell. Her husk had been commandeered by Nodens. She was transport. Nothing more.

The entity standing before him now was different. Levi probed silently, reaching out with his mind. Although the thing—because Levi could no longer think of it as a man—radiated evil and contempt, it wasn't the encompassing, overwhelming nihilism projected by a deity like Nodens. This was a lesser adversary. An avatar, perhaps. A psychic projection. Maybe even a minor demon. But none of those would account for the level of chaos and destruction that had been visited upon Brinkley Springs. Such lesser supernatural beings would be incapable of such transgressions—at least, without being discovered. But then again, perhaps their actions had been discovered. Perhaps they *had* been noticed, and that was why he'd been placed here tonight.

"You stink of magic." The thing's voice was a raspy, grating whisper, as if its throat were filled with gravel or dirt.

"And you stink of blood and offal."

"Indeed. And now I'll add yours to the stench, little thing, as well as the blood and innards of those behind you."

"You can try, but I warn you, these two are under my protection. You will fail."

"Don't be ridiculous. You are weak. You may know the art, but that will not save you."

"That remains to be seen." Levi struggled to keep his voice calm and his expression serene. "Tell me, whom do I have the honor of addressing?"

"So polite, you are. I'm impressed. Most of these creatures have simply run away from me, or screamed or tried in vain to fight back, but you seek dialogue. You, sir, are a gentleman. Since you asked politely, My name is Samuel."

Levi paused. "Samuel?"

The creature laughed. "You pitiful bag of meat. Of course my name isn't Samuel. Did you actually think I would give you my real name?"

"I suppose not, but it certainly never hurts to try." Dispensing with the charade, Levi recited a passage from *The Long Lost Friend*, issuing a challenge of sorts. "Enoch and Elias, the two prophets, were never imprisoned, nor bound, nor beaten."

"Is that a fact?"

Levi ignored the interruption. His voice rose to a

shout as he continued. "Thus, no one of my enemies must be able to injure or attack me in my body or my life, in the name of God the Father—"

"Don't you mean God the Destroyer?"

"—the Son and the Holy Ghost. *Ut nemo in sense tentat, descendere nemo. At precedenti spectatur mantica tergo.*"

The challenge completed, Levi's shoulders went slack. He stood, panting, covered with sweat, and waited for the adversary's reaction. When the reply came, it wasn't at all what Levi had expected.

"Are you quite finished, little magus?"

Levi's stomach fluttered. He suddenly felt very cold. The creature wasn't evil—at least, not in an earthly sense. He had faced evil countless times. He'd seen its effects, the damage it caused. He'd seen evil reflected in both human and inhuman beings. This creature, while certainly evil in both its intent and the acts it committed, wasn't an agent of hell, nor had it been spawned in one of the nether regions. If it had originated in the Pit or been satanic in origin, it would have reacted strongly—perhaps violently—to his challenge. The fact that it had merely taunted him told Levi that this was something else, something beyond the Judeo-Christian pantheon or any other of the world's major religions. This wasn't just evil. This was something much worse. Levi knew of only one pantheon that fit that description: the Thirteen, a race of beings that were neither gods nor demons, but holdovers from a universe that had existed long before this one. They were the ultimate in antiquity, older than the stars. Concepts like good and evil were beneath them, inconsequential, as was human life.

Only one of the Thirteen would have reacted to Levi's challenge as this being had. But that made no sense either. Levi knew all of the Thirteen, and none of them matched this entity's description. He quickly ticked them off in his mind. Ob, Ab and Api. Leviathan and Behemoth. Kandara. Meeble. Purturabo. Nodens. Shtar, Kat, Apu and—

Levi heard footsteps sweeping through the grass behind him as Donny and Marsha slowly backed away.

"Is there anything else you'd like to say?" The creature's condescending tone dripped with impatience and boredom. "Anything at all that you'd like to add before I eviscerate you and decorate yon trees with your innards?"

"Actually, yes there is. Donny? Marsha?"

"Y-yeah?" Donny sounded as terrified as Levi felt.

"Run!"

The shadow surged forward, roaring. Marsha screamed. Levi took one step backward and then braced his feet, squaring off against the onrushing attacker. Meeting its furious stare, Levi kept his eyes wide. He did not blink. He did not dare. His heart pounded as he recited an enchantment to spellbind an enemy.

"Thou horseman and footman," he cried, making a motion with both hands. "You are coming apart under your hat. You are scattered. With the blood of the five holy wounds, I bind thee. In the name of the Father and the Son and the Holy Ghost, you are enchanted and bound."

"No, little magus, I am not."

Levi scampered backward, dismayed. In truth, he'd suspected the spell would be ineffectual against this enemy, but at the very least, it should have bought him some time. Even if only to flee. Like his challenge, the creature just ignored it.

Its terrible mouth curled into a garish smile. "Now it is my turn. Your soul will feed me well."

"Levi!"

The shout came from behind him—Donny's voice. What were they still doing here? He'd told them to run. Not wanting to risk taking his eyes off his opponent, Levi yelled, "Get out of here. Please, you don't—"

The creature slashed at him with one hand, sprouting long, black talons from its fingertips as it struck. Levi grunted. The air rushed from his lungs as the sharp claws raked across his chest, shredding the fabric of his shirt. As they tore through his shirt pocket, one of the nails slid against Levi's copy of *The Long Lost Friend*. There was a sharp, crackling sound, accompanied by a spark of blue-white light. The attacker yanked its hand away as if it had been shocked. Grinning, Levi breathed deep. The air smelled bitter and electric. He glanced down at his chest. The shirt was torn but his skin remained unbroken.

The shadow-man growled. "How?"

Still smiling, Levi patted his now-frayed pocket. "Whoever carries this book with him is safe from all enemies, visible or invisible; and whoever has this book with him cannot die without the—"

The entity struck at him again, this time aiming its talons at Levi's eyes. Levi sidestepped the charge and delivered an uppercut to the being's abdomen. Pain raced up his arm, and his fist went numb. It was like punching a block of ice.

"C-cold . . ."

"Not nearly as cold as your corpse will be in death. And that is all that will exist of you—an empty husk of decaying flesh. And then, not even that. You will return to the dirt that spawned you. Your soul is mine to consume. You will not exist beyond this level."

"Well, you'll have to succeed in striking me first, and I don't intend to let that happen."

They stepped away from each other. Levi panted for breath. His adversary scowled, clearly unhappy with the stalemate.

"I order you to leave this place," Levi said.

"You order me to do nothing, bearded one. My brothers and I will deal with you later. For now, I am content to turn my attention to your companions, instead."

The thing rushed past Levi, unleashing a powerful swipe with its forearm. The blow didn't connect, but Levi stumbled backward anyway, more from instinct than fear. The entity raced past him and charged toward Donny and Marsha, who were still standing at the edge of the yard, seemingly mesmerized by the battle.

Levi steadied himself and pointed his right index finger at the creature. Winded and half-nauseous from the adrenaline surging through his body, he took a deep breath and closed his eyes. His finger wavered in the air. His arm shook.

Marsha shrieked.

"Get the fuck back," Donny shouted. "What are you doing? Get out of there."

Levi opened his eyes again, and in a calm, clear voice, said, *"Hbbi Massa danti Lantien."*

The entity slowed, as if running through wet cement. It glanced over his shoulder at Levi.

"What is this?"

"Me, going to work." The trembling in Levi's finger became more pronounced.

Donny grabbed Marsha's arm. "Come on. Let's go while we can."

"No." She pulled away from him. "We're not leaving anybody else. Not again."

"Marsha—"

"I said no, goddamn it!"

The man in black turned back to them and slogged forward. It hunched over, grunting with effort, clearly exerting itself with each step.

Levi took another deep breath. With his finger still upraised, he exhaled.

"I, Levi Stoltzfus, son of Amos Stoltzfus, breathe upon you. Three drops of blood I take from you. The first from your heart. The second from your liver. The third from your vital powers. In this, I deprive you of your strength and vitality. Now crawl on the ground like the worm you are. You'll raise no hand against us."

The enemy collapsed on its belly, indignant with rage. It thrashed on the wet grass, but its movements were slow and lethargic.

"That will slow him down," Levi yelled at Donny and Marsha, "but it won't last long, and it cost me something. Go. Go now!"

"What about you?" Marsha asked.

"I'll be fine. Like I said before, I've had experience in these matters."

Donny grabbed Marsha's arm again and pulled, leading her away. Levi saw them both glance over their shoulders as they cut across the neighboring backyard and disappeared into the darkness. Then he was alone with the thing.

"Now," he said, his smile returning, "where were we? I believe you said something about taking my soul?"

"I'll devour it," the creature groaned. "If not me, then one of my brethren."

"Tell me about them."

"Surely you jest. You have given me your name, and you have not the sigil nor the power to make me talk."

Levi sighed. "Fine. We'll do this the hard way, then. *Dullix, ix, ux.*"

Powwow hadn't worked against this being, and the charm to still-bind it, while effective, was already weakening—otherwise it wouldn't have been able to thrash and roll about. Levi racked his memory, searching for something that might work. Making sure he remained out of the thing's reach, Levi quickly tried several different spells and charms, running the gamut from snippets of the traditional Catholic Rite of Exorcism to obscure Haitian voodoo recitations, Enochian chants and various rites of the Golden Dawn. All were ineffective.

"Is that your best, little magus? You are well versed in the art. Of that I can attest. But still, you are weak. *Weak!*"

The creature's movements increased. It flopped back and forth like a fish on dry land, struggling to sit up. Levi grew desperate. There was no time to create a binding circle or to invoke the Greater Banishing Ritual of the Pentagram, although Levi had his doubts now that even that would work against this enemy. Nor did he have time to construct a spirit trap. Even if he'd had time, he didn't have a luminol light or anything else that he could use to force the entity into the trap. And again, he wasn't sure that would work either. Spirit traps were only useful against incorporeal spirits, and whatever this thing was, it had certainly felt corporeal enough when he'd punched it in the stomach.

The entity lifted its head free of the ground, looked up at him and smiled. "Soon, bearded one. Soon."

Levi nodded. "I'd prefer later, if you don't mind. We'll get together and do lunch."

Turning, Levi fled in the same direction Donny and Marsha had gone. His enemy's laughter followed him. Levi cringed at the sound. His ears burned with shame and embarrassment.

"You have given me your name," the dark figure called.

As he ran past the church where he'd tried to communicate with the spirit of the dead man, Levi noticed that the corpse was no longer there. The chalk outlines and the bloodstains were still present, but where the body had been, there was now just a small pile of ashes. The dog's corpse, which he'd left impaled on the wrought-iron fence, was gone, too. More ashes sprinkled the ground beneath where it had dangled.

Nothing left, Levi thought. *They're consuming souls, and their victims are reduced to dust within hours. No decay. No decomposition. They just turn to nothingness. This is bad magic. This is very bad magic, indeed.*

He found Donny and Marsha easily enough. They'd made no effort to hide the signs of their passage. Both were breathing hard. Their footfalls slapped the pavement as they dashed across the street. Levi caught up with them on the other side, just as they were ducking behind a vacant apartment building.

"Wait."

Donny spun around, fists raised, his jaw twitching. When he saw that it was Levi, his shoulders went slack.

"Holy shit! We thought for sure you were dead."

"Not yet." Levi wiped the sweat from his brow with his ripped shirttail. "I appreciate the two of you sticking around back there, but I really wish you hadn't. You could have been killed."

"What the hell happened back there, anyway?" Donny asked. "What are these things?"

"I don't know yet."

"I thought you said this was your job? That you deal with things like this?"

"It is my job. I've just never dealt with something like this—or at least, something in this particular form."

Donny frowned. "What's that supposed to mean?"

"It means I have an idea—a few ideas, actually—of what we might be facing here, but I'm still not one hundred percent sure. I need to do more, in order to be positive. I need to see more."

"Why?"

"Because I need to learn their identity. Until I do that, I'm afraid I can't fight them."

Marsha paled. "Then what are you going to do?"

"Get the two of you to safety first. I can do that much, at least. After that . . ."

Donny nodded. "Yeah?"

"After that," Levi repeated, "then I guess I'll have to face them again. And this time, alone."

"Are you crazy? I watched that fight back there. He nearly punched your head off."

"But he didn't. He wanted to, but if you remember correctly, his blows didn't actually connect with me."

"I noticed that," Marsha said, nodding. "He clawed your shirt. How is it that he didn't cut you?"

"You wearing body armor?" Donny asked.

"No." Levi smiled slightly. "He couldn't hurt me because I carry something on my person that prevents attacks like that. Something much better than body armor. His claws cut my clothing, but they were ineffective on my body."

"Even so," Donny said, "you might not get so lucky a second time. You go back, then I'm going with you."

Levi shook his head. "I'm afraid that's out of the question. I told you, I have to face them alone."

"I can't let you do that."

"You don't have a choice. I'm going to make sure the two of you are hidden away. I'll provide you some safeguards that should prove effective. But then I'm going back out again, and you're not coming with me. Your responsibility is to your girlfriend here."

"I'm not his girlfriend," Marsha said, glancing at Donny.

"Oh. I'm sorry. The two of you seemed so close, I just assumed."

"She's . . ." Donny paused, floundering for words. "I just don't—"

A crow screeched overhead. All three of them jumped.

"Come on," Levi said. "Let's get under cover while we still can."

"Get the hell away from here or I'll blow a goddamn hole in your belly!"

The threat was accompanied by the sound of a shotgun being pumped. The noise was muffled through the heavy wooden door, but still identifiable enough that both Paul and Gus jumped out of the way. Standing on either side of the door, safe from any potential shotgun spray, they looked at each other and shook their heads.

"Go on!" The person inside the house was clearly terrified. His voice quavered as he shouted. "Get out of here now, goddamn you. I ain't telling you again."

"Greg," Gus called out. "Put down the shotgun. It's me."

"Me who?"

"Your brother, dumb ass. Gus. Who'd you think it was?"

Gus kicked the door with the toe of his boot, which he'd wisely changed into after taking off his Spider-Man bedroom slippers. The door rattled in its frame. An ugly brown wreath that hung askew near the top of the door swayed back and forth slightly, shedding leaves and bits of bark.

"You didn't say it was you," Greg hollered. "All you said was 'it's me.' How the hell was I supposed to know who 'me' is?"

"Never you mind that. I've got Paul Crowley out here with me. Now hurry up and let us in before somebody sees us."

"Paul's here with you?"

"Hi, Greg. Yeah, I'm here. Now open up. Bad things are happening and it's not safe out here."

There was silence on the other side of the door for a moment. Then they heard a thump as Greg sat the shotgun down. A moment later, the locks clicked and a chain rattled as it was slid across its hasp. Then the door creaked open. The battered wreath shed more twigs and leaves. Greg peered out at them.

"Take a picture," Gus said. "It'll last longer. Now let us in, damn it."

The door opened the rest of the way and Greg stood to one side, letting Paul and Gus rush by him. Greg was clad only in a pair of black sweatpants and mismatched socks. He quickly shut the door behind them and then locked it again. The shotgun leaned against the wall, next to a woven floor mat piled high with work boots and dirty shoes. Greg picked it up and eyed them warily.

"Would one of you boys mind telling me just what in the hell is going on? I hear shooting all over the place and folks screaming, and the power is out and the phones are off, too. Hell, I can't even get my weather radio to work, and that runs on batteries."

"We don't know," Paul admitted. "Something bad, obviously. Like you said, there's people shouting and lots of gunfire. The big propane tank behind the firehouse may have gone up. We've seen some dead folks, just lying in the street. But nobody seems real sure who's causing it or even what exactly is happening. One fella told us it was dark people, but we don't even know what he meant by that."

"Dark people? Who told you that?"

"You'd recognize him," Gus said. "Used to bring his car into the shop. I can't remember his name. Always seemed nice enough, but Paul seems to think maybe he meant black folks."

"Dark people?" Greg frowned. "That don't make any sense. Why would black people want to shoot up Brinkley Springs?"

"That's what I said, too," Gus exclaimed.

Paul shrugged. "I ain't saying they are. I'm just telling you what the other guy said to us. None of it makes any sense to me."

"Come on. Let's sit a spell. Figure this thing out."

Greg motioned with the shotgun for them to follow him. He led them into the living room and beckoned to a brown, worn-out couch. Paul and Gus both sat down, grateful for the respite. The couch springs groaned beneath them and the cushions sagged. Greg crept over to the window and pulled the faded curtains shut, stirring up a cloud of dust. The room, already gloomy, grew pitch-black.

"Hang on a minute," Greg said, stumbling around in the darkness. "Let me light a candle."

They sat in silence, listening as he fumbled his way to the kitchen and searched through drawers until he found what he was looking for. Then he returned with a long red candle in a tarnished brass holder. The flame glinted off the three bottles of Rolling Rock beer he clutched by the necks in his other hand. He placed the candle on the coffee table and then handed each of them a bottle. Both men accepted them without pause. The glass was cold and wet, and the sound the caps made as they twisted them off was somehow comforting—but not as much as the first sips.

Paul sighed. "I needed that."

"I reckon so," Greg agreed. "You both looked pretty shook-up."

"It's hell out there," Gus said. "And to be honest, big brother, I was a little worried about you. Glad you're okay."

"Shit." Greg patted the shotgun almost lovingly. The flickering candle flame reflected off the barrel. "I'll tell you what. I'm the last person in Brinkley Springs they want to mess with."

Paul took a long drink of beer and then pressed the bottle against his forehead. He leaned forward, sighed again and then looked at them both. "So, what are we gonna do? You boys got any ideas?"

"I was thinking on this while I was in the kitchen," Greg said. "I reckon that fella you met was wrong. It ain't black people that are doing this."

"Who do you think it is?" Gus asked.

"That's easy. The NWO."

Groaning, Gus rolled his eyes. "Oh, Greg. Now ain't the time to start with that goddamn New World Order nonsense again. I swear to God, you're worse than that crazy Earl Harper wing nut who lives up above Punkin Center. Always with the NOW bullshit."

"N-W-O, not N-O-W. And it ain't bullshit, little brother."

"The hell it ain't. First you thought Y2K was gonna kill us all. Then you said nine eleven was an inside job. Then there was all the crap about how President Obama didn't have a birth certificate. And then you—"

"And all of that stuff is connected. Bush and Obama are pawns of the same people. But that ain't my point. You guys ever hear of eugenics?"

"No," Gus said, "and neither did you until you got on the Internet. Swear to God, somebody ought to take away your computer access."

Greg ignored the comment. "They want to control humankind through what they call selective breeding. The Nazis started it, but the NWO are continuing it. See, the only way to control the population is to first get it back down to a manageable size. They're culling the herd, same way the game commission does when the deer population gets out of control. That's why we've got diseases like cancer and AIDS. You telling me that we can put a little goddamn skateboard-looking robot on Mars and have it send back pictures, but we can't find a cure for cancer? There's a cure. You can bet on that, boys. There's a goddamn cure. They just won't release it because cancer helps cut down the population."

Paul drained his beer and belched. The Pheasant brothers both fanned the air and frowned.

"Seems like cancer would take a long time to cull the population," Paul said. "Wouldn't they try something that worked a little quicker?"

"Don't encourage him," Gus said.

"Well, they ain't just using cancer. That was just one example. Look at the world! We've got a high child-mortality rate among the poor. We've got war everywhere. These are all ways of whittling down the population. Another way to do it is shooting sprees. See, the CIA are in on it. So is the KGB."

"There ain't no KGB anymore, Greg."

"So you say, Gus. Me, I don't believe everything I hear from the mainstream media. I'll tell you something. That old Putin ain't no dummy. The KGB are still around. They're just called something different now."

"Look," Paul said, "I've never been one to tell a man what he should or shouldn't believe, Greg, but I just don't understand what any of this has to do with what's happening outside. I don't reckon Vladimir Putin declared war on Brinkley Springs."

"The CIA and the KGB both developed ways to control people's minds. One morning, you could wake up and everything could be fine, and then, all of the sudden, you grab your rifle and start shooting. Haven't you guys noticed how things like that are on the rise? Every week, we hear about a school getting shot up or some nut killing all his coworkers. It's all just another method of population control."

"Goddamn it, Greg." Gus slammed his bottle down on the coffee table, sloshing beer all over his hand. "The NWO aren't shooting up Brinkley Springs any more than that Amish fella staying at Esther's is. That's stupid talk, and it ain't helping us any right now."

"Then tell me why we haven't heard any sirens. Tell me why the cops haven't shown up yet. Why are the phone lines down? And none of the electronic stuff is working. This is a controlled situation, Gus. Hell, they've probably got the town cordoned off. Nobody gets in or out, I bet."

Paul stood up. "I think we should put that theory to the test."

The Pheasant brothers stared up at him.

"What do you mean?" Gus asked.

"Personally, I don't believe in this NWO stuff, but one thing's for sure, you're right about the police and firemen. Nobody has shown up to help, but maybe that's because nobody knows about our situation. I think we should try to leave, try to go for help."

"I don't know," Gus said. "It's like a war zone out there. Maybe we'd be better off just staying put."

"Screw that. People are dying outside. *Our* people! We saw it. I've lived here all my life, and I'll be god-damned if I'm gonna let it end this way. Brinkley Springs may have been dying, but it doesn't deserve to get murdered. I'm going. On foot, if I have to, but I'm going, either way. It would mean a lot to me if you guys came along. I could use the backup."

The brothers glanced at each other for a moment and then stood up as one.

"You're right," Gus said. "This is too big for us to handle on our own, but that doesn't mean we should just hide out like a bunch of kids. Let's go."

"Hang on a second." Greg glanced down at his sweatpants. "I reckon I ought to change first. And maybe we should all drink another beer, just to get ourselves ready."

"You've got five minutes," Paul said. "Chug the beer while you get dressed. You ain't gonna come back downstairs in a pair of Spider-Man slippers, are you?"

Greg and Paul began laughing. Gus shook his head.

"Fuck you both."

Paul grinned. "I'll remember you said that if it turns out your brother was right about the New World Order."

"If he's right, then I hope the NWO shoots you first."

Melanie Candra peeked through her curtains and watched in terror as a tall, looming figure dressed entirely in black chased a fat man in flannel boxer shorts down the sidewalk. As she stood there trembling, the pursuer caught up with his prey, grabbed the man's hair with one hand and yanked him off his feet. The fat man uttered a short, surprised squawk and then his attacker swung him through the air. His scalp tore free. The loose flap of skin and hair dangled from the black figure's hand. Its owner soared halfway across the street and then slid across the asphalt on his face and chest. He quivered, but did not rise. The dark shape then raced over to him and knelt beside the body. Melanie let the curtains fall shut again and backed away from them, biting her lip to keep from screaming.

She'd moved to Brinkley Springs from New Jersey a year ago, hoping to open an equestrian center and horse farm. Real-estate prices were cheap and she'd found the small-town sentimentality a refreshing change from that of the Mid-Atlantic suburbs. She hadn't counted on the economy changing so drastically, however, and now her dreams of running a horse farm were just that—dreams. Instead, she was stuck in a dingy little farmhouse that was drafty in the winter and filled with insects in the summer, in a town that seemed to die a little bit more each day. And if Brinkley Springs hadn't been dying before, it certainly was now. Judging by the sounds outside, it was being murdered. Exterminated.

The street fell silent again. Still shaking, Melanie tiptoed into the kitchen and pulled a large butcher knife out of the top drawer. She'd thought that having a weapon—any weapon—might make her feel better, but instead, she wanted to puke. She crossed the kitchen and back into the living room. She glanced down at the cordless phone. The light was still off. The power was still dead. She found herself longing for the days of rotary phones. They still worked during a blackout. She wondered, however, if that would be the case in this instance. Earlier, when she'd tried dialing 911 on her cell phone, it had been dead, as well. She couldn't even get it to come on, let alone dial for help.

She stood there in the silence, wishing for a sound. The ticking of her cuckoo clock. The ring of a phone. The engine of a car driving by. A bird chirping. A dog barking. Anything would be better than this oppressive stillness that seemed to have suddenly settled over the street. Well, except another scream, of course. She didn't think she could handle another one of those. Maybe the man in black was gone. Maybe the fat guy in the flannel boxer shorts was dead. Maybe that was why it was so quiet out there now—the murderer had moved on to find another victim.

What if he'd moved on to her? What if she was next? What if he'd seen her at the window and was now standing on her front porch or peering in her windows? Still clutching the knife, she pulled her pink knit bathrobe tighter around her and glanced at all the windows, verifying the curtains were drawn on each.

If he's out there, she thought, *I can look through the peephole. I'll be able to see him but he won't be able to see me.*

No, but he'd hear her. The floorboards around the door tended to creak when stepped on. She'd have to be quiet. She had a vision of some black-clad maniac driving an ice pick through the peephole right into her eye.

Trembling harder, she crept to the front door and slowly brought her face to the peephole. Then she peered outside. Melanie breathed a sigh of relief when she saw that her front porch was empty—a sigh that was stifled a moment later when she saw the man in black breaking down the door of the house across the street. He raised one black-booted foot and kicked the door in on the first try, reducing the heavy oak to kindling. Then, with a sweep of his cloak, he stepped through the wreckage and went inside. She held her breath, waiting for him to come back out or waiting for the screams to start—but neither happened. She tried to remember if the house was occupied or not. So many of them stood vacant, and more seemed to end up on the market every month. Not that they were selling. She'd pretty much had her pick when she bought this place. Melanie had intended it to be temporary—a place to live in and keep her stuff until she got the horse farm operational. Then she'd planned on fixing this place up and using it as a rental property.

Restless, she rocked back and forth on the balls of her feet, stopping suddenly when she spotted a blur of movement from the open doorway across the street. She'd been expecting the killer, or perhaps a fleeing resident, but what exited the home was a large black bird. Flapping its wings, it soared up above the roofs and disappeared from her sight.

She noticed that the fat man's corpse was gone. In its place was a small pile of dirt or ash. She couldn't tell which from her vantage point. She wondered if someone had dragged the body away, or if perhaps the man hadn't been dead after all. Perhaps he'd crawled away, wounded.

Moments later, three men armed with guns crept past her home, moving from car to car, using the parked vehicles as cover. They seemed very intent. Their expressions were grim and serious. Melanie recognized two of them as the men who ran the local garage—they were brothers, she thought. The Pleasants? The Pheasants? She couldn't remember which. She didn't know the other man who was with them, but he looked like someone who could handle himself; he had a big, burly frame. She reached for the doorknob, intent on calling out to them for help, but then she paused. What if they were working with the other killer? She'd heard gunshots sporadically through the night. It had sounded like more than one person was shooting and more than one type of firearm was being used. What if these weren't the good guys? Maybe they were some kind of domestic terrorist group or just a bunch of crazies.

She stood there, debating with herself and hating her indecisiveness, until they'd moved on, and then was overwhelmed with a sense of regret. Clenching her jaw, she decided to risk it. She reached for the doorknob again when there was a soft rustling sound from the corner of the living room. Eyes wide, Melanie spun around so fast that she almost lost her balance. Teetering, she reached out with one hand and pushed against the wall for support. The noise was coming from the chimney. It grew louder as she stood there. Dirt and flecks of debris drifted down from above. Melanie whimpered. She realized the flue wasn't closed, but surely that didn't matter. The chimney wasn't wide enough for a human being to fit through.

Was it?

A black form burst from the opening, and Melanie screamed. She flung the butcher knife at the shape, realizing too late that it was nothing more than a bird—a crow, just like the one she'd seen fly out of the house next door. The knife spun end over end and then thudded softly onto the carpet. The bird paid it no notice. Instead, the crow flew up onto the mantel and perched there, staring at her with its beady eyes.

"Jesus Christ . . ."

The bird croaked in response. A second crow emerged from the fireplace and landed on the recliner. Then a third appeared and lit on the couch, followed by a fourth and a fifth.

A gathering of crows, she thought. *A murder. A gathering of crows is called a murder . . .*

Melanie backed up to the door. Keeping her gaze on the birds, she reached down and fumbled for the umbrella she kept in the corner next to the coatrack. Her fingers closed around the handle. She raised the umbrella and shook it at the birds. As she did, the umbrella ballooned open, momentarily blocking her view. She caught a whiff of something that smelled rotten.

"Get out of here," she yelled, wrestling with the open umbrella. "Shoo!"

When she lowered the umbrella, the birds were gone. In their place were five identical men, each dressed all in black. They varied only in height. One of them raised his hand and spoke. His voice was like a rusty, squeaking hinge.

"Hello."

She didn't even have time to scream.

* * *

Randy woke up cold, wet and confused. His head throbbed. The pain seemed to be centered in his temples. He opened his eyes and saw the night sky. Pinprick stars stared back at him. He was lying on something hard. Pavement? Asphalt? He shivered in the damp air. What was he doing outside? And what was that smell?

Groaning, he pushed himself into a sitting position. His hands, pants and shirt were sticky. Frowning, he glanced down at the wetness and saw that it was blood. Then he looked up at the wreckage.

The blood wasn't his. He was shocked by how much there was. It had come from the car, running out onto the road and . . .

And then it all came back to him.

Randy gulped cold air, buried his face in his bloodied hands and screamed—mournful, unintelligible shrieks that left his throat raw. He wished he would pass out again, but that didn't happen, so he continued screaming. He didn't stop until he heard something flutter overhead. Startled, Randy looked up and saw a small bat swoop overhead. Randy had seen bats in his backyard plenty of times, but he hadn't realized they could fly so fast. This one zipped right along. Seconds later, it crashed into the invisible barrier. The bat dropped like a stone and landed on the road. It twitched once and then lay still. Even from where he sat, Randy could tell that the collision had killed it. The bat had been going too fast, just like Stephanie and Sam.

Wiping his nose, he choked down a sob. There was nothing he could do for them now. Not for Stephanie. Not for Sam. Not for his parents. Not for anyone.

As Randy watched, a tiny smokelike wisp escaped

from the bat's corpse and rose into the air. The shapeless, ethereal form hovered for a moment and was then pulled toward the barrier, as if by a magnet. There was a brief flash of light and then the white stuff—whatever it was—disappeared. He considered this for a moment and then decided that he'd probably been better off passing out. Otherwise, he could have blundered into the same thing that had just killed the bat.

"What the fuck is going on? What is this shit?"

Randy stared at the dead bat and realized something. It wasn't the only dead animal around the base of the barrier. The ground was littered with dead birds—robins, woodpeckers, sparrows, crows, pigeons, finches and even a white duck. Not just birds either. He saw a red fox, two groundhogs, a skunk and a mother possum with several babies still clinging to her back. All of them were stiff and lifeless. Stranger still were the small piles of ash between the bodies. He wondered what the dust was and where it had come from.

Obviously, this was not an exit. He had never been one for science fiction. He'd never read many comic books or watched horror movies, preferring NASCAR and football instead. But he'd played enough video games to know that whatever was happening, it wasn't normal. Something had sealed off the town. If you touched it, or got too close, it sucked out your energy—or whatever those white wisps had been. He had no doubt that the barrier stretched far overhead. He wondered if it extended underground, as well, but he lacked the tools to dig down and find out. He was pretty sure such an effort would be a waste of time. They were trapped here.

He thought back to when he was younger. He and Marsha would spend their summer nights running around in the backyard, capturing lightning bugs and putting them in one of their mom's mason jars until it was time to go to bed. Now he knew how those bugs had felt, except that he didn't think the men in black would let everyone go once it was time to go to sleep.

He climbed to his feet and picked bits of gravel from his palms. Then he gingerly felt his scalp. He had a knot at the back of his head and another on his forehead, but the skin didn't feel broken, and as far as he could tell, he wasn't bleeding. Making a concerted effort not to look in Stephanie and Sam's direction, Randy limped back to his truck and climbed inside. He took a few deep breaths and forced himself to calm down. The only thing left to do was find his sister. If he couldn't protect their parents or his friends, the least he could do was make sure Marsha was safe. Once he found her, maybe they could try the old logging road on the back end of town. He'd taken his truck four-wheeling up into the mountains many times, and he knew that the rugged 4×4 could handle the harsh terrain. If they were lucky, maybe the force wouldn't extend that far. Maybe it was a way to escape. They had to try, at least, because the only alternative Randy could see was to sit down and wait to be killed—and that was no alternative at all.

Another bird slammed into the shield and was snuffed out. As with the bat, a smoky form drifted up from the corpse and was absorbed by the barrier. Randy rubbed his temples. The throbbing had subsided somewhat, but his head still hurt. He put the truck into gear. As Randy pulled away, his headlights spotlighted the still-steaming wreckage of Sam's car. Randy swallowed the lump in his throat and forced himself to look away.

They stood over Melanie Candra's mutilated body, which had been torn limb from limb. Her blood seeped into the carpet and decorated the walls, mantel, furniture and ceiling fan.

"I have met our adversary," said the first. "A magus, schooled in the ways of old. His knowledge was impressive, if ineffectual. He tried a number of different schools and workings against me, and failed."

"And you killed him?"

"No. He escaped me, but he won't remain free for long. I'll kill him last."

"Are you certain of his abilities?"

"He is strong, but he cannot stand against us. He'll be no problem. A minor annoyance, nothing more."

"How can you be sure?"

"Because the fool gave me his name. He performed a rather rustic binding spell. Simplistic and crude, but it worked . . . temporarily."

The others interrupted with coarse laughter. "And this was how he escaped? He slowed you down?"

"I tell you it matters not! During the spell, he invoked his name and the name of his father. We have all that we need to defeat him now. Our magic is stronger."

The fifth, who had remained quiet until now, spoke. "If what you say is true, and I have no reason to doubt that it is, then there are two magi in this town."

The others gasped and hissed.

"Two?"

"Indeed. Two, for I encountered one as well."

"Perhaps you were confronted by the same magus."

"No, this was a young man who does not have knowledge of the gifts he possesses. He escaped me quite by accident. I let him go, content to save him for later."

"I have seen this young man, as well," said the third. "Did he flee from a home when you saw him last?"

"Yes." The fifth nodded.

"Then it was him. I saw three young people run from a home. Are you certain he doesn't understand his gift?"

"I am positive. Why?"

"When I saw him, he was able to start two vehicles and the three of them drove away. I assumed then that he was the magus we had sensed. I was unaware of the second."

They fell silent and bowed their heads in thought. After a moment, the first spoke.

"Two adversaries. We must be very careful, brothers."

"It is of no consequence," said the second. "One does not know how to use his abilities and the other has given us his name. We will save their souls for last, and then be sated and ready to sleep again."

"Then that will be soon," the fourth replied, "for I sense the town is almost emptied. There are only a few left. Most are hiding together in groups, which should expedite things."

The first raised his arms. "Perhaps we will have time to enjoy the night and revel before the dawn comes. Let us finish this task."

CHAPTER EIGHT

"Look over there." Gus nudged his brother with his elbow and nodded his head toward Axel's house.

The three of them were huddled together behind Ray Dillinger's old chicken coop. Ray had passed away two years earlier from diabetes-related complications and his property had stood vacant ever since, including the coop. It still smelled faintly of chicken shit. They had encountered more dead bodies as they made their way through the streets, but not as many as they had expected. Instead, they'd found small mounds of ashes scattered along the streets and sidewalks and in yards. None of them had an explanation for it, but the sight disturbed them. Even more disturbing was the silence. They hadn't heard a scream in several minutes.

"What?" Greg frowned, glancing around in confusion.

Gus pointed again. "There's a light on down in Axel Perry's basement."

Greg and Paul glanced at the small house. Sure enough, the ground-level cellar window was lit with a dim, soft glow.

"But the power is out," Greg whispered. "How's he got light?"

"It's candlelight," Paul said. "See how it changes and flickers?"

"You reckon he's okay?" Gus asked. "I like old Axel."

"I like him, too," Paul agreed. "He's a good old boy. They broke the mold when they made him."

"We should check on him," Greg said. "Make sure he's alright. I mean, he's an old man and all. He might be scared. Don't want him having a heart attack or anything."

"That's a good idea," Gus said. "Maybe we can take him with us. Get him the hell out of here."

Paul shook his head. "We'll check on him, but we can't take him with us. I hate to say it, but he'd slow us down. I ain't exactly a spring chicken anymore, and my heart's beating so fast it's fit to pop right out of my chest. I can't imagine what shape Axel is in right now."

"It don't seem right," Greg said, "leaving an old man behind."

"I don't like it either," Paul replied, "but think about it. We may have to move fast. Run. We might have to fight or think on our feet. There's no telling what could happen. At the very least, he'd slow us down, but if he got hurt, we'd be screwed. Better to leave him inside the house than to leave him in a field somewhere."

Gus nodded. "That's a good point."

"I still don't like it," Greg said.

"Your vote is duly noted." Paul stood up. "If it helps, I don't like leaving my dogs behind either, but there it is. Now come on. We're wasting time. Let's check on Axel, make sure he's okay and let him know we're going for help, and then move on."

They hurried over to Axel's house, weapons at the ready, watching the nearby homes and yards for any sign of movement. Gus stepped in one of the mysterious piles of ash. It clung to his boot and pants leg and swirled in the air around him. Gus coughed.

"Goddamn," he wheezed when the coughing fit subsided. "Whatever that stuff is, it tastes nasty."

"I've got an idea what it is," Paul said.

"What?"

"Trust me. You don't want to know."

"Now that ain't fair, Paul. Tell me what you think it is."

Paul kept his voice low as they crossed the yard. "Think about it. We've been seeing these piles everywhere, right?"

The Pheasant brothers nodded.

"But they weren't around before tonight. And earlier, when me and Gus were sneaking around, we saw a lot of dead bodies. Not so many of them now though, are there? Instead, there's just those little piles of ash."

Gus gagged and began coughing again. He doubled over, clutching his stomach.

Greg's eyes grew wide. "You don't mean . . . that stuff is dead people?"

Paul shrugged, and then glanced around the neighborhood. He stepped up onto Axel's front porch and approached the door. Greg put a hand on his brother's shoulder, but Gus shoved him away and retched again. Greg decided to look in the other direction and stand watch. There was no answer to Paul's repeated knocking. After a few tries, he came back down into the yard.

"That's fucking disgusting." Gus wiped his mouth

with his shirtsleeve. "Why did you have to tell me that shit, Paul?"

"Hey, you asked. Don't ask questions you don't want answered. Didn't your mother ever tell you that? Now quit dicking around and come on."

Paul started around the side of the house, his rifle at the ready. Gus and Greg stared at him in confusion.

"But nobody answered when you knocked," Greg whispered. "Where are you going now?"

"To tap on one of those basement windows. Maybe we can get his attention that way."

They hurried along behind him. Gus continued furiously wiping at his mouth and nose, his expression one of horrified disgust.

"Jesus," Greg whispered. "Jesus fucking Christ, what a mess this whole thing is."

"You reckon it was death rays?" Gus asked.

"What?"

"All the bodies. What do you think it was that turned them into ash? I mean, it couldn't have been fire. I smell smoke, but that's from somewhere across town. If somebody had burned the bodies, we'd see little fires all over town. We'd smell gasoline and stuff. So what do you think did it? There's no bones, no jewelry or bits of clothing left behind. What could do that to a person?"

"How the hell would I know?"

"I'm just saying, it's mighty odd. Thought maybe you'd have one of your theories."

"Will you two be quiet?" Paul handed Gus his rifle. Then he got down on his hands and knees and peeked through the window.

"What do you see?" Gus asked. "Is Axel down there? Is he okay?"

"He's down there, and he's got company. Can't see for sure, because of the light, but I think that's Jean Sullivan and her little boy down there with him."

"Well, let them know we're up here."

Paul reached forward and rapped on the glass, eliciting frightened screams from inside the house.

"It's us," he called. "Paul Crowley and the Pheasant Brothers! Open up, Axel."

After a moment, Paul stood up and brushed grass clippings from his hands and knees.

"He coming up?" Greg whispered.

"Yeah. At least, I think so. He motioned toward the stairs."

They crept back around to the front of the house, arriving just as the front door creaked open.

"You bunch of idiots," Axel said. "You darn near gave me a heart attack. And I think little Bobby Sullivan might have just peed himself. What were you thinking?"

"We were thinking about you," Paul said as Axel let them into the house. "How you holding up, old-timer?"

Axel shut the door behind them and locked it. "We're scared and we don't know what's going on. Any news?"

"Yeah," Paul replied, "but none of it is any good."

"Come down to the basement and tell us about it. It's safe there, if a little chilly. Damn kerosene heater is on the fritz, just like everything else tonight."

Paul hesitated. "We can't stay, Axel. We saw your light and thought to check on you. Maybe you should blow out the candles, by the way. You can see them from the street. But like I said, we can't stay. We're going for help."

"I've got a bottle of whiskey down there. Don't usually drink it myself, but I might be so inclined if you boys would do a shot with me."

Gus grinned. "I reckon we can stay for a little bit, at least. Right, Paul?"

Sighing, Paul shrugged and followed the others down into the basement. He thought, not for the first time, of his dogs and hoped that they were okay.

Joel Winkler sat cross-legged in his big, plush recliner and looked around his darkened living room. It seemed so different, so strange, without the lights on. Joel always had at least one light on twenty-four hours a day, even if it was just the small night-light in the bathroom next to the master bedroom. He didn't like stumbling around in the dark.

The lights had been just one of the things Richard liked to complain about.

He missed Richard. Not a day went by that Joel didn't think about him, but right now, he was thinking about him more than ever.

They'd met in college. Before his freshman year, Joel had never been out of Brinkley Springs and the surrounding vicinity. Richard was from California and had traveled all around the world. They sat next to each other in psych class, formed a friendship and began spending time together. Within days, that friendship had turned romantic. After graduation, Richard had gone back to California and Joel, unable to find a job, had ended up back in Brinkley Springs. He'd been depressed and despondent until two months later, when Richard showed up at his door. The moving van was parked outside.

They'd lived together for just over a decade. Joel knew what people said behind their backs, but he didn't care. Yes, some of the people in town were blatantly homophobic, even in this day and age, but most were just curious. As far as he knew, Brinkley Springs didn't have any other gay couples. Not that they'd let it officially be known that they were indeed a couple. Joel had balked at revealing that, preferring instead to tell people that Richard was just his roommate. In the end, that was why Richard had left a second time—Joel's steadfast refusal to come out of the closet and openly embrace and acknowledge their relationship.

Joel died a little more each day without him.

Feeling melancholy, Joel began humming Gordon Lightfoot's "If You Could Read My Mind." It had been their song.

He stared at the picture on the end table. It had been taken four years ago at the beautiful Cass Scenic Railroad State Park, near Bald Knob. In it, he and Richard were smiling, arms around each other. Behind them was a colorful kaleidoscope of fall foliage. Joel had taken the picture himself, using the timer on his camera. They'd been laughing about the mountain's name—Bald Knob—and it had led to playful innuendos that lasted throughout the day and ended in a slow, passionate bout of lovemaking in a rented cabin atop the mountain later that night.

The shadows swallowed everything else in the living room. Once-familiar objects like the grandfather clock and the potted plants and the coffee table became unidentifiable shapes. The book he'd been reading, a lurid paperback called *Depraved*, was all but invisible in the darkness. Everything had changed. Muted. But the picture remained clear. Richard's smile, his hair, his eyes, were unaffected by the gloom. Joel buried his face in his hands and could still see his lover's face.

The town had fallen silent. The screams and gunshots had subsided. Somehow, the silence was worse. Joel hoped that it would all be over soon.

"The feeling's gone," he whispered, "and I just can't get it back."

When the window shattered and a dark-cloaked man leaped into the room, Richard didn't jump or scream or try to run away. He simply looked up, wiped the tears from his eyes and sighed.

"You are not afraid?" The figure loomed over him, arms outstretched.

Joel shook his head. "I'm too tired to be afraid. I saw what was happening. Earlier, out in the street. I watched two of you pull a family from their car. Nobody came to help them."

"Nobody could."

"Is this the end of the world?"

The intruder laughed. The sound reminded Joel of a whistling tea kettle.

"No. Merely the end of *your* world."

"Will it hurt?"

"I could make it very painful indeed. Agonizing and slow. Now are you afraid?"

Joel shook his head.

The man's shoulder's slumped. "It is better when you are afraid. It improves the taste of your soul. But no matter."

The man in black reached for him and Joel leaned forward into the embrace.

"Thank you," he whispered as the darkness engulfed him.

Kirby Fox cowered in his tree house, reading his Bible (a red, faux-leather-cover King James version that he'd been given at church after completing catechism classes a year before) and begging the Lord not to let what had just happened to his parents happen to him, as well.

He'd been camping out in the backyard, sleeping in the tree house—or at least that was what his parents had thought. In truth, there had been very little sleeping, as Kirby's tree house contained a folder full of pictures printed off from a porno site. He kept the folder in the middle of an old Trapper Keeper left over from elementary school, and hid the Trapper Keeper inside a long white box of comic books. His parents had never been inside the tree house—at least, not that he knew of—but Kirby saw no reason not to be cautious at all times.

Like now, for example. He looked up from the book of Psalms, his finger frozen over a random passage. He'd had to squint to read it because his flashlight wasn't working. The tree-house roof had a hole in it so that he could stick his telescope out of it on clear nights. Each spring, his father trimmed the branches away from the hole, providing an unobstructed view of the stars. Kirby kept a five-gallon bucket beneath the hole to catch rainwater and had a tarp he could pull over the top of it. He realized now that he'd forgotten to pull the tarp closed. The leaves rustled softly as the breeze picked up. Wind gusted down through the hole, ruffling the naked pictures, his comics and the Bible pages. The printouts fluttered across the floor. Naked women stared up at him from a dozen different poses. Kirby felt sick and guilty. The pictures had been provided by Gary Thompson. Kirby had given him ten bucks and his copy of *Modern Warfare 2* in exchange for them. Gary's parents had a color printer and unlimited Internet access. The kid had a nice business as a middle-school pornographer.

Kirby had beat off twice, guiltily wiping himself with paper towels and then tossing the evidence in the corner, and then snuggled into his sleeping bag and read some back issues of *Gold Digger, Naruto, Green Lantern* and *Ultimate Spider-Man*. At some point, probably during the issue where Doctor Octopus proposes to Peter Parker's Aunt May, Kirby had fallen asleep.

His father's screams were what woke him, although Kirby hadn't realized it actually was his father at first. The cries were too high-pitched. Too strange. It was only when his father was flung through the bedroom window and landed in the yard, shards of glass sticking out of his face, that Kirby had realized the shrieks belonged to him. His father had lain there, thrashing and quivering and squealing. Then parts of Kirby's mother had followed him out of the broken window. First had come her head. Then her arm. Then something from inside of her. Then another arm.

Kirby had been too frightened to scream. He'd simply cowered there in the tree-house door, watching in shock and horror as his father bled to death with his mother's decapitated head and various internal organs lying upon his chest. The ground around him was soaked with blood.

After his father fell quiet and quit moving, Kirby became aware of the screams from elsewhere in town. There were too many of them. He'd sat with his back to the wood-plank wall, pulled his knees up to his chest, grabbed the Bible—and prayed. His mother had insisted he keep the Bible in the tree house; it was her idea of good luck. In hindsight, maybe she'd been right. His parents were dead but Kirby was still alive. He turned his attention back to the book and focused on a random psalm.

"He giveth to the beast his food, and to the young ravens which cry . . ."

Kirby was unaware that he was reading aloud and equally oblivious that he was crying.

"He delighteth not in the strength of the horse: he taketh not pleasure in the legs of a man. The Lord taketh pleasure in them that fear Him, in those that—"

Something warm and wet plopped onto the page and splattered against the crook of skin between Kirby's thumb and index finger. A raindrop? Frowning, he looked up and saw two eyes staring back at him through the hole. It was a crow, he realized. A big black crow—the biggest he'd ever seen. The bird had shit right through the hole and onto the Bible.

Kirby wiped the offending substance away with his shirttail. Sniffling, he turned his attention upward again, but the bird was gone. In its place was a man, perched on the roof of the tree house and grinning wide enough that his teeth flashed white in the darkness.

Then the darkness flowed through the hole, and whatever good luck Kirby's Bible had brought him finally ran out.

* * *

"Is that yours?"

Levi glanced up and saw that Donny was pointing at the buggy.

"Yes, it's mine."

"Where's your horse?"

"She is safe. I have her stabled down near the river."

"How do you know they haven't fucked with her, too?"

"Dee has certain protections. Similar to mine. No harm will come to her."

Marsha smiled. "Your horse is named Dee?"

Levi nodded. "Yes. And my dog, who is back home in Pennsylvania, is named Crowley."

"Those are unusual names. Don't get me wrong—I like them, but they're not ones you hear every day. Around here, not too many people even bother to name their horses or dogs."

"I named them after old friends of my family." He paused, surveying the street. "It looks okay to cross. We'll be safe once we get inside Esther's house."

"How?" Donny asked. "I mean, no offense, Levi, but I don't see how we're any better off inside that old bed-and-breakfast. We ought to get the hell out of town."

"I don't think we can leave. I don't think they'll let us. And as for the house, I can protect us once we're inside."

"The way you protected us back there, you mean?"

Marsha gasped. "Donny!"

"It's okay." Levi raised his hand. "He's right. I did miserably back there. I almost failed. That won't happen again."

"But how are you going to protect us? I mean, no offense, Levi, but how can I be sure that Marsha is going to be safe?"

Levi smiled. "You're a soldier. So am I. The only difference is our methods and the weapons we choose. I give you my word that she'll be safe inside. Now come on. Let's go, while the coast is clear."

They hurried across the street. Marsha and Donny trotted behind Levi, hand in hand. They had just made it to the opposite side when a truck engine shattered the silence. Marsha and Donny jumped, startled by the sudden noise. Levi merely turned in the direction of the disturbance.

"Now *that* is odd."

A four-wheel-drive pickup truck rounded the corner and raced toward them. Levi frowned, staring at the onrushing headlights, and raised a hand to shield his eyes from the glare.

"That's Randy," Marsha yelled. "That's my little brother!"

Marsha and Donny waved their hands at the approaching truck. As it neared them, Marsha released Donny's hand and ran toward the curb. The truck skidded, the brake lights flashing red in the darkness, and then slid to a stop. Randy leaped out of the cab, leaving the engine running, and dashed toward his sister. The two embraced fiercely, as Donny and Levi hurried toward them.

"Are you okay?" Marsha gasped. "You've got blood all over you."

Randy nodded. "I'm okay. It's . . . it's not my blood."

He pulled back from her, and they all glimpsed the tears on his cheeks.

"Come with me," he said. "I can get us out. The old logging road—"

"That won't work," Levi said. "We need to get inside."

Randy stared at Levi, then glanced at Donny and Marsha. "Who's this?"

"You can call him Levi," Marsha said. "It's okay. He's a friend."

Donny stuck out his hand and Randy shook it. They embraced quickly, and Donny slapped him on the back.

"Good to see you," Donny said.

"You, too. Thanks for taking care of my sis, yo."

Randy reached his hand out to Levi, but Levi hesitated. He seemed deep in concentration.

"What's up?" Randy frowned. "Do I have a booger hanging out of my nose or something?"

"Your aura," Levi whispered. "It's interesting, to say the least."

Randy's frown deepened. He glanced at his sister and Donny, but they only shrugged.

"What's up with him?"

"Apparently," Donny said, "he sees auras. And yeah, I know how that sounds, but after some of the shit we've seen tonight, I'm inclined to believe it."

Marsha took her brother's hand. "Where's Mom and Dad?"

Randy's expression clouded. He took a deep breath, tried to speak and then sagged forward. Donny and Marsha caught him before he could collapse.

"Jesus," Donny grunted.

"Randy?" Marsha patted his cheek with her hand. "Randy!"

"He's passed out," Donny said. "I'm guessing shock. I've seen this before."

"Is he going to be okay? He's got a lump on the back of his head. And all this blood! What's happened to him? Where are my parents?"

"We need to get him inside," Levi said, stepping forward to assist them. "Quickly."

Donny picked Randy up and gently placed the teen over his shoulders.

"Hurry." Levi's tone was insistent. He stared up into the sky.

"Why?" Donny glanced around but didn't see anything.

"Because they're coming."

"Shit."

"Yes."

Donny carried the unconscious teen toward the house. Marsha trotted along beside him, stroking Randy's hair and begging Donny to be careful with him. Levi ran over to the truck, shut off the engine and the headlights and then closed the door. The wind picked up and the tree limbs rustled in the breeze.

"Your will be done, Lord. All I ask for is time. For their sakes as well as mine."

Turning, he hurried after the others. As they reached the bed-and-breakfast, the door opened and Esther stepped outside. Myrtle bustled around behind her in the doorway.

"What's happening?" Her eyes widened when she saw Randy. "Oh, goodness! Is he hurt? Is he . . . dead?"

"He's okay," Donny panted. "Just passed out."

"Well, get him into the sitting room." Esther moved aside and let them pass. Then she beckoned at Levi. "What is happening, Mr. Stoltzfus?"

"I'll explain what I can," he said, slipping past her and into the foyer. "But first, I want to make sure we're safe. I don't have much time. Do you have a Magic Marker I can borrow, or even a pen or pencil?"

"Oh, yes. I have some in the kitchen. Which would you like?"

"It doesn't matter. But I need one quickly."

Nodding, Esther hurried into the kitchen. Myrtle shut and locked the door, and then she and Levi joined the others in the sitting room, where Donny had laid Randy on the sofa. The teen's cheeks were pale in the candlelight, and his breathing was steady but shallow. His eyes flickered beneath the lids. Marsha sat beside him, stroking his hair.

"Is he going to be okay?"

Donny lifted Randy's wrist and checked his pulse. He nodded. "He'll be fine. His pulse is strong, and his breathing is steady—if shallow. Just let him rest for a bit."

Esther returned from the kitchen and handed Levi a black Magic Marker. He dashed back into the foyer. Esther, Myrtle and Donny followed him. Levi uncapped the marker and then glanced over his shoulder at Esther.

"I apologize in advance for doing this, but it's the only way to keep us safe. This will protect us. I'll pay for the paint and repairs later, if you wish."

Before she could respond, he stood on his tiptoes and began to write on the wall just above the closed door. He didn't talk, didn't explain to them what he was doing. He seemed totally absorbed in the task. The three could only watch him and look at one another in confusion. He wrote,

> *I.*
> *N. I. R.*
> *I.*
> *SANCTUS SPIRITUS*
> *I.*
> *N. I. R.*
> *I.*
> *Ito, alo Massa Dandi Bando, III.*
>   *Amen J. R. N. R. J.*
> *SATOR*
> *AREPO*
> *TENET*
> *OPERA*
> *ROTAS*

When he was finished, Levi stepped back and studied his handiwork.

"Oh my . . ." Esther's hand went to her chest.

"What is that stuff?" Donny asked. "Is that Latin or something?"

"I recognize some of it," Myrtle said, sounding excited. "It's a powwow charm. Isn't that right, Mr. Stoltzfus?"

"Three different charms, actually." Levi turned to them and smiled. "You are partially correct, Mrs. Danbury. But I must hurry. Please excuse me one moment. While I'm doing that, it might be best if you snuffed out the remaining candles."

"But then we'll have a hard time seeing."

"Yes, but perhaps those outside will have a hard time seeing us, as well."

"But you said that inscription above the door would protect us," Esther said. "Why do we care if they know we're in here?"

"Because I don't want them surrounding the house. When we're done, after I've rested a bit, I need to go back out there. That's easier to do if I can sneak outside, rather than running a gauntlet."

He turned away and repeated the inscription process over every door and window in the house, while the others returned to the sitting room. When he was finished, Levi joined them. To the others, he seemed exhausted.

"Mrs. Laudry—"

"Call me Esther, dear."

"Very well. Esther, would you be so kind as to grant me a drink of water?"

"Certainly. We have bottled water in the refrigerator. I would imagine it's still cold, even with the power being out. I'll get some for everyone. Myrtle, would you help me?"

"Sure. Good thing our eyes have adjusted to the dark. I don't fancy breaking a hip on top of everything else tonight."

"Oh, hush."

The two old women bustled off to the kitchen again. Marsha hovered over her brother, seemingly oblivious to anything else in the room. Donny and Levi studied each other.

"You look beat, Levi."

"Not yet."

"No, I mean you look tired."

"Oh." Grinning, Levi scratched his beard. "That I am. But it will be a long time before I sleep. I don't think any of us will sleep before dawn—except for the boy there. His name is Randy?"

"Yeah."

"He has . . . abilities." Levi's tone was flat—a statement rather than a question.

Donny shrugged. "He's pretty good at fixing cars, but other than that, I don't know. Why?"

"It's . . . Never mind. We have more urgent matters to discuss. I just find him fascinating, is all."

Donny looked over at Randy and Marsha and then back at Levi. "Fascinating?"

"He reminds me of . . . someone else at that age."

"Who?"

"Here we are," Esther said as she and Myrtle came back into the room, juggling plastic bottles of water. "It's still cool. I'm sorry we didn't pour it into glasses, but these seemed easier, given the circumstances."

Levi smiled as he accepted one. "I'm sure this is fine. Thank you both."

He unscrewed the cap and took a long sip while they handed bottles to Donny and Marsha. Marsha opened hers, but rather than drinking, she raised her brother's head slightly off the couch, put the bottle to his parted lips and poured a small amount into his mouth. Randy swallowed and then smacked his lips. His eyes remained closed.

"I hope he's okay," Marsha said.

"Here." Levi stood up, crossed the room and knelt by him. "Allow me."

He took Randy's hand in his and lightly pinched the skin between the thumb and index finger. A moment later, Randy's eyes opened. He glanced around in bewilderment and then relaxed when he saw his sister and Donny. Levi gently released his hand and then returned to his seat.

"Thirsty," Randy rasped, licking his lips.

"Here. Don't try to sit up." Marsha gave him another sip of water.

"Where are we?"

"We're at Mrs. Laudry's bed-and-breakfast," Marsha told him. "You passed out on the sidewalk. Do you remember? You were getting ready to tell me something about Mom and Dad."

His expression darkened. "Oh."

"Randy, what happened? What's wrong?"

He sat up slowly and stared at his hands in his lap. Marsha put her arm around him. Donny sat down next to her on the other side of the couch and took her free hand in his. When Randy looked up at her again, fresh tears brimmed in his eyes. He spoke slowly at first, halting between words. His voice was monotone. Emotionless. But then the words began to spill out of him. He shuddered and his throat worked as if what he had to say was choking him. He told them everything that had happened—the power going out, the crow on the patio that had turned into a man, the murder of his parents, the strange effect the spilled salt had on the killer, his escape with Stephanie and Sam, what they'd seen driving through town, the strange graffiti on the hanging tree, Sam and Stephanie's death, the invisible barrier and the dead birds. When he was finished, he broke down into uncontrollable sobs, leaned forward and buried his face in his sister's lap. She wrapped her arms around him, lay her cheek against his back and shared his grief. Donny rubbed her back and tried to comfort them both.

"That poor boy," Myrtle whispered. "Those poor children. Randy and Marsha are good kids, and their parents were fine people. This is such a shame."

"It's terrible." Esther nodded in agreement. "What do you think really happened, Levi?"

He glanced up at them, appearing distracted. "I'm sorry?"

"Out there. What do you think really happened with Randy tonight?"

"I think it happened exactly like he told us."

Esther flinched. "But some of the things he said, birds changing into humans and invisible force fields . . ."

"You haven't been outside. We have. I believe the boy is telling the truth. In fact, I know he is. We've seen some of the same things he saw."

Myrtle grew pale. "Is it the apocalypse? Are these demons?"

"I don't know what they are yet. That's what I need to figure out."

They fell silent again and listened to Marsha and Randy weep.

Levi folded his fingers into a steeple, closed his eyes and concentrated. Randy's sudden appearance outside had badly distracted him. The youth clearly had the gift, but seemed almost completely oblivious to it. In some ways, Levi envied him for that. He thought back to when he was Randy's age—that fateful summer when everything had changed and he'd learned just what high a price magic had—and wished that he'd been oblivious, as well. Maybe if he hadn't known, things would be different. Maybe the girl he had loved would still be alive. Maybe he'd still have a home, a real home, with people who welcomed him and a family that he could always turn to, no matter how bad things got.

He needed to focus. Growing maudlin over the past wouldn't help their present situation. What did he know so far? Brinkley Springs had been attacked by supernatural entities with the ability to change shape. They had appeared as both a crow and human. In their human guise, they appeared clad in antiquated, Puritan-style clothing. Their speech was a curious mix: outdated colloquialisms mixed with more modern terms and slang. They had inhuman strength, speed and abilities. They were systematically slaughtering every living thing. They devoured their victims' souls, leaving an empty husk behind, as a locust in summer leaves its desiccated shell clinging to a tree. Their victims' bodies turned to dust shortly after death, leaving no trace save for a small pile of ash.

Levi shuddered at the thought of such a fate. To have one's soul eaten, to lose all sense of self or being, to not travel to the levels and planes of existence beyond this one, to become the sum total of null with no chance of ever being reborn or reconstituted—that was the worst fate he could imagine. Better to end up in hell than to be completely eradicated.

What else did he know? The entities seemed impervious to various workings and magical disciplines. His binding spell had been only partially effective, serving to slow his antagonist down rather than actually binding it to his will. They'd sealed off

Brinkley Springs from the outside world by means of a mystical barrier, which would have taken an enormous force of will and an incredible amount of energy to construct. It was possible that the barrier was some sort of soul cage, though Levi had never heard of one so massive in size. It was a stunning achievement. And then, finally, there was the word Randy had seen carved into the trunk of a tree— *Croatoan*. It was obvious from their reactions that Randy, Marsha, Donny, Esther and Myrtle hadn't recognized the word or its significance, but Levi did. He just didn't know how it fit into all of this.

Yet.

Croatoan. The word had several different meanings, and not all of them were related to occult lore. At best, it was a location and nothing more, but Levi was fairly certain its association with tonight's events was something more sinister.

He opened his eyes, unfolded his fingers and cleared his throat. The others all turned to him.

"The highway leading into town . . . How many cars and trucks use it at night?"

"Not many," Donny said. "Traffic is usually pretty light at night. Maybe one or two cars and a few tractor trailers all night long. That's it."

"But a few will pass through?"

"Yeah, probably. Why?"

"I'm thinking about this barrier that Randy told us about," Levi said. "We can't leave—can't contact the outside world. But if an oncoming car hits it, and the driver is uninjured or able to call for help, others might become aware of our situation."

Myrtle sat up straight. "Can we hold out until then?"

Levi shook his head. "I don't think so."

"Does that mean you have a better idea of what's going on?"

"Perhaps," Levi answered. "At the very least, I'm starting to connect the dots. How many of you have heard of Roanoke?"

"I've been there many times," Esther said. "They have some lovely antique shops."

Marsha nodded. "It's not that far from here. Just over the border in Virginia."

"I don't mean the city of Roanoke. I'm talking about the original version—Roanoke Island. Are any of you familiar with it?"

Donny, Marsha and Randy shook their heads. Esther frowned.

"Oh." Myrtle snapped her fingers. "That's where all those people disappeared, back during the colonial days, right?"

"Correct. At least, partially. This Roanoke, unlike the Roanoke you were all referring to, is an island off the coast of North Carolina."

"I know that place," Donny said. "It sits right off of Highway 64. We passed through there on our way to the Outer Banks."

"And if you blinked," Levi replied, "then you probably missed it. In many ways, Roanoke is much like Brinkley Springs. It's small—about eighteen square miles—and it's fairly remote, even with the highway access. I'd guess less than seven thousand people live there, and many of them are probably seasonal."

"I don't know," Donny said. "I seem to remember there were a lot of tourists there when we went through. Of course, it was summer and all."

"Oh, no doubt there were tourists. Roanoke is a historical site, after all. As Myrtle said, it was a place of some importance in this country's past. But . . . I also think it might have some significance concerning tonight's events."

Marsha leaned forward. "What do you mean?"

"Bear with me. It's a long story, but I'll do my best to be brief. Near the end of the sixteenth century, the English tried several times to establish a permanent settlement on Roanoke Island. Had their attempts been successful, Roanoke would have been the first English colony in the New World. Keep in mind that this was before the American Revolution, of course, and the English had claimed the area as their own. In fact, at the time, there was no North Carolina as we know it today. Roanoke Island was simply a part of Virginia. They named it after Queen Elizabeth I, who was also called the 'Virgin Queen.'"

"And was she?" Donny asked.

"Who knows?" Levi shrugged, and then continued. "Sir Richard Grenville was the first person to attempt to create a permanent settlement on the island. In 1585, at the behest of Sir Walter Raleigh, Grenville transported a group of English colonists to Roanoke Island. He left them under the guidance of a man named Ralph Lane, and then he sailed back to England for more supplies. At first, things went well, but Grenville's return was ultimately delayed, and the settlers reportedly found themselves running out of supplies. Soon, they were in pretty dire straits. They eventually had to abandon the colony altogether and return back to England with Sir Francis Drake, who had anchored at Roanoke after attacking the Spanish colony of Saint Augustine."

"So the settlement failed," Marsha said.

"Indeed. But a second attempt to colonize the island

was made in 1587, and many of the original settlers returned with that second group of their countrymen, determined to make a go of it. Men. Women. Children. Families. Sadly, they fared no better. They brought livestock with them, but many of the animals died in transit. They brought seeds and tools but had trouble raising enough crops to sustain themselves. The seeds withered. The tools broke. Once again, they began to run low on supplies, so a man named John White sailed for England to retrieve more. He left behind his daughter Eleanor and her daughter, Virginia, who was the first English child to be born in the New World. She was named after the queen, I would imagine. It couldn't have been easy for White to leave his friends and family behind, let alone his granddaughter, but apparently, he only expected to be gone three months. He told his fellow colonists that if the situation grew dire, and they had to abandon the settlement for any reason while he was gone, that they should carve the name of their new destination, and mark it with a Maltese cross under the carving so that he'd be sure to notice it. That way, he'd know where to find them upon his return. And with that final instruction, he left."

Donny tilted his head from side to side, cracking his neck and shoulders. "No offense, Levi, but I don't see how this helps us."

"You will in a moment. Patience. White made it back to England safe and sound, but when he got there, he found his country embroiled in a war with Spain. Despite his protestations, White's ship was confiscated by the authorities for use in the war effort. White was full of despair, and he argued for the ship's return, but to no avail. The settlers were on their own. He didn't make it back to the colony until 1590—three years after his departure."

"Three years instead of three months," Esther said. "Those poor people. They must have thanked God when he finally arrived."

Levi shook his head. "On the contrary, as Myrtle said earlier, the settlement was empty. There was no one left to thank God. When White stepped off the boat, he found that all of the colonists had simply vanished. Their valuables and money and clothing still remained. Indeed, in many homes, rotting food sat on cobweb-covered plates, as if the inhabitants had left halfway through their meal. But there was not a single living soul to be found. None of the inhabitants remained behind. There were no bodies and no signs of foul play. It was as if they'd disappeared into thin air."

Esther made a noise in her throat.

"Desperate to find them," Levi continued, "White and his men searched the colony for clues to their whereabouts. Remember what White had told them before leaving—that if they had to abandon the settlement, they were to carve the name of their new destination somewhere and mark it with a Maltese cross? Well, White didn't find any signs of a Maltese cross, but he *did* find two carvings. The first was the letters c-r-o, which had been etched into a tree. The second word was carved in a fencepost. That word was *Croatoan*—the same word Randy saw carved into a tree tonight."

"Cro," Marsha said. "Crow?"

"Perhaps," Levi said, "or maybe we're seeing connections where there are none. But it is curious, don't you think?"

"But what's Croatoan?" Randy asked, sitting up. "What does it mean?"

"It is a name for many different things. White knew it as the name of an island to the south of Roanoke. Today, that island is called Hatteras, but back then, it's name was Croatoan, and it was inhabited by a friendly tribe of Native Americans. Based on this, White logically assumed that his people had decided to take shelter with the natives until his return, though his assumption didn't account for the half-eaten meals and other signs that the colonists had left in a hurry. Convinced they were at Croatoan, White intended to go after them, but he was delayed yet again. Several hurricanes prevented him from reaching the island, and he had to return to England instead. He never made it back to the New World, and the settlement remained abandoned. It's said that he went mad with grief and guilt."

"So the lost colonists settled Croatoan . . . Hatteras?" Myrtle asked.

"No. White, and all of the historians, archeologists and scientists who have come along since then and assumed the same thing, were wrong. The truth is not widely known, other than to certain individuals like myself, but it's a truth nonetheless."

Esther frowned. "Individuals like yourself?"

"Magicians. Powwow doctors. Priests. Warlocks. Witches. Call us what you will. They are different names for the same thing. Our disciplines and methods may differ, but in the end, we're all on the same path."

"So, you're not Amish?" Esther's expression was one of disappointment.

"No, I'm not Amish. I was at one time, but not anymore."

"I see." Her frown deepened. "Myrtle and I discussed it, when you were upstairs in your room. I just assumed, judging by how you dress and the buggy outside, that you were either Amish or Mennonite. I would certainly never have pegged you for a . . ."

"A what? A pagan?"

"That's a nice way of saying it." Esther looked away. "Sounds like Devil worship to me."

"I'm not a Satanist, Esther. I was once a part of the Amish faith, but I was forced to leave the community many years ago. What you need to understand is that the decision wasn't mine. I still hold on to my moral upbringing. I'm not Amish or Mennonite, or Protestant or Catholic. But really, those are just labels. If you need me to explain my beliefs, I'm just trying to live my life right and do God's work, the way that feels right to me."

"By using witchcraft."

"I told you before," Myrtle said, "it's not witchcraft. He's using powwow."

"Not just powwow," Levi corrected her. "Powwow is ineffective against the things outside. The wards I placed over the door, for example, are powwow based but infused with other disciplines, as well."

"What kind?" Myrtle's eyes shone, and Levi cringed at the eagerness in her voice.

"I'd rather not say."

"Powwow," Esther said. "Witchcraft. Seems like the same thing to me."

"Be that as it may," Levi said, "right now, it's the only thing keeping us alive."

"God is keeping us alive, Mr. Stoltzfus."

"You're a religious woman, Esther. I'm sure you prayed tonight. Has it occurred to you that perhaps God sent me to safeguard all of you? Perhaps I am the answer to your prayer."

"I don't—"

"Look," Donny interrupted. "I don't reckon this is the time for a religious debate. Those things are still out yonder, and I for one would like to know what we're dealing with. I don't know shit about magic, but I do know what I saw tonight, and I do know that Levi saved our asses. I'd like to hear him out."

"Yeah," Marsha agreed. "Me, too. Finish the story. What happened to the colonists, and what does it have to do with tonight?"

"The settlers never went to Croatoan. In fact, they never abandoned the colony. Something else happened to them—something far worse than simply running out of supplies. I told you that *Croatoan* has different meanings. Among them, it is also one of the names of an entity known as Meeble."

"Meeble . . ." Donny frowned. "I've heard that name before. In Iraq, I think. Can't remember where or why, exactly."

"It's certainly possible," Levi said. He was about to continue, when his attention was drawn to the window. He sensed a presence outside. He stood up, walked to the window and looked into the darkness. Seeing nothing, he returned to the chair and sat down again.

"What is it?" Esther asked. "What's wrong? Are they out there?"

"I believe so. At least one of them was. If my theory is correct, then they're searching for us, and they won't leave until they've killed us all. But I've taken steps to mask our presence inside these walls. We'll be safe. They can't enter. Not without my permission."

"But why do they want to kill us?" Marsha's tone was exasperated. Panic flashed in her eyes. "I don't understand this."

"I don't either," Levi admitted. "At least, not all of it. At this point, I'm still just connecting the dots and seeing what picture they make. All I have is a theory, and that theory is tied into Croatoan, Meeble and the lost colony of Roanoke. As I said before, the settlers never abandoned the island. What White didn't know—and couldn't have known—was that after his departure for England, five of the colonists began dabbling with the occult. Keep in mind, they were in an already-bad situation. The crops were failing, much of their livestock was dead or sick. Things looked grim. Perhaps these five men prayed to God for help. Perhaps, when their prayers weren't answered to their satisfaction, they turned to other means and methods. Other gods. Perhaps they prayed to someone else, all in an effort to help their fellow man."

"How is that any different from what you and I do?" Myrtle asked.

Levi hesitated. He wanted to tell her that there was a world of difference between what he did and her crystal-gazing, pseudo–New Age nonsense, but this was neither the time nor the place. Instead, he simply smiled as politely as he could and continued.

"It's not any different, except that these men were amateurs. They didn't understand the forces they were dealing with, nor how to bend them to their will. In the end, they didn't even invoke the right entity.

Instead of summoning a nature spirit or something helpful, they accidentally began worshipping something else, and eventually, they brought that something else into our world."

"A demon," Donny guessed. "Meeble."

"It was indeed Meeble, but Meeble is not a demon. He's something different. And here is where things might get difficult for you to believe—especially for you, Esther. All I can say is that I believe them with the utmost sincerity."

Randy laughed. "Shit, dude. I saw what these fuckers could do with my own eyes. I'll believe pretty much anything at this point."

Donny and Marsha nodded. Esther scowled. Myrtle leaned forward, staring at him with rapt attention.

Levi took a deep breath and exhaled. "Much of what we think we know about the history of our planet and the development of the human race is wrong. Our history books and oral traditions are full of inaccuracies. This is especially true of our religious texts. The primary doctrines of Judaism, Christianity, Islam, Buddhism, Jainism, Hinduism, Shinto, Satanism, Wicca and all of the others have been tampered with and rewritten by mankind so much over the years that none of them reflect the original works. Instead, they are filled with inaccuracies and falsehoods. It takes many years of study and searching to learn the real truths. You might believe, for example, that the Bible is the inspired word of God, but it isn't. You've been taught to believe that it is, but what you believe is a lie. The Bible is not God's word. Neither is the Koran or the Torah or any of the other holy books."

"Then whose word is it?" Esther challenged.

"They are the words of men, edited, parceled, snipped and changed countless times to reflect the will of the men in charge, rather than God's will. If you truly want to know God's word and seek His will, then you've got to look beyond the Bible, because the book we've been taught to call the Bible is *not* the complete text. Do you know how many books and scrolls and interpretations were excised over the years? Hundreds. It's not the inspired word of God. It is composed only of the books men decided should be in it. It doesn't give us the complete picture. For that, you have to turn to other texts. Perhaps they aren't in the canon, but they were written at the same time and they are just as valid. Those texts give us a *true* understanding of God. For example, the Bible we all grew up reading tells how God created the universe, but it says nothing about the universe that existed before ours, or about the enemy that came from that other universe."

"You mean Satan?" Myrtle asked.

Levi shook his head. "No, I mean the Thirteen. In the beginning, the entity we know as God or Yahweh or Allah, or hundreds of other names, created the heavens and the Earth. That much is in the Bible. What the Bible doesn't tell us is that in order to create this new universe, He needed a lot of energy. So God destroyed the universe that existed before ours. He reduced it down to the very last atom and utilized the harvested energies as building blocks to create our universe. The old universe ceased to exist and ours was born. However, in addition to God, there were thirteen other denizens of that previous universe who somehow escaped the destruction. Nobody knows how. Suffice it to say, when our new universe sprang forth, they were still here, and they were enraged by what had happened. These entities are collectively known to us as the Thirteen, and they've been the enemies of God and all of His creations—human and otherwise—ever since. They've sworn to destroy anything created by God. After all, He destroyed their universe. Perhaps they merely seek revenge, or maybe they plan to build a universe of their own—a third universe, in which they are the ones in charge. Whatever the case, they are not gods or demons, though they've often been mistaken for such. They are not susceptible to all of the same magicks, workings and laws that govern, banish or bind demons, angels and other supernatural entities. Very specific—and dangerous—magic must be used when confronting them. That magic is known only to a few, of which I am one."

"And this Meeble dude is one of the Thirteen," Randy said. "Right?"

"Exactly!" Levi couldn't hide his enthusiasm. His impressions about the boy, founded when he first saw Randy's aura, had been correct. Despite having no teaching, or indeed, any inkling of his gifts, the boy was attuned.

Randy grinned, clearly pleased with himself despite the evening's grim events.

"Meeble is indeed one of the Thirteen," Levi continued. "He is not as calculating as Ob, the Obot, who commands the Siqqusim, nor is he as big as Leviathan, Lord of the Great Deep, or as powerful as He Who Shall Not Be Named, but Meeble is just as dangerous, cruel and committed to our eradication as any of them. His physical form is bestial. He appears as a hulking, white-furred cross between a cat and an ape and stands almost sixteen feet tall, according to those few who have seen him and lived to tell about their encounter. While the rest of the Thirteen seem to focus their destructive energies on a global scale, Meeble seems to delight instead on destroying humanity one town at a time. That's what happened at Roanoke. And until tonight, I and many others like me assumed that's what was happening in many of the cases where entire populations seemingly vanished overnight—ghost towns out west and such. Now, I'm not so sure."

"But I thought you said Meeble was behind this?" Marsha clenched the sofa cushion tightly with both hands. "Now you're saying he might not be?"

"Perhaps not directly. This is still all just a theory. There's one more piece of the puzzle to put into place." He stood up and placed his hat back on his head. "And so, I've got to go back out for a little while."

"Like hell," Donny said, jumping to his feet. "If you're going back out there, then I'm going with you."

Marsha reached up and grabbed Donny's arm. "Oh no you're not."

Donny pulled away. His eyes remained focused on Levi. "Seriously. You can't face those fuckers by yourself."

"I'm not. God is on my side."

"You just got done telling us that God blew up an entire universe of people to make this one instead."

"Indeed. Can you think of a more powerful ally to have standing with you?"

"Even so, I'm coming along."

Marsha protested again, and the others all began to talk at once. Levi whistled, getting their attention.

"It's not open for debate, Donny. I appreciate your offer. I really do. But somebody needs to stay behind and watch over the others. Randy is still weak, and—"

"I am not." Randy swayed as he tried to stand. "Look, I'm fine."

Myrtle wagged a finger at Levi. "That's a very sexist thing to say."

"I'll have you know," said Esther, slowly rising to her feet, "that I knew how to shoot a rifle before I learned to read. I used to go hunting with my father all the time, Mr. Stoltzfus. That was how things used to be in these parts. I reckon I'm capable of defending myself. Myrtle and Marsha, too."

"You people seem to think I'm making a request. I'm not. This is an order."

"I'm not in the army anymore," Donny said. "And I don't take orders."

"No?" Levi glanced at Marsha and then back to him. "Would you like to know what I think, Donny? I think you're afraid to be left alone with Marsha. I think there's something unsaid between the two of you, and whatever it is, it scares you to death."

Donny opened his mouth to respond, but said nothing. He stared at Levi. The tips of his ears turned red.

"I want all of you to remain here. Remember, as long as you stay inside the house and don't try to leave, you'll be safe. You have my word on that."

Before any of them could argue anymore, Levi turned and hurried into the foyer. Sensing nothing outside, he opened the door, stepped outside onto the porch and closed the door behind him. The coast was clear. He whispered a fervent prayer, reciting from memory a benediction against enemies, sickness and misfortune that his father had taught him long ago.

"The blessing that came from Heaven, from God the Father, when the true living Son was born, be with me at all times. The holy cross of God, on which He suffered His bitter torments, bless me today and forever. The three holy nails which were driven through the holy hands and feet of Jesus Christ, bless me today and forever. The spear by which His holy side was pierced and opened, protect me now, today and forever. May the blood of Christ and the Holy Spirit protect me from my enemies, and from everything which might be injurious to my body and my soul. Bless me, oh you five holy wounds, in order that all my enemies may be driven before me and bound and banished. All those who hate you must be silent before me, and they may not inflict the least injury upon me, or my house or my premises. And likewise, all those who intend attacking and wounding me either spiritually or physically shall be defenseless, weak and conquered. The cross of Christ be with me. The cross of Christ overcomes all water and every fire. The cross of Christ overcomes all weapons. The cross of Christ is a perfect sign and blessing to my soul. Now I pray that the holy corpse of Christ bless me against all evil things, words and works."

When he was finished, Levi made the sign of the cross four times, to the north, south, east and west.

"Guide my hand. Your will be done, as always."

He took a deep breath and stepped off the porch. He felt naked and exposed. The prayer was the last of his powwow. From this point on, to defeat his enemy, he'd have to rely on methods and benedictions that were far older and far less holy than the one he'd just used.

Marsha slowly unclenched her fist and let go of Donny's arm. He winced. She glanced up and gasped. She hadn't realized it until just now, but her fingernails had dug into his skin, leaving angry red marks.

"I'm sorry."

He shrugged. "It's okay."

The group stared at each other in silence for a moment. Then Myrtle tiptoed over to the window and cautiously looked outside.

"Is he gone?" Esther asked.

"I think so," she whispered. "I don't see him, at least."

"Well, good riddance then."

Myrtle let the blinds fall closed and spun around. "Esther! There's no call for that. He's your boarder."

"And he can leave here come sunup. I won't have him under my roof another night."

"Oh, for God's sake!" Marsha bristled at this. "He's fighting for you. For all of us. How can you say that about him?"

"Because he's not doing this for us. You get to be as old as me, Marsha, and you'll see. I know how people are. I see through them. That man may think he's fighting for us, but if you really look at him, you'll see he's fighting for himself—and the way he's doing it is simply un-Christian. I won't have it here. Better to end up dead than in concert with the Devil. I know that you've been through a lot tonight, but trust me. Levi would sacrifice every single one of us if it meant defeating the enemy. I can see it in him."

"Listen to you," Myrtle said. "Do you hear yourself?

This is a far cry from what you were saying about him earlier."

"Earlier, I didn't know. He's not what he seems."

Myrtle shook her head. "But he was praying, right before he left. I heard him whispering a prayer to God—the same God you believe in."

"Not my God."

"Fuck this shit." Donny started for the foyer. "I don't need to hear this crap."

"What are you doing?" Marsha grabbed for him again, not caring if she hurt him or not, but Donny shrugged her off. When he responded, he didn't look at her.

"I'm going with him. Somebody needs to watch his back."

Marsha put her hands to her face and stared at him, the realization sinking in.

"He was right, wasn't he? Levi was right. You're afraid to be left here with me."

Without a word, Donny strode toward the foyer. Seconds later, they heard the door open and close.

"It doesn't matter," Randy said. His tone was sullen. "None of us are gonna escape anyway. Nobody ever gets out of this town. Not before, and especially not now."

With Donny's silent departure confirming her question, Marsha collapsed onto the couch and put her arm around Randy. They comforted one another as best they could and waited to see who would return—Levi, Donny . . . or the crows.

CHAPTER NINE

The darkness deepened. The moonlight dimmed. Thick, sluggish clouds crawled across the sky, blocking the feeble stars. Gone were the gunshots and screams. Gone, too, were people fleeing down the streets or across yards and vacant fields. All across Brinkley Springs, the dwindling number of survivors huddled in their homes and basements, tool sheds and root cellars, storefronts and barns, cars and trucks, praying for help and waiting for the inevitable.

And one by one, the inevitable found them. The shadows arrived . . . hungry.

Stu Roseman was pulled, kicking and screaming, from beneath his queen-size bed before being disemboweled. Mara Dobbs was yanked from her closet, where she'd hidden beneath a pile of blankets and towels, and was then drowned in her own toilet. Don and Jamie Mahan cowered inside their Ford Explorer, desperately trying every few minutes to start the unresponsive vehicle until both it and them were torn apart. Jerrod Hintz and Scott Balzer were discovered hiding in the butcher shop's walk-in freezer and were clubbed to death with half-frozen slabs of meat. Candy Winters ended up with her head sticking out of her vagina. Toby Paulson was suffocated with his own severed penis. Bob Parker was strangled with his own intestines. Rocky Quesada and Joy Oliva had their heads repeatedly bashed together until both were nothing but paste. Aaron Milano was impaled on a flagpole. His two cats were impaled above him. Jeremy Garner, Peggy Stanfield and Michelle Broadhurst were discovered cowering in a far, dark corner of Herb Swafford's hayloft. They were stabbed, cut, chopped and impaled by a variety of Herb's farm tools—pitchforks, axes, shovels and rakes. Herb's head and entrails lay in the mud outside the barn. His pigs would probably have eaten the scraps if the pigs hadn't been killed, too. So were his cows, sheep and one lone horse.

No matter where they hid, no one was missed. No matter how desperately they tried to escape or how valiantly they fought to save their lives, the end result was the same. Everyone had their turn. Everyone died. The shadows were as methodical and precise as they were ravenous and cruel. Human candles were snuffed in the night, never to shine again, and after their souls were devoured, the shadows moved on, leaving corpses in their wake.

A small few died of natural causes. Keith David, Rebecca Copeland and Bobbi Russo all died of heart attacks brought on by fear and stress. Tim Draper and Perry Wayne suffered massive strokes that left them paralyzed and unconscious, and ultimately breathless. Don Hammerton tripped while running down the street and cracked his head open on the curb. Robin Clark suffered a seizure, bit through her tongue and bled to death. In each of their cases, their souls drifted slowly upward, flaring brightly but briefly as they were absorbed by the invisible barrier.

Regardless of how they had died—murder or something more natural—the corpses didn't last long. There was no slow progression of decay and decomposition. Shortly after their death, the people of Brinkley Springs returned to the ashes and dust from which they had originally sprung.

And then, eventually, even the dust disappeared.

Donny stood beneath the tree in Esther's front yard and looked both ways down the dark street, trying to figure out which direction Levi had gone. Nothing moved. Even the wind had stopped. He listened for footsteps, or any other sound that would give away Levi's presence, but there was nothing. The silence made the tiny hairs on the back of his neck prickle. He'd been scared and nervous many times in Iraq. Hell, he'd been scared every day. But those fears were nothing like what he felt tonight.

And not all of it had to do with what was happening in the town.

He glanced back at the bed-and-breakfast, hoping to see Marsha peeking out the window at him, but the curtains remained closed. His heart sank, but what had he expected? He wished he could tell her how he felt, wished desperately that he could find the words to explain his revulsion from Brinkley Springs and his steadfast refusal to linger here any longer than he had to—even if it meant never seeing her again. But every time he tried to tell her, all it did was lead to miscommunications and further hurt feelings. It would be better for her if he just left again. She was stronger now. It wouldn't affect her the way it had the last time he'd left. She'd get through it. She was older now, and she had Randy and her—

Well, she didn't have her parents anymore, did she? After tonight, she didn't have anybody left at all, other than her little brother . . . and him.

Something twisted in Donny's gut. He felt a hot flush of anger and resentment that his decision to leave had now been made even more difficult. How could he abandon her now, in the aftermath of all this? He hated himself for feeling that way and would never have admitted it out loud to anyone, but the emotions were there all the same. What the hell was wrong with him? Had the last few years fucked him that goddamned bad? Was he so self-fucking-centered that when his ex-girlfriend's parents were murdered, the only thing he could think of was how inconvenient it was for him?

Ashamed, he had a sudden urge to run back inside, take Marsha in his arms and apologize to her. What was he doing out here, anyway?

"I was about to ask you the same thing."

Donny gasped but did not scream. He was too startled to scream. He spun around quickly, pulling his arms in tight over his midsection and kicked out with his foot. The blow swept by Levi but didn't faze him.

"Jesus fucking Christ, dude! You scared the shit out of me. Don't you know not to sneak up on someone like that?"

"Language. I don't mind cursing, but neither do I appreciate you taking the Lord's name in vain."

"Sorry. You just really spooked me." Donny straightened to his full height again. "So, what . . . ? You can read minds, too? How did you do that?"

"I have my ways."

"Well, you shouldn't have crept up like that. I mean, damn . . . I could have killed you just now, Levi."

"No, you couldn't have."

"You sure are a cocky bastard, Levi."

"I'm not cocky. I'm confident. Arrogance is a sin. Being prepared isn't. Now what are you doing out here? I told you to stay inside the house."

Donny grinned. "And I told you I don't take orders anymore."

Levi stepped closer, until his forehead was only inches from Donny's chin. As he stared up into the younger man's eyes, Donny saw the anger in his expression—and something else, too. Fear. Levi was afraid, he realized, and that only increased Donny's own uneasiness.

"Do you think this is a game? This isn't some comic-book or movie fantasy, where we defeat the bad guys with no consequences during the battle. I meant what I said, Donny. I can't protect you out here. I need you to go back inside, for my own sake as well as yours."

"I can handle myself, Levi. Trust me on that."

"I know you can. I have no doubts about your abilities, and I'm sure you'd be good to have at my side in a tough situation, but that's not what I'm talking about."

"Then what are you talking about? What do you mean when you say for your sake as well as mine?"

Levi's voice softened. "I . . . I have enough blood on my hands. Enough ghosts following me around. I don't need to add any more."

"Me either, Levi. You think I don't know about guilt? You think I don't know what it's like to kill

somebody—I mean, what it's *really* like? That feeling
you get in your stomach. The way it follows you
through the day. Or how it feels to lose a friend—to
watch them die right in fucking front of you—
while you go on living? I reckon I know how that
feels better than you think."

Levi stared at him for a moment. His expression
changed, and for a moment, Donny thought the older
man was going to cry. But then his features smoothed
out again.

"Okay," Levi said. "I'm still not sure I understand
your motivations, especially when you have a fine
woman waiting inside who clearly loves you. In truth,
though, I appreciate the company. It's not often
somebody walks this road with me. But understand
me, Donny. Your fate rests squarely on your shoulders. I can't protect you beyond the house. I can mask
our presence somewhat, so that we can move about
unmolested. But we're not going to be evading them
for long. I need to confront them. That's the only
way I'll get the information I need to stop this."

"Well, let's get to it, then. We can go find them or
we can stand around here talking all night long.
Which is it going to be?"

"You're not afraid?"

"Of course I'm afraid, Levi. I'm fucking terrified.
And so are you. I can see it on your face. But if you
think you've got a way to stop these . . . whatever
they are, and I can help you do it, then I say we do it
already."

Levi nodded. "Let's go. I have to find something
first."

Donny followed him across the street, resisting
the urge to glance behind them and see if Marsha

was watching. A part of him hoped that she wasn't, but an even bigger part of him would have been disappointed if he turned and didn't see her. He hesitated, his steps faltering. His legs felt heavy.

"Do you happen to know which—?" Levi paused, noticing Donny's discomfort. "Are you okay?"

"Yeah."

"Having second thoughts?"

"No," Donny insisted. "I'm fine. What were you doing out here, anyway? Myrtle looked outside right after you left, and said she didn't see you. We thought you'd gone."

"I was, but then I remembered that I had to do some shopping first."

Donny frowned. "Shopping?"

"Yes, in a way. I was trying to figure out which one of these homes belonged to Myrtle. I'm certain that, given her proclivities, she probably has what I need."

"Proclivities? You mean all that New Age stuff?"

"Yes."

"So why not just knock on the door and ask her?"

Levi shrugged. "At the time, I was worried that if I returned, I'd have to argue with you about not coming with me again. But now that you're here anyway . . ."

Donny pointed across the street. "That's her house, over there."

"You don't want to go back to Esther's either."

"Is it that obvious?"

"It is to me," Levi said as they crossed the street. "And to Marsha, I would assume. And to anyone else who has eyes and has ever been in love."

Donny's ears began to burn. His skin felt flushed.

"I don't mean to pry," Levi continued, "but it's

clear to me that you love her as much as she loves you. What's the problem?"

"I don't want to hurt her anymore."

"You hurt her once? Infidelity?"

"No, nothing like that. I'd never do that to Marsha. It's just . . . it's complicated. I don't like it here. I never have. This town . . . it weighs on you. It eats away at people. You know what I mean? It just never felt like home to me."

"So you ran away?"

"Yeah, I reckon so—if you call joining the army and going to Iraq running away."

"And did you find what you were looking for overseas? Did war feel like home?"

"No. It felt like hell."

"So you returned."

"Not by choice. Believe me, this was the last place I wanted to come back to. But my mom got sick. Cancer."

"Where is she now?"

Donny sighed. "She passed. I stayed long enough to take care of her estate. Put the house on the market. Made sure the funeral director was paid. I was leaving tonight, in fact. A few minutes earlier and I wouldn't have been here when all this started. I'd have been on the road and miles away."

"Where were you going?" Levi asked as they approached Myrtle's front door.

"I don't know. I hadn't thought that far ahead, to be honest. Anywhere, I suppose. Anywhere that felt right, you know? Some place where I could find myself."

"Well, you're here now."

"What's that supposed to mean? You telling me this is all fate?"

Levi shrugged. "Fate. God's will. Call it what you want. Some people think the universe is chaotic—that there's no rhyme or reason to why things happen. I think they're wrong. There's a specific order to things. We don't always like how things turn out, but they turn out that way for a reason. You were going out to find yourself, but maybe your self was here all along."

"Whatever."

"I'm still not sure I understand your hesitation to get involved with Marsha, though."

"The first time I left, Marsha got so depressed that she dropped out of college and tried to kill herself. That's my fault, you know? I don't want to let her in, because I'm gonna leave again and I don't want to put her through that once more."

"I see. That's a heavy burden for a young man like yourself."

"You're telling me."

Levi fell silent and cocked his head, as if listening.

"You hear something?" Donny whispered after a moment.

"No, I was just making sure the coast was clear, and it is. Let's go inside."

"I reckon the door is locked. Brinkley Springs may be a small town, but folks still tend to lock their doors when they leave."

"That's okay. I have a key."

"Myrtle gave you her keys?"

Levi shook his head. Then he grasped the doorknob with his right hand and closed his eyes. As Donny watched, he took a deep breath, held it for ten seconds or so, and then exhaled. Levi opened his eyes as the latch clicked. He turned the knob and the door swung open.

"How the hell did you do that?"

Levi winked. "How do you think? Come on."

They went inside, Levi first, with Donny following close behind him. Myrtle's house was a dusty, spider-webbed monument to clutter. Every inch of available shelf space or tabletop was piled high with a bewildering array of items—stacks of magazines and paperback books, vials of scented oil, votive candles, potpourri, incense burners, crystals, beads, pewter fantasy figurines, tarot cards, ceramic unicorns and dolphins, assorted knickknacks and more. One bookshelf was stuffed with Myrtle's self-published books, and next to the shelf were six open cardboard boxes filled with more. A large angel figurine perched precariously atop the television. Donny didn't like it. Rather than being comforting, the angel seemed somehow sinister, as if it were watching them reproachfully. The air in the house was thick with the competing smells of various incense that made him half-nauseous.

"Crap," he muttered.

"Yes," Levi said, eyeing a shard of quartz that was lying on the coffee table. "A lot of it is. Most of it, in fact. But hopefully she has a few things here that are worthwhile."

"So what are we looking for, anyway?"

"Two things. Why don't you go into the kitchen and find us some salt. Doesn't matter what kind. Table salt. Sea salt. Iodized salt. They're all fine. Get all the salt she has—as much as you can carry."

"Salt?" If not for the seriousness of their situation, Donny might have thought that Levi was fucking with him. "What do we need salt for?"

"It's a weapon. You heard what Randy said. The

thing that killed his parents had an aversion to salt. Many supernatural entities do, at least when they're in corporeal form. Salt is always a good magical fail-safe."

"And here I just thought it made food taste better."

"It does that, too. Now, go on. I'll poke around in here and see if I can't find us some sage."

"Sage?"

"Yes. I have a small quantity with me, here in my vest pocket. But we'll need a lot more."

"Personally, I'd be more comfortable with an M16."

"But we already know such a weapon would be useless against our foe. Salt and sage are what we need."

"If you say so."

Levi nodded, his attention focused on the clutter.

Shaking his head, Donny went into the kitchen and poked around in the dark. He found a salt shaker on the table and slipped it into his pocket. Then he opened the pantry door and found a large canister of salt on the top shelf. When he returned to the living room, Levi wasn't there.

"Levi?"

"I'm upstairs," he called. His voice was faint. "I'll be down in a second."

Donny waited. He sat the salt canister down on the table and flipped through a towering stack of magazines that leaned against the wall in one corner of the room. The titles were ones he'd never heard of before—*Fate*, the *Fortean Times*, *Angels*, the *Coming Changes*, *Conscious Creation*, *Lightworker Monthly* and others. Levi bustled around above him. Donny heard footsteps creak across the ceiling, followed by the sound of a drawer opening. He picked up an issue of the *Fortean Times* and flipped through it. There was a lengthy feature article about mermaids, including a report of a supposed mermaid sighting off the coast of Haifa, Israel, the previous year. Most of the other articles seemed to be culled or clipped from various newspapers and magazines from around the world. All of them focused on the odd or paranormal— ghosts in London's Highgate Cemetery, a man in Beijing falling seventeen stories and living, sightings of everything from Bigfoot to panthers in Manhattan, a rain of fish in a small French town, a Vietnamese man who had grown horns from his head and more. Each story was stranger than the previous, and all of them were supposedly true. Although Donny had never heard of the magazine, he certainly recognized some of the credited sources for the reports— the Associated Press, the *Times* of London, the *Washington Post* and others.

Donny suddenly felt light-headed. The room began to spin. His pulse throbbed in his ears. He took a deep breath and steadied himself. It was all so bizarre. Most of the time, he felt like a young old man. He'd seen things—done things—that the rest of his former friends in Brinkley Springs would never do or understand, but even after seeing as much of the world as he had, he was faced now with the realization that he knew nothing and had seen nothing. There was an entire other world that existed in the shadows of the real world, a world populated by people like Levi and creatures like the ones outside. Skimming the articles in the magazine had just made the realization more concrete.

"Jesus Christ," he whispered, breathless. "Jesus fucking Christ . . ."

He heard footsteps on the stairs. Donny composed himself. Seconds later, Levi appeared, carrying a small bundle of what looked like dried-up hay. He waved it as he approached.

"I found some. I just knew she'd have some on hand. Even an amateur knows about the properties of sage. Now we're ready." His gaze darted down to the magazine still in Donny's hands. "Oh, the *Fortean Times*. That's one of my favorite magazines."

"Really?"

"Oh, yes. I read it every month."

"I should have figured you would."

Levi feigned offense. "I'll have you know that I also read everything from *National Geographic* to *Soldier of Fortune*."

"How about *Penthouse*?"

"Only for the articles." Grinning, Levi pointed to the magazine in Donny's hand. "That's an old issue. If I remember correctly, there's an interesting article about Namibian bloodsuckers in it. Very thought provoking, since the classic *chupacabra* legends originated in South America."

"I don't know about that." Donny's mouth felt like it had been stuffed with cotton. "I didn't read anything about bloodsuckers. I saw a big piece on mermaids."

"Ah, mermaids." Levi nodded. "Leviathan's handmaidens. Beautiful and utterly evil. They're vampiric, as well, though not in a sense that you'd probably understand. Nasty creatures, to be sure, but not nearly as bad as what we're facing tonight."

"Are . . . are the crows vampires?"

Levi frowned. "No, I don't believe so. They've given no indication of such. Something similar to vampires, perhaps, given that they seem to feed on the souls of living things, but I'm not sure yet."

Donny didn't respond. With one trembling hand, he put the magazine back on top of the pile.

"What's wrong?" Levi asked. "You're sweating."

"Levi . . . how long have you been involved in this?"

"In what?"

"This." Donny made a sweeping gesture with his hand. "All of this fucked-up occult stuff."

Levi lowered his head and stared at the floor. When he looked up again, his voice was softer and his air of self-assuredness was gone. He looked and sounded tired.

"All of my life. I was born into this. My father, Amos, practiced powwow, as did his father before him."

"So, your dad taught you how to do these things?"

Levi shrugged. "Some of them. He certainly taught me powwow, but his lessons—and tolerance—stopped there. He didn't approve of the other methods I learned. He didn't see that they were essential for battling the very things we were supposed to be taking a stand against."

"He wanted you to grow up to be just like him."

"In a sense. Although, to be honest, I think my father would have been happiest had I grown up to be just another farmer like my brother. I couldn't, of course. Magic would have found me whether I'd been taught or not. The same can be said of Marsha's brother."

"Randy? Is that why you were acting so weird

about him? But Randy's not magic. Trust me, I've known that kid since he was little. He's just a yo-boy. There's nothing magic about him, unless you count how he can keep his pants from falling all the way down when he walks."

"I'm not sure what a yo-boy is," Levi said, "but trust me when I tell you that Randy has the gift. He was born with the abilities. They've just never been awoken in him. Probably because there's been no one in his life who recognized his talent. I would guess that he's had moments of luck—like tonight, when the vehicles started after he touched them. Little bits of synchronicity such as those are very much part of what we do. The trick is to recognize them when they happen and harness or control them, bending them to your will. Had he been properly taught, he'd be formidable against our foes."

"Is that what you're going to do? Train him?"

"No!"

Levi said it so strongly that Donny took a step backward. At first, he was afraid that he'd somehow offended Levi. The older man stood stiffly, his expression serious and grave.

"No," Levi said again, softer this time. "I'm sorry. That came out sounding harsher than I meant. But no, I won't teach Randy. I won't teach anyone."

"Why not?"

Levi paused. At first, Donny didn't think he was going to answer the question. He stuffed the sage in his pocket and glanced around the room. Then he looked back up at Donny.

"When I wanted to learn about other disciplines—other workings—my father balked, so I went elsewhere. In my former faith, young people are given a year to explore the outside world and determine if they really want to commit to the Amish way of life. I used my year to learn. I went outside of our community on a pilgrimage of sorts and sought out the training of others. I was young and arrogant and brash, and so certain that I was better than my father or anyone else."

"You said earlier that arrogance is a sin."

"And it is," Levi said. "I was sinful. I didn't see it that way at the time, though. I was so righteous in my desire to be one of God's chosen warriors, using the enemy's own tricks against them. And I was right. Powwow wouldn't have been effective against some of the foes the Lord has led me to face over the years. I've had to use other methods. My father thought that me learning those methods was a blasphemy against God, but I disagreed. I learned those methods to further God's will. Eventually, my insistence led to my downfall. I was cast out of my community, disowned by my family and forced to leave the only home I'd ever known. Sent out to live among the English—our term for the outside world. I was just about Randy's age when this happened."

"When what happened? They disowned you just for learning magic?"

"No. At least, not just for that. Something else happened."

"What was it?"

Levi didn't respond.

"Levi, why did they kick you out?"

"There was a girl. Her name was Rebecca. I . . ."

"Yeah?"

"I loved her. I'd known her all my life. We grew up together, much like you and Marsha. She was . . .

impacted . . . by something I did. Something decid-edly darker than powwow. Something I'd acciden-tally unleashed. And when I tried to undo what had happened, Rebecca . . . she . . ."

"Go on," Donny urged. "I'm listening."

"Never mind. We don't have time for this now."

Levi strode toward the door. His expression was grim and purposeful. Donny reached for him as he passed by, but Levi shrugged him off. He reached the door, paused, tilted his head and then opened the door. He hurried outside. Donny rushed after him.

"Hey." He grabbed Levi's elbow. "Listen, man. I'm sorry if I pissed you off back there."

Levi smiled sadly. "You didn't. It's just been a very long time since I've had to talk about it—Rebecca and everything else. Doing so feels like ripping a scab off before the wound has healed. Does that make sense?"

"Yeah, it does. Believe me, I know the feeling. And for what it's worth, Levi, I'm sorry you lost your home."

Levi patted his hand. "Well, let's just make sure we save yours. I know you said that you don't think of Brinkley Springs as your home, but ask yourself this: If this isn't home, then why are you fighting for it? If you're not fighting for the town, then who are you fighting for? Are you doing this for Marsha? If so, then perhaps she is your home?"

Donny opened his mouth to respond, but Levi si-lenced him with a finger.

"No," he said. "Don't answer me. Just think about it. It's like the old saying goes—home is where the heart is. What you need to ask yourself, Donny, is where does your heart lie?"

* * *

Once Greg, his brother and Paul were safe in Axel's cellar, they'd recounted everything they knew, sparing Jean's son the gorier details. After that, they'd grown quiet. Greg kept expecting Paul to urge them back outside again, but he seemed to have abandoned his insistence that they go for help, opting instead to just stay where they were. So they did. Bobby huddled in his mother's lap. Jean kept one arm wrapped protectively around her son. Axel hummed a tuneless version of "Big Rock Candy Mountain." Gus just stared straight ahead at the wall. Paul breathed heavy through his nose, and at one point, Greg thought the mountain man had fallen asleep.

Eventually, Greg broke the silence by saying, "I reckon the Mountaineers are going to have a good season this year. Might go all the way."

He paused, waiting for a response, but Gus, Paul, Axel, Jean and Bobby only stared at him. He couldn't really see them all that well in the darkness because Paul had made Axel blow out the candles after their arrival. But Greg didn't need to see them to know that they were staring at him. He could feel their eyes upon him. He cleared his throat, suddenly feeling foolish.

"Well, that's what I think, at least. They got a fella from New Jersey. A good Christian boy. Come out of the ghetto in Newark and has one hell of an arm on him. Studying to be a horticulturist or some such thing."

Gus stirred. "What the hell is wrong with you?"

"Me? I'm just talking college football. What the hell's wrong with *you*?"

"How can you be talking sports at a time like this?

How in the world would you think that's appropriate, Greg?"

Greg shrugged and propped his feet up on the kerosene heater. Axel had told them that the unit wasn't working, so Greg wasn't worried about burning his shoes.

"I don't know," he said. "It was just so quiet. We're all sitting here and ain't none of us talking. I just thought some conversation might lift our spirits."

"He's right," Paul murmured.

"You want to talk sports?" Gus sounded incredulous.

"No, I don't mean that. I couldn't care less about football right now. But Greg is right about it being quiet. There hasn't been a sound from outside in quite a while."

"Do you think it's over with?" Jean asked. "Could they be gone?"

"Maybe," Gus said, "but I ain't sticking my head out there to see."

"One of us should," Axel replied. "It doesn't make much sense for us to be sitting down here freezing our butts off in the dark if the danger is over with. At the very least, we've got to alert the authorities like you boys had originally planned."

"Still do plan on it," Paul said. "Soon as we get out of here."

"You didn't seem in a hurry to leave," Greg pointed out.

"Neither did you," Paul snapped. "And besides, I figured we could use a rest."

"Well . . ." Greg sighed. "We got one. And our situation ain't changed none while we were sitting here on our asses. I reckon Axel is right. We should go check."

"You go right ahead," Gus said. "I'm staying down here."

Paul stood up. "We'll all go. That's the safest way."

Jean hugged her son tighter. "Bobby's not going anywhere until we know for sure it's safe."

The men glanced down at her and then back to Paul.

"She's right," Greg said. "Don't seem right to send the boy outside with us."

"No," Paul agreed. "I don't guess it does. Jean and Bobby, you stay here. We'll let you know if the coast is clear."

Gus and Greg got to their feet. Groaning, Axel did the same. He put his hands on his hips and arched his back. His joints popped loudly.

"Damn arthritis," he muttered. "Sitting around in this damp basement hasn't improved it at all."

Bobby reached for Axel. "Mr. Perry, I don't want you to go. I want you to stay here with me and Mommy."

Greg noticed the emotion on the old man's face as he turned to look at the boy. Axel looked happy and sad all at the same time. He shuffled over to where Jean and Bobby sat and handed the boy his gnarled old walking stick.

"Here." Axel handed the boy the cane. "You take this. You remember what I told you about it, right?"

Bobby nodded emphatically. "Yes, sir. You said it was magic because it came from Mrs. Chickenbaum."

Axel laughed. "That's right. Mrs. Chickbaum. Now, we'll only be gone for a minute. We're just gonna creep upstairs and have a look-see—make sure all of the bad men are gone. While we do that, you just hold onto this old stick. It will keep you and your mother safe. Okay? Can you do that for me?"

"Yes, sir."

"Good boy." Axel patted his shoulder and then turned toward them. "All right, let's go see what's what."

The four of them hesitated at the bottom of the stairs, each one waiting for someone else to go first.

"Age before beauty," Greg said to Axel and Paul as he made a sweeping gesture with his hand. "You two were the ones who wanted to go."

Grumbling to himself, Paul started slowly up the stairs. Gus followed him. Greg and Axel stared at each other.

"Go ahead," Axel said. "I insist. I'm old and I'll only slow you down."

Greg followed along behind his brother. He heard Axel creeping along behind him. The wooden stairs creaked beneath their feet and the handrail shook slightly. Greg worried that the stairs might collapse under their combined weight. After all, the house was nearly as old as Axel was. There was no telling how much damage time and insects had done over the years. That would be a hell of a way to go— surviving the massacre outside only to break their backs in Axel Perry's basement.

When they reached the top, Paul opened the door. They turned around and glanced back down the stairs. Jean and Bobby stood at the bottom, staring up at them from the darkness. Greg raised his hand and waved.

"You guys be careful," Jean called. "And please hurry back?"

"We will," Axel said. "And Bobby, you just hold on to that walking stick. Okay?"

"Okay, Mr. Perry."

"We'll be right back. I promise."

As they crept through Axel's house, Greg turned to the old man.

"You shouldn't tell the boy that old stick is magic."

"Why not? It makes him feel better—safer. Where's the harm in that?"

Greg shrugged. "I guess."

"And besides," Axel continued, "how do you know it's *not* magic?"

Greg shook his head. "Crazy old man."

"I'm not the one who thinks the NOW controls the world."

"It's NWO, not NOW. How many times do I have to tell you people that before you'll listen?"

Paul and Gus crossed to the windows and peeked outside.

"See anything?" Greg asked.

"Nothing," Paul said. "Even the bodies are gone now. It's like nothing happened."

"Well, that's the worst part, isn't it?" Gus turned away from the window. "Not really knowing what's happening? I mean, if this was a tornado or a blizzard or a flood, we'd know what to do. We'd know how to protect ourselves. But after everything that's happened tonight, we still don't have the faintest fucking clue what we're dealing with here."

Greg walked to the front room. The others followed him. When he began unlocking the front door, his brother stopped him.

"You sure about this?"

"Sure I'm sure," Greg replied. "You and Paul

looked through the windows and didn't see anything, and it's quiet now. I reckon that whatever happened, the worst is over now."

The locks clicked open. Greg turned the doorknob and opened the door—

—and something tall and black and foul-smelling grabbed his face and yanked him outside. Smothered, Greg was unable to scream.

The others did it for him.

"So," Donny asked as they walked along, "if you're not Amish anymore, then what's up with the clothes and the beard and the hat? Couldn't you dress a little more . . . I don't know, modern? Stylish?"

Levi sighed and tried to conceal his annoyance. He'd been asked questions like this hundreds of times, and his answers always remained the same.

"I'm single," he said. "I thought that women might be attracted to the beard. All of the magazines and talk shows say that beards are back in style now. And as for the hat, I wear it for the same reasons anybody else wears one—to keep the sun out of my eyes and the rain off my head. And to hide my bald spot."

"Shit, Levi. Just get hair plugs."

"Haven't you ever read the story of Samson? Mess with a man's hair and you take away his power."

Donny chuckled nervously. Levi could tell that the younger man wasn't sure if he was joking or not, and that was fine by him. In truth, Levi privately wished that Donny would stay quiet. Even though they were currently shielded from the enemy, there could be other dangers around, and there was no sense in advertising their presence. Plus, he needed to think and he could do that better if Donny was silent.

"What about the buggy? Why do you drive a buggy if you're not Amish?"

"Have you seen the price of gas lately?"

"Good point."

Finally, Donny stopped talking. Gritting his teeth, Levi tried to focus. He sensed the soul cage overhead, just as Randy had said it was. The boy hadn't known its true name or purpose, of course. He'd thought it was merely a prison to keep them from leaving the town. In truth, it was a construct of great willpower and malice, a mystical barrier designed to capture the souls of all living things that came into direct contact with it. Judging by the amount of energy it was giving off, the cage had captured many souls indeed. Levi wondered if he could dispel it before the soul cage's creators had a chance to feed off its contents, but then decided against doing so. Better to save his strength for the main task, rather than wasting it on the cage. If he was successful, the souls trapped in the cage would be free. He only wished it wasn't too late for those the entities had already fed on directly.

The corpses that had filled the streets earlier were missing now. A few small piles of dust remained behind, but most of these had vanished, as well, eradicated by the cool, swift breeze. Levi slowed their pace as they passed by the hanging tree that Randy had mentioned. The carving was still there, stark against the bark: CROATOAN.

How was it connected to what was happening here? The methods and goal—eradicating every living thing in an entire town—were those of Meeble, but their adversaries obviously weren't him. What did it all mean? Levi couldn't help but picture their dilemma as a puzzle spread out on a tabletop. In the center of the puzzle was a hole, and until he found that missing piece, the full picture wouldn't be revealed. Somehow, the entities stalking Brinkley Springs were connected to Meeble and the Thirteen. The question was, how?

His thoughts turned to revenants and shades. Could the black figures be one of those? Shades were spirits, the shadowy ghost of a dead person. The term stemmed from several sources, including Homer's *Odyssey* and Dante's *Divine Comedy*. In Greek mythology, the dead lived in the perpetual shadow of the underworld. The Hebrew version of the shade— the *tsalmaveth*—translated as death-shadow. While the entities certainly had shadelike attributes, he didn't think that was what they were. Likewise, they didn't seem to fit the definition of a revenant. But then again, many of those definitions were faulty. The term had been assigned to creatures that were not revenants, but Siqqusim, a race of beings able to inhabit the bodies of the dead. In Akkadian literature, when Ishtar and Ereshkigal threatened to "raise up the dead to eat the living and make the dead outnumber the living," they were referring to casting Siqqusim into corpses. They were zombies, rather than revenants, but it was a distinction that was lost on most.

Medieval revenants were more similar to what he faced now. Levi considered the Anglo-Norman legends and folklore of that time—the documented accounts of William of Newburgh, the chronicler Walter Map, the Abbot of Burton and the bishop Gilbert Foliot, and the later writings of Augustus Montague Summers. Though the accounts varied, all had agreed that revenants who returned from the dead were wicked and evil while alive, and that the only way to destroy one was through exhumation, followed by decapitation and the removal and subsequent immolation of its heart.

Was it possible that his foes were some new form of revenant, a type thus far unknown to occultists? If so, how was he supposed to defeat them?

He was still thinking about it when they heard the screams. Without a word, Levi and Donny ran toward the sound. Their footsteps pounded on the asphalt, punctuating the cries. They rounded a corner, emerged onto another street and found a house under siege.

"That's Axel Perry's place," Donny said.

The five dark figures had surrounded the home. Two of them were in the front yard. One had just torn the face off an unfortunate victim. The man's body lay jittering and twitching on the wet grass. Three other men stood on the front porch, watching in terror. Levi recognized one of them as one of the two owners of the local garage.

"Oh, shit," Donny moaned. "I think that's Greg Pheasant lying on the ground. But what's wrong with him? He doesn't look right."

Levi reached into his pocket and pulled out his copy of *The Long Lost Friend*. He kissed it and then handed the book to Donny.

"Here. I'm about to drop our concealment. Keep this on you and don't let it go. And Donny, for God's sake as well as our own, stay here and do exactly what I tell you."

"What are you going to do?"

Levi gritted his teeth. "I'm going to pick a fight."

Without another word, he inched toward the house. The injured man was still twitching, but his movements had slowed. As Levi crept closer, the man's killer leaned over and thrust a hand into his back. He could hear the flesh rip from where he stood. The killer fished around inside the body and then wrenched the spine free, snapping it off at the base of the skull and then holding it in one hand like a dead snake. The man's movements abruptly ceased.

The man in black held the grisly trophy high over his head. "Now we'll feed on the rest of you."

"No," Levi said, stepping forward. "You won't."

CHAPTER TEN

The shadowy figures turned toward the sound of his voice. When they saw the source of the interruption, they shrieked. Levi imagined that the sound was probably like what one would hear if standing beneath a jet engine. Donny dropped Levi's copy of *The Long Lost Friend*, slapped his hands over his ears and shouted something, but Levi couldn't understand him. The words were lost beneath the cacophony. Levi tried his best to ignore the noise and focus.

Levi's heart beat once. Twice.

Then, still shrieking, three of the creatures swept forward in human form. The other two shape-shifted into crows and soared toward him. Levi stood with his feet spaced at shoulder width and his hands in his pockets. His demeanor was grim but calm. He did not speak or flinch as they closed the gap. One of the birds pecked at his cheek. The sharp beak drew blood, but Levi didn't flinch. Its feathers brushed against his skin as it passed. They were ice cold.

The other crow swooped at Donny. He dropped to his knees and scrabbled in the yard for Levi's copy of *The Long Lost Friend*, picking it up at the last instant. The bird's attack missed. Screeching, both crows circled around again.

"Leave the youth alone," Levi shouted at them. "Your fight is with me now. Face me as men."

The three human-shaped figures stopped before him, laughing.

"But we are not men, little magus," the tallest said. "We have not been men for quite some time."

Which means that they once were, Levi thought, fighting the urge to grin. *I might have been right. They might be some form of revenant—ones with the ability to change shape.*

The two birds joined their brothers and resumed human form. The five figures surrounded him, hovering only an arm's length away.

"Your quarrel is with me," he told them. "I bested you earlier. Let the others go unharmed and face me again."

The tallest gnashed its teeth. "You do not give orders to our kind, Levi, son of Amos. We will do as we wish."

"Cowards."

"Still your tongue, bearded one. We'll feed until there is nothing left."

"Levi," Donny shouted, "look out!"

The shortest of the five slashed at Levi with its talons. He sidestepped the attack and pulled one of his hands free from his pockets. In his fist was a handful of salt. Levi tossed it into the creature's snarling face and yelled, "*Ia, edin na zul. Ia Ishtari, ios daneri, ut nemo descendre fhatagn Shtar!* God, guide my hand."

The effect was immediate and remarkable. Hissing, the shadow-man recoiled as if Levi had splashed battery acid in its face. Levi grinned as his opponent flung its clawed hands into the air and screeched—a long, warbling, teakettle sound that rose in intensity and seemed to have no end. The dark figure stumbled backward, colliding with its brothers, and violently shook its head from side to side.

Levi held up another fistful of salt. "Come on, then. I have plenty to go around."

The creatures held their ground, staring at him with unbridled hate.

Levi backed up slowly, not taking his gaze from them. He stopped when he reached Donny. Without turning around, he whispered, "Move with me toward the house. Don't panic. As long as you have the book, they can't touch you."

"It's not me I'm worried about, dude. It's you."

"I'm fine. Now come on."

He and Donny moved as one, shuffling toward the house. The three men in the doorway—Levi couldn't remember if Donny had given him their names or not—had watched the confrontation and stalemate in horror, as if not quite believing what they were seeing. Levi and Donny moved slowly, circling around their foes. The dark figures turned with them, watching. Then, just as Levi and Donny had almost passed them, all five charged at once, flinging themselves at the men.

"Go!" Levi shoved Donny forward. The younger man stumbled but did not fall. For one terrifying second, Levi thought he might try to stay and fight, but he obeyed, running toward the house—a soldier to the end, following orders.

Heat flared in Levi's back as one of the attackers slashed at him. The claws ripped through his clothing and into his flesh. Levi responded by tossing salt over his shoulder, and felt a vicious, satisfying thrill as the creature screamed in obvious torment. A blow landed on his left shoulder and Levi's entire arm went numb. Moving quickly, he grabbed another fistful of salt with his good arm and spun in a circle, flinging it in a wide arc. Again, the attackers fell back.

"You don't have an unlimited supply," one of them croaked. "Already the bulge in your pockets lessens."

"I have enough," he said through gritted teeth, trying to ignore the pain in his back and shoulder. His left arm still had no feeling. It hung limp and useless. "Try me, if you like."

"Bah." The tallest of the five spat on the ground and the grass withered where the saliva landed. It took a tentative step toward him and Levi feinted with the salt. The creature stopped.

"You are a worthless adversary," it taunted. "Gone are the days when any of your kind provided us with a worthy challenge."

"Oh, I'm sure there have been many of my kind who defeated you easily enough. We're a resourceful bunch, us humans."

"Only the red men. Their shamans were worthy. Even still, they retreated when we carved our master's name in a tree to glorify him. That is because they feared us—and him."

The red men! It took all of Levi's will to keep from smiling with glee. The entity obviously meant the Native Americans. Another vital clue and a further piece of the almost-completed puzzle.

"You are from Roanoke." It wasn't a question. "Your master's true name is Meeble."

The creature sounded surprised. "Well done, little magus. You know Croatoan's real name, and therefore, I must surmise that you know what he is capable of, as are we, his faithful servants. And yet still you stand against us. Perhaps you are not so worthless an adversary after all."

It all made sense now. Levi was overwhelmed by a sudden sense of frustration. How could he have not seen it before? Five shadowy figures—the five Roanoke colonists who had worshipped Meeble, now turned into some sort of psychic vampires, eating the souls of the living and carrying on their master's work. His theory had been correct. They were revenants of a kind, and although he still didn't know their names (he would have, if he'd had access to his library back home) he knew how to stop them. It was important, however, that they *not know* that he knew. Not until he was ready.

"You're wrong," he said. "I can't stand against you after all."

He turned and fled. Laughing, the five figures raced after him, sliding to a halt as Levi abruptly wheeled around and faced them again.

"And now, for my next trick . . ."

"What—?"

He pointed his index finger and focused his will. "*Hbbi Massa danti Lantien.* I, Levi Stoltzfus, son of Amos Stoltzfus, breathe upon thee."

"No! He seeks to trick us, brothers, as he did me, earlier tonight."

Levi scattered the rest of his salt at his feet in a wide arc, holding them back just long enough to finish. "Three drops of blood I take from you. The first from your heart. The second from your liver. The third from your vital powers. In this, I deprive you of your strength and vitality. Now crawl on the ground like the worm you are. You'll raise no hand against me."

All five of the creatures collapsed on their bellies, faces pressed against the wet grass and dirt. They roared in anger, struggling as their movements slowed.

"That never gets old." Levi winked at them. Then he turned and ran for the house. "Thank you, Lord. That was close. A little too close for comfort."

"You know this is pointless," one of the creatures howled. "It didn't work before. It won't work now. You will only delay us."

"A delay is all I need."

Levi leaped over the dead man lying in the yard. His face was missing, and grass clippings stuck to the glistening musculature covering his skull.

One of the men standing at the front door called to Levi as he approached. His ruddy cheeks shone with wetness and his eyes were bloodshot.

"That's my brother." He pointed at the body. "Help him."

Levi slowed as he approached them. He recognized the distraught man as Gus Pheasant, one of the brothers who operated the town's automobile-repair shop. They'd directed Levi to Esther's boardinghouse when he first arrived in Brinkley Springs—a moment that now seemed as if it had happened in the distant past.

"I'm sorry," Levi said. "But your brother is beyond my care. He's dead."

"Bullshit. Donny told us you're some kind of voodoo doctor. Make him better. Do some witchcraft or whatever it is you do."

"I can't. It's beyond my ability. I really am sorry."

Gus began to weep again. He leaned against the grizzled mountain man.

"This is Axel," Donny said, introducing an elderly man standing in the doorway. "And that's Paul. And you already know Gus."

Levi nodded, rubbing his still-numb arm. "Gentlemen. I'm sorry we couldn't meet under better circumstances."

"Donny says you can help us," Paul said. His voice was gruff and serious—and tired. "I'd ask you if it was true, but I saw how you just handled yourself against those . . . whatever the hell they are. I reckon you can hold your own."

"I can help," Levi said. "But you need to do exactly what I tell you, and we need to move quickly. That won't hold them for long."

Donny handed Levi his book. "What's the plan?"

"We need to run."

"That's what we were going to do," Axel said. "Gus, Greg and Paul had a plan to get out of town."

"You wouldn't have been able to," Levi said. "This town is enveloped in a soul cage."

"I don't know about any of that," Axel replied. "But I'm all for going wherever you think is best."

"Good. We must leave right now."

"I need to check on my dogs first," Paul said. "We left them in the pen back at my place, before we knew exactly what was happening. I've been gone too long. I need to make sure they're okay."

Levi stared into the mountain man's eyes and realized that, despite his no-nonsense demeanor, Paul was in shock.

"I'm sorry," Levi apologized, "but if your dogs

were alive when you left them, then they aren't any longer. Our foes aren't content to just kill us. They seek to snuff out every living thing in this town. I suspect that they can track us simply by our life force. They can see it the way some creatures can see in the infrared spectrum. That's how they've ferreted out the survivors in hiding."

"You don't know my dogs. They've faced down black bears."

"Our foes are not bears. I'm sorry, but your dogs' fate is certain."

Gus straightened up and wiped his nose with the back of his hand, smearing his face with snot. He seemed oblivious to it. "Why are they doing this?"

"Because they can. Because it pleases them to do so. And because this is what they were created to do." Levi glanced over his shoulder and was alarmed to see that the five revenants were already moving. "We've got to go. *Now.*"

"Where?" Donny stared at the creatures.

"Back to the boardinghouse. I can deal with them there."

"I can't run that far," Axel said. "You boys will have to go on without me."

Donny turned to him. "No offense, Mr. Perry, but fuck that. We're not leaving you behind."

"Not to mention Jean and her boy," Paul said.

"Who?" Levi asked.

"Jean Sullivan," Axel said, "and her young son, Bobby. They're hiding down in my basement."

"Can the boy run?"

"They can both run," Axel said, "but I'll just slow you down. I can't walk ten steps without my arthritis flaring up, let alone run all the way across town."

Donny gripped Levi's arm. "Whatever you plan on doing, can't you just do it here? Why do we have to go back to Esther's?"

"I need to trap them," Levi said. "The boarding-house is already prepared. All it will take is a minor alteration. There's no time to set a trap here."

"Levi, son of Amos!"

They all stared at the revenants. One of them had regained his feet, and stood—hunchbacked and crooked, but standing nevertheless. It pointed at him.

"They'll be free soon," Levi said. "I'm very sorry, Mr. Perry. If we had more time."

Axel waved a hand. "Don't apologize, son. Just get the others to safety. I'll fetch Jean and Bobby."

"We ain't leaving without you," Paul said. "Bad enough I left my dogs behind. I daresay the same won't happen to you."

"Damn straight," Gus agreed, staring at his brother's corpse. "We ain't gone through all of this just to leave you behind, Axel. That wouldn't be very neighborly. Wouldn't be very Christian either."

Donny turned to Levi. His eyes were pleading. "There has to be something you can do. We can make a stand here."

Levi glanced back at their foes and sighed long and mournfully. Then he turned back to them. His expression was grave.

"Take me to the woman and her child."

"And?"

"And then do exactly as I say."

Axel shut the door behind them and led the group back through the house and down into the basement. A lone candle burned. A young, pretty woman and a young boy who looked exactly like her sat huddled in the corner. The woman was stroking the boy's hair and whispering in his ear. They looked up as the men entered, and stared at Levi in confusion.

"You can call him Levi Stoltzfus," Donny said. "He's here to help. Levi, this is Jean and Bobby Sullivan."

"Nice to meet you," Jean said. Then she turned to Donny. "And I'm sorry about your mom. I haven't had a chance to see you since you came back."

"Yeah," Donny said. "Hell of a homecoming."

"That it is, hon. That it is."

"You lit a candle?" Paul pointed.

"I had to," Jean explained. "Bobby was scared. I figured one wouldn't hurt."

Levi focused on their surroundings, studying the layout of the cellar and quickly inventorying its contents. He talked as he walked around the room.

"The universe is a lot bigger—and a lot more complex—than any of you know. Consider for a moment that the universe is infinite. Then consider the number of planets that infinite space must contain. Staggering, yes? And yet, that is only a very small part of what makes up the universe. There are other dimensions and other realities, and each of them are infinite, as well."

He paused in front of a door and peeked inside. It opened into a shallow closet, inside of which were three shelves overflowing with old board games and forgotten winter clothing. He closed the door and continued.

"There is a way to move between all of these different worlds in all of these various dimensions and realities. It's called the Labyrinth. Think of it as a dimensional shortcut of sorts. It weaves through time and space, nowhere and yet everywhere all at once. It connects to everything. *Everything*. Many supernatural beings—creatures beyond mankind's knowledge—use it to travel between worlds and traverse dimensions. Some humans have traveled though it, as well. Sadly, for them, such an endeavor usually leads to tragedy. Normally, the only time we're meant to see the Labyrinth is when our spirit has departed our body and we travel to the realms of existence beyond this one. But there are ways to pass though it while still alive. Safe ways. All it takes is the knowledge of how to open one of the doorways."

"Sounds like an episode of *Doctor Who*," Donny said.

Levi frowned. "I've never heard of it. I don't watch much television."

"I hadn't heard of it either until I went to Iraq. A buddy of mine used to watch it on his laptop. Guy flies around in a phone booth and goes to different worlds and stuff."

"A friend of mine," Levi said, "a reporter named Maria, told me that scientists call this string theory—different dimensions stacked up against each other like membranes. They are partially right. It sounds like this doctor program is partially right, as well."

"Not for nothing," Paul said, "but how does any of this help us?"

Levi pulled out his compass and studied it. To his dismay, the needle simply spun in a circle, not settling on any one point. He wondered if this could be some sort of residual effect of the soul cage, or if the compass was simply faulty. He put it back in his vest pocket and turned to Axel.

"You wouldn't happen to own a compass, would

you Mr. Perry, or anything else that I could use to determine direction?"

"No," Axel replied, "but if you need to know which direction is which, I can help you there. If you turn round, back to that broom closet you were just snooping in, you'll be facing due north."

"Excellent." Levi glanced at the ceiling. "And there are no eaves or decorations over our heads. Were it not for everything else, this would be absolutely perfect."

Donny shook his head. "Everything else?"

"Normally, I would fast before attempting this working. Also, I'm missing some of the ingredients. Understand, I'm not a novice. I can do this without them. It just makes me uncomfortable—uneasy—to do so. These are forces that it's better not to tamper with."

"I don't have a fucking clue what you just said."

Levi chuckled. "That's okay, Donny. It's probably better that you don't."

"Just do whatever it is you've got to do," Paul said.

"I need a minute to myself."

"Do we have another minute?" Gus asked. "Will those things stay stuck outside that long?"

"Let us hope so. Could one of you snuff out the candle?"

Paul did as he'd asked. Levi fell silent. He stood in front of the closet door, bowed his head, folded his hands in front of him and then closed his eyes. His breathing grew shallow. He remained like that for a moment, feeling their gaze upon him.

"The hell is he doing?" Gus whispered.

"I don't know," Paul said. "Heck of a time for a nap."

"Maybe he's praying," Jean said.

"Leave him alone, guys." Donny's tone was stern. "I've seen him do things tonight that . . . well, you wouldn't believe me if I told you, even with everything that's happened."

"None of this seems very Christian," Gus said. "I thought Amish folks were Christians."

Donny groaned. "You sound like Esther. She gave him shit earlier about that."

"Oh," Gus replied, "I ain't saying there's anything wrong with it. It just surprised me, is all. As for Esther, well . . . she's old. Old folks are like that. Set in their ways."

"Hey," Axel said. "What's that supposed to mean?"

"No offense. I didn't mean nothing by it."

Levi opened his eyes again, and the others fell silent. His arm was no longer numb. His senses were once again sharp and alert. Without speaking, he walked over to the couch, pulled off the red blanket that had been draped over the back of it, and returned to the closet door. The blanket smelled of dust and disuse, and he idly wondered how often Mr. Perry used this basement before tonight. He spread the blanket out in front of the door and smoothed it out with his hands. Then he reached into his pockets and pulled out the rest of the salt. He poured this on the floor in a circle around the blanket. Finished, he motioned them over.

"I need you all to stand together, as close as possible. It's very important that you be on the blanket from this point on. Whatever happens—even if our enemies break in here—do not go beyond this circle of salt. Don't reach beyond it for anything. Don't stretch beyond it, not even an elbow or the tip of your toe. If we are attacked, stand where you are. Don't flee. If you have to sneeze, cover your mouth. Don't even spit beyond the circle."

Paul stared at him, clearly puzzled. "Why not?"

"Because nothing must break the circle. Do all of you understand?"

One by one, they nodded.

"In a moment," Levi said, "I'm going to tell all of you to close your eyes. When I do that, you'll need to keep them closed until I tell you to open them again. I can't stress this enough. It's even more important than not breaking the circle. We'll walk together, hand in hand. I'll lead you. It will be very quick, but it might not seem that way to you. You may hear things. Smell things. Even feel things. Ignore them. Whatever happens, do not open your eyes."

"What happens if we do?" Gus asked.

"Remember how I said that traveling through the Labyrinth has adverse effects on people?"

Gus nodded.

"Keep your eyes closed and you won't find out why. Now come. I sense our attackers are almost free."

They moved onto the blanket and huddled together, jostling one another in order to fit. Jean picked up Bobby and held him. Levi checked the floor, making sure all of their feet were within the circle. Then he collected four candles from across the room and sat them down beyond the edge of the line of salt at different positions—north, south, east and west. The wax was still warm and pliable. He pulled a lighter from his pocket and relit them.

"Don't do that," Paul cautioned. "The dark men will see the light."

"In a moment, that won't matter. This procedure

requires candles. Technically, they should be red, like the blanket, but I think I can make do."

"But you just had me snuff one out."

"Correct. And now I need some that are lit."

He stepped into the circle, and they had to crowd together even tighter in order to make room for him on the blanket.

"Don't anybody fart," Gus said.

Bobby giggled at this until Jean shushed him.

Levi stuck his thumb in his mouth and bit down hard until he tasted blood. The others gasped and groaned, but held their positions. Taking his thumb from his mouth, Levi held his hand out over the blanket and squeezed out three drops of blood. As each drop fell, he repeated the same phrase.

"*Ia unay vobism Huitzilopochtli. Ia dom tergo Hathor.*"

"If that don't beat all," Gus whispered. "I think I'm gonna be sick."

"Quiet," Donny said.

Levi bowed his head and pressed his thumb against his pants leg until the bleeding stopped. When he spoke again, it was in a strong, authoritative yet apologetic tone.

"I stand, rather than sit in the appropriate and required manner, but I am safe inside a circle of protection, and I humbly ask that you not molest me. I come with great humility. I cannot pay proper homage, for my enemies are beset against me, yet I pray I do not offend. I come here to open a gate. Despite my meager offerings, I come with awe and respect. I come seeking passage. I call upon the Gatekeeper, who gave to us the Nomos, which is the Law. I call upon the Doorman, who is the Burning Bush and the Hand That Writes and the Watchman and the Sleepwalker. I call upon the voice of the Tetragrammaton. I call upon him who is called Huitzilopochtli and Ahtu; him who is called Nephrit-ansa and Sopdu; him who is called Hathor and Nyarlathotep. I call upon him whose real name is Amun. And thus, by naming thee and offering my blood thrice, I humbly request an opening. Those with me in the circle are under my protection. By following the Law to the best of my abilities and with limited resources, and by naming thee, I humbly ask that you grant us safe passage from this place. I humbly ask that you protect us, and that we not be harmed or molested by those who dwell between the walls or within the halls, or the denizens of Heaven nor hell, or the realms between them, or the Thirteen, or the things that live in the wastes beyond the levels. I humbly ask that you guide us so that we do not end up wandering and lost in that realm beyond the Labyrinth, the lost level, in which there are no exits save death. I beg of thee, and hope that so shall it be."

Levi paused, aware that the others were holding their breath. Outside, the revenants howled, free of the binding spell.

"Okay," Levi said. "I'll need to get to the door, so make a little room for me—without breaking the circle. Everyone hold hands and close your eyes. Stay together. Don't let go of each other and whatever you do, don't open your eyes until I tell you it's okay. I'll lead the way. Donny, you'll bring up the rear."

Donny nodded. "That's better than taking point."

"Can you shut the door behind us? Remember,

you can't open your eyes, so you'll have to do it by feel."

"I'll take care of it."

Jean put Bobby down beside her and held his hand tightly. He reached up and took Axel's hand. Axel smiled down at him.

"I forgot the Mrs. Chickenbaum stick, Mr. Perry. I'm sorry. Maybe we could go back and get it?"

"That's okay, Bobby. I think Levi might have some better magic of his own."

They carefully changed positions until Levi was closest to the door. Outside, the sounds of fury increased. Levi grasped Jean's hand. Axel took Paul's. Paul grabbed on to Gus's hand and Gus took Donny's.

"Won't they be able to follow us?" Donny asked.

"No," Levi said. "They can't cross the circle."

"But we can't either."

"We'll be walking through a door. We'll only step out of the circle for an instant. Now, everyone close their eyes. We have company."

Upstairs, the front door crashed open, followed by the sound of breaking glass. Gus moaned and Bobby whimpered. To Levi, it sounded as if every window in the home had just imploded. Making sure that their eyes were indeed closed, Levi grasped the doorknob and opened the door. Gone were the shelves and the games and the winter gear. The door no longer led into a closet. Instead, it opened into a long, straight hallway that seemingly had no end. Each side of the corridor was lined with doors as endless as the hall itself.

"Now we have you, little magus! No more games."

The door at the top of the basement stairs was wrenched from its hinges by a powerful blow. Footsteps pounded down the stairs. Levi felt Jean squeeze his hand, hard.

Taking a deep breath, he stepped out of the circle and led them forward.

"Somebody's coming."

Marsha's eyes snapped open. She was amazed that despite their predicament, she'd almost dozed off on the couch. She'd been thinking about Donny—how angry she was with him for going with Levi, and how indicative it was of their entire relationship, and how she hoped, despite everything, that he was okay. Then her brother's voice had roused her. She sat up quickly. Randy, Myrtle and Esther sat in the darkness. Randy was next to her on the couch. Esther and Myrtle occupied high-backed chairs across from them. Outside, the street was quiet.

"What do you mean, dear?" Esther leaned forward in her seat, staring at Randy intently.

"I don't know," he replied. "It's just a feeling I've got all of the sudden. Someone is coming."

"The killers?" Marsha reached out, took his hand and squeezed it.

Randy squeezed back. "I don't know. Never mind. I don't know what the hell I'm talking about . . . Oops. Sorry, Mrs. Laudry. Didn't mean to curse."

"It's okay."

"You could be right," Myrtle said. "Perhaps you're sensitive to these things. Levi seemed to think that you had hidden abilities."

Esther rolled her eyes. "The boy would be much better off without Levi's influence."

Myrtle ignored her. "Did you ever notice anything before tonight, Randy?"

"Like what?"

"Feelings? Intuition? Maybe you knew what the questions were going to be on a test at school before you took it? Or maybe someone in your family lost or misplaced something, and you were able to tell them where to look?"

Randy stared at her as if she were crazy. "No. I'm just . . . me, you know? I don't believe in that stuff."

"It doesn't matter if you believe in it or not. It's still real."

"I'm not special. That Amish dude is smoking crack or something. I'm just a normal kid. Brinkley Springs is my home."

Myrtle pressed on. "But maybe you—"

"I'm not special!"

Marsha jumped, startled by her brother's tone. He released her hand and sprang to his feet.

"If I was fucking magic, then my mom and dad would still be alive. Sam and Steph . . . oh my God, Steph. You guys didn't see her. She . . ."

He trailed off, unable to finish. Marsha stood and tried to comfort him, but Randy pushed her away. For a moment, she thought he was going to burst into tears again, but instead, her brother ran for the bathroom. They heard him bumping around in the darkness. A moment later, the toilet lid slammed against the tank and they heard him vomiting.

Marsha glared at Myrtle. "I think that will be enough, Mrs. Danbury."

"I'm sorry, Marsha. I didn't mean any harm."

"I know you didn't, but my brother has been through enough tonight. We all have. I don't want you upsetting him any more than he already is."

"Of course, dear. Of course. I'm sorry about that. I just . . ."

"What?"

"Well, if Levi is right about your brother, then maybe Randy can help us. Maybe he can safeguard us, just in case Donny and Levi don't return."

Marsha fought to keep her emotions in check. She wanted to race across the room and pull the old woman from her chair and scream at her.

"Donny will come back." She was aware of how cold and clipped she sounded, but at that moment, Marsha didn't care. "He'll be back."

"I'm sure he will, dear."

Marsha assumed that Myrtle was aware she'd hit a nerve, because she fell silent again after that. Esther hummed tunelessly and rocked back and forth. Her hands fretted with the hem of her blouse. Myrtle stared at the floor. Marsha sat back down again. The couch springs squeaked beneath her. After another minute, they heard Randy leave the bathroom and begin making his way through the dark.

"Are you okay?" Marsha called.

"Yeah, I'll be alright. I just . . . Hey. What's this light in the kitchen?"

The women glanced at each other, puzzled. Frowning, Esther stood up.

"What light is that, Randy?"

"Right here." His voice grew muffled as he moved toward the kitchen. "It's coming from inside your pantry. Did you leave a light on?"

"No. The power is still out."

Esther, Myrtle and Marsha made their way to the kitchen. Randy was standing next to the refrigerator. He pointed as they entered.

"See?"

Sure enough, a yellow-white light was shining beneath the pantry door. It was bright enough to illuminate the linoleum floor beneath their feet.

"My word," Esther said. "What in the world is that?"

The four looked at each other in concern. Esther took a step toward the pantry door but Marsha pulled her back, put a finger to her lips and shook her head.

"Don't," she mouthed.

They turned back to the pantry and stared at the light. As they watched, it grew brighter, creeping out from beneath the door and spreading across the kitchen floor like a miniature sunrise. Marsha noticed that she could see the others clearly now. The illumination was enough for her to notice the dark circles under her brother's eyes and the dried blood on his skin. The light continued to grow, glinting off the appliances and the collectible-spoon rack hanging above the dining table.

Then they heard the footsteps—quiet at first, but growing steadily louder. Impossibly, they sounded as if they were coming from inside the pantry. Esther began to tremble. Whimpering, Myrtle reached out and took her friend by the arm. Behind them, Randy and Marsha clustered close together. None of them spoke.

The footsteps came closer, and now they heard a murmured voice. It sounded as if it were coming from a great distance away, perhaps out in the street or from one of the neighboring houses. Marsha held her breath and listened harder. No, the speaker wasn't outside. The voice was coming from inside the pantry. Soon she realized that there were other voices with it.

And one of them was screaming.

The footsteps were now right on the other side of the door. The light grew brighter still.

"Get back," Randy said. He stepped in front of them, placing himself between the women and the door. "They're coming!"

The doorknob turned. The breathless screams grew louder. The door rattled. Marsha, Esther and Myrtle clung to one another. Randy stood with his fists clenched, but Marsha saw his knees shaking. The door opened, crashing against the wall with a thud and flooding the kitchen with a dazzling, blinding light. Marsha threw a hand over her eyes and squinted. There were figures in the middle of the light and a long hallway behind them.

Myrtle shrieked.

Levi stepped out of the open door, followed by a group of people. Squinting, Marsha looked for Donny. She didn't see him. She was surprised to see others with Levi instead. Jean Sullivan came first, followed by her son, Bobby, who was followed by old Axel Perry and Paul Crowley. They were all holding hands, and all of them had their eyes closed. Paul's arm trailed behind him, as if he was holding someone else's hand.

"Where's Donny?"

If Levi heard her, he gave no indication. Instead, he turned and faced the new arrivals. "Hurry. Jean, Bobby and Axel, you can all open your eyes. Paul, just a few steps more and then you can, too."

"I can't," Paul said. "He ain't moving."

"Levi," Marsha called. "Where is Donny?"

"Marsha?"

She squealed when she heard him call her name, but she still didn't see him. His voice sounded muffled and far away.

"Gus," Levi shouted, "you have to keep moving. Come on!"

Marsha realized that it was Gus Pheasant who was screaming. She glimpsed him right behind Paul, on his knees and clinging to the mountain man's hand. His other arm was outstretched behind him, as if holding someone else's hand, as well, but the light was too bright for Marsha to see who that person might be.

"Donny?" She stepped closer.

"Gus," Levi urged. "Come on!"

"They aren't doors," Gus screamed. "They're windows on worlds. Windows on goddamn worlds!"

"Goddamn it, Gus!" Paul faced straight ahead, his eyes squeezed shut. "I'm very sorry about what happened to your brother, but we don't have time for this shit. Quit fucking around and get a move on!"

Levi brushed past Jean and Bobby, who rushed over to Esther and Myrtle and embraced them. Randy shoved forward, trying to help Levi as he grabbed onto Paul and pulled.

"Don't let go of him, Paul."

The fear in Levi's voice filled Marsha with dread.

"I won't. What do you want me to do?"

"Look toward the sound of my voice," Levi told Paul. "You can open your eyes now, as long as you don't turn around. Just don't let go of Gus."

Paul did as Levi commanded. His face was pale and sweaty. He looked exhausted.

"Levi," Donny yelled from inside the light. "Something's coming up behind me. I think they got through."

"It's not them, Donny. They can't come through this way."

"Then what the hell is it? It's growling."

"Just hang on a moment longer."

"I saw a city," Gus ranted as Paul teetered forward. Gus's eyes were wide open and blood leaked from the corners of them and ran down his cheeks. "I saw a big city with tall, silver buildings. The city covered an entire planet. There were robots living there instead of people. And there was another city, a different city, and it was made out of light."

"Levi." Donny's voice was tinged with panic. "It's getting closer. Do something, damn it!"

Levi turned to Randy. "Help me with him. Just don't look directly into the light, okay? It's like staring into the sun."

Randy nodded, his mouth agape. Together, they grabbed Gus and dragged him forward. He reached for them with both hands. Levi gasped.

"Levi," Donny shouted. "I lost my grip on Gus!"

"It's okay. Don't panic, Donny. You're close now. Just walk straight ahead."

Randy and Levi pulled the struggling auto mechanic out of the hallway. A moment later, Donny emerged from the light. Marsha ran to him and flung her arms around him as he stepped out of the pantry. His eyes popped open and he stared at her in disbelief.

"Marsha? Where . . . where are we?"

"Esther's kitchen," she said. "What happened? How did you . . . ?"

"We took a shortcut," Levi said, and reached for

the door. As he did, the light faded. The corridor was still visible, but now it seemed to be superimposed over Esther's pantry. Shelves of canned goods lined the walls, but they seemed transparent, as if both locations—the corridor and the pantry—were occupying the same space at the same time.

"There were zombies." Gus rocked back and forth on the kitchen floor. "Zombies, just like in the movies. Zombies and clowns and dinosaurs. And there was something in the middle of it all. Something dark, like tar, except that it didn't have any shape."

Levi slammed the door and said, *"Ut nemo in sense tentat, descendere nemo. At precedenti spectaur mantica tergo. Ia Amun traust nodrog. Amun, Amun, Amun."*

The light vanished. To Marsha, it felt as if a great, invisible weight had been lifted off all of them. Her skin tingled. She looked down at her arms and saw goose bumps. Then Donny put his arm around her and she forgot all about them.

"You left," she whispered. "Just like before. Goddamn it, Donny. You left again."

"I know, but I came back. This is where I belong, Marsha. With you. You're my home. Levi helped me see that. And I promise you that I won't leave again. Not ever."

She stood up on her tiptoes and kissed him. She wasn't sure how long they remained like that, but eventually, she became aware that the others were looking at them.

Randy grinned. "So are you two back together or what?"

Gus's rambling litany continued. "Goat men and lizard men and snake men and elephant men. There were creatures made out of fire who lived in the sun, and a whirlpool in space and a giant monster with a fucking squid for a goddamn head."

"What's wrong with him?" Axel asked. "Is he . . . crazy?"

Panting, Levi leaned against the wall, removed his hat and wiped his forehead with the back of his hand. "He opened his eyes and saw beyond the doors."

"Everything is connected," Gus moaned. "All of it. It's like this big old puzzle, and everything is a piece. I was on a beach and these things crawled out of the ocean and they were part crab and part lobster, but they had scorpion tails."

"Hey, buddy." Paul knelt next to Gus and squeezed his friend's shoulder. "Settle down, okay? It's all over. We're safe now. Levi got us out."

"The moon blinked. We were in there a long time, you know? We walked and walked and it watched us the whole time."

"What?"

Gus leaned close, his face inches from Paul's. "The moon. It blinked at me. It's an eyeball. It was watching us."

Paul looked up at Levi. "Is he going to be okay?"

"I honestly don't know. In truth, probably not. His mind has snapped."

"How? What happened to him in there?"

"There are some things that aren't meant to be seen. He opened his eyes and saw them. That was why I cautioned all of you before we left."

"What is all this?" Esther raised her voice. "Where did you all come from? How in the world did you get inside my pantry? Is it all over? Where are the killers?"

Levi sighed. "If I had to guess, I'd say they're tearing the town apart looking for us."

"But they can't find us, right?" Donny asked. "This place is safe."

"Correct. As long as the wards I drew earlier are still in place, we remain hidden from them as long as we're inside the bed-and-breakfast."

Paul stood up. "So what happens now?"

"Now?" Levi put his hat back on his head. "Now, you pray the dawn arrives, while I prepare to make a last stand."

CHAPTER ELEVEN

Donny didn't want to move. Marsha felt good against him, warm and soft. She felt *right*. But when Levi urged them all back into the living room, he didn't argue. Most of the others went quietly, too stunned and confused to question their unlikely champion. Only Gus remained behind, sitting on the floor, scratching at the linoleum with his fingernails and babbling about sea monsters that were part crab, part lobster and part scorpion. Paul and Randy pulled him to his feet and helped him along behind the others.

Levi put his hand on Donny's shoulder and motioned for him to come closer. When the rest of the survivors were out of earshot, he leaned close.

"I'll need your help."

"You've got it," Donny said. "Just tell me what you want me to do."

"First, we need to get everyone upstairs. The wards and glyphs will protect them, but I need them all in one place, so that they don't get in my way."

"I don't think anyone will argue with that."

"I don't either."

"What happens after that? What's the plan?"

"Let's get them upstairs first."

Donny followed Levi back into the living room.

Was it his imagination, or did the magus seem taller? Certainly his voice was more grim than it had been before. Even his stride seemed to have become stronger. His boots clomped on the wooden floor, despite the thick carpeting and rugs.

"Okay," Levi addressed the group. "With luck, and God's help, this will all be over soon."

"God isn't there," Gus interrupted. "He's been split in three, and one part of him is stuck in a loop. He is born again. And again and again and again, over and over. Poor guy."

"Hush." Paul ruffled Gus's hair as if he were one of the mountain man's beloved bear hounds.

"Can you stop them?" Marsha asked.

Levi nodded. "I believe so, yes. But again, I'll need all of you to do exactly as I say. Otherwise . . ."

He didn't have to finish, Donny noted to himself. They'd each seen enough horror for one night, and they had Gus as a living example of what could happen.

"I need all of you to go upstairs," Levi continued. "Trust me when I tell you that you'll be safe there. Certainly safer than you would be down here. Remember, our enemies can't find you as long as you remain within this house. I want you to stay there until it's safe to come back down."

"And how will we know that?" Myrtle asked.

"Because I'll still be alive. Donny is going to stay down here and help me—"

"No," Marsha said.

Levi held up his hand. "He won't be here the whole time, and he won't be in any immediate danger. The same safeguards that protect the rest of you will be protecting him, as well. But I'll need him to do something for me before he can join you upstairs. It's something important. Indeed, without his help, my plan will fail."

"I can help." Randy stepped forward.

"No, you can't." Marsha grabbed her brother's arm.

"So can I," Myrtle said. "Don't forget, I know about this stuff, too. Tell me what you need me to do, and I'll do it."

"I appreciate your offers, but that won't be necessary."

"Bullshit," Randy said. "Those fuckers killed my parents and my friends, yo. If you're gonna kick their ass, then I want a piece, too."

"The best thing you can do for your loved ones," Levi said, "is to stay alive. That's what they'd want. That's all that matters now."

"He's right," Donny told Randy. "Think about your sister, dude. You've both lost enough people tonight. She doesn't need to lose you, too."

Randy sneered. "Says the guy who keeps running out on her."

Marsha gasped, and Randy shrugged her off. Donny opened his mouth to respond, but then thought better of it. In truth, the kid was right. He'd deserved that.

Gus took advantage of the momentary silence. He turned to Paul and said, "You know that Teddy Garnett fella? Old boy who lives up in Punkin Center?"

Paul nodded.

"I saw him. While we were in there. He passed by us in the hall. Except that it wasn't him. It was a different him."

Paul looked like he was ready to cry. When he spoke, his voice was hoarse with emotion.

"I reckon you had a bad dream is all, Gus. You'll be okay. Just quiet down."

"No, it wasn't a bad dream. I'm not stupid, Paul. I know what I saw. It was Teddy, but it wasn't. He had some other folks with him, too, but I didn't recognize any of them. A real pretty black girl and some young guy dressed up like a mobster in one of those Tarantino movies and a fella our age. Looked like a farmer, maybe? He reminded me of Levi a little bit."

Donny noticed Levi twitch at this, as if startled.

"Did they speak to you?" Levi asked. "Did this man give you his name?"

Gus turned to Levi and smiled. A thin line of drool hung from the corner of his mouth. "What?"

"This man. This farmer who reminded you of me. Did he give you his name? Was it Nelson LeHorn?"

Gus suddenly glanced down at his feet with a look of concern. "I want my Spider-Man slippers. Where did my Spider-Man slippers go?"

"Who's Nelson LeHorn?" Donny asked.

"Someone from my past who disappeared a long time ago." Levi shook his head. "Never mind that. It's not important right now. I think we should begin. I'm anxious to end this, and I'm sure all of you are, as well."

"You're damn right," Paul muttered.

"I can't go anywhere without my Spider-Man slippers!"

Talking among themselves, the group headed upstairs. Marsha stopped halfway up and looked back at Donny. Her eyes shone in the darkness.

"I'll be okay," he said, trying his best to smile.

"You'd better be." She started to turn away.

"Marsha?"

She paused. "Yeah?"

"I love you. I always loved you. I know that now."

"I love you, too, you asshole."

Marsha grinned. Donny grinned back. Then she turned and was gone.

"You should hold on to that one," Levi said. "You're meant to be together."

"Did you read that in some tea leaves or tarot cards?"

"No. I read it in your eyes. And in hers. You're soul mates."

"I never believed in that stuff before."

"I haven't," Levi said. "Not in soul mates, at least. Not in a long time."

"So what changed your mind?"

"The two of you did. Now, let's get started. We've got a lot to prepare."

Levi returned to the kitchen. Donny followed him. When they got there, Levi stood facing the front door. He seemed to be studying the layout of the first floor. Donny remained silent while he did. The kitchen and front door were connected by a short hallway. One side of the dark hallway led to the living room. The other side led to the stairway, as well as the first-floor bathroom and a small bedroom. Apparently satisfied by what he saw, Levi turned and looked behind them, studying the rear door on the far side of the kitchen. He walked to it, parted the curtains and peered outside.

"Good. Only two entrances on this floor. I thought that was what I remembered from before, but we were pressed for time earlier, and I needed to make sure."

"What do you need me to do?" Donny asked.

"Check the cupboards. I need bowls, coffee mugs—anything that I can burn sage in."

While Donny did this, Levi opened the pantry door. Donny froze, half expecting to see the dark men leap out, but instead, the space was filled with shelves of dry and canned goods. Levi hunted around inside until he found a large canister of salt. He pulled it from the pantry and closed the door again. Then he grabbed the salt shaker from the counter and unscrewed the top of it. Thus armed, he began sprinkling lines of salt in front of the kitchen window and the back door. Donny grabbed an armload of blue ceramic bowls from the cupboard and sat them on the counter. Levi looked up and nodded.

"Those will be fine."

"I don't think Mrs. Laudry will be too happy with us. These are nice bowls."

"I think she'd be even less fond of the alternative." Levi reached in his vest pocket and pulled out the two dried bundles of sage. He tossed it to Donny. Donny caught it with one hand. "Put some of that in each bowl."

"How much should I use?"

"All of it, but in even amounts, if possible."

Donny spread the bowls out on the counter and began dividing up the sage. The smell was not unpleasant. He found it strangely soothing. While he did this, Levi left the room. Donny finished just as he returned.

"What now?"

Levi picked up two bowls. "We place these around the first floor and light them."

He placed one bowl beneath the kitchen window and another next to the back door. Then he picked up two more. Donny did the same and followed along behind him. They put the bowls all over the house, and Donny noticed that Levi had salted most of the house. All of the doors and windows had a line of salt beneath them. The only areas that didn't were the front door and the stairwell.

"Don't we need salt there, too?" Donny nodded toward the front door.

"Not yet. Remember, I placed a ward above the door before we left earlier."

Squinting, Donny looked above the door. Sure enough, the words were still there, written in black Magic Marker and almost unnoticeable in the gloom.

"What about the stairs?" he asked.

"That comes next. Listen carefully. They'll be coming soon."

"Wait—I thought you said they couldn't find us as long as we're in the house."

"They couldn't," Levi said. "But now I want them to."

"So you're using us as fucking bait?"

Levi didn't respond. "I'll remove the ward over the front door. When I do that, they'll be able to sense our presence. I imagine they'll waste no time in coming here. The rest of the house will remain sealed, so they'll have no choice but to enter through the front door."

"And kill every one of us. This plan sucks, Levi."

"They won't hurt the others. It's me they want most of all, and perhaps Randy."

"All the more reason not to lead them here. We're sitting ducks. Talk about a fucking ambush!"

"It is an ambush," Levi agreed, "but we're the ones

ambushing them. They'll go after me first. Trust me on this."

"But there's no salt in front of the stairs. What's to stop them from going up there first and slaughtering everybody?"

"You. You're stopping them."

"How?"

Levi pulled out his copy of *The Long Lost Friend* and handed it to him. "All you have to do is stand firm. They can't hurt you as long as you have this. If they go for you first—and understand, that is unlikely—then you'll only need to stall them long enough for me to get their attention. But I don't think that will happen. I think they'll come in the front door, see me and let their anger and hatred consume them. In fact, I'm counting on it."

"But without the book, they'll rip you to pieces."

Levi smiled. "They didn't get me back at Axel's house, and I'm confident that they won't get me here. I still have a few other tricks up my sleeve. And again, that's where you come in. I need you to hide on the stairwell. When they come in, wait until all five have gone past you. Then, I need you to sneak down the stairs behind them and salt both the front door and the bottom of the stairwell. Do the door first. Then the stairs."

"And they won't be able to get upstairs."

"Exactly. Nor will they be able to leave."

Donny shook his head. "I don't know, Levi. This sounds like suicide to me."

"I need to have them all in one spot. This is the only way to do that."

"What happens after you've got them in here? What are you going to do? A big magic battle?"

"Hardly. Nothing so cinematic. That only happens in Harry Potter. The truth is, I still don't know how to fight them."

Donny's heart sank. He gaped at Levi, speechless. After a moment, he ran a hand across his head, feeling his scalp tingle beneath his buzz cut.

"So . . . all of this is what? A bluff? A lie? Something just to make the others feel safe? Are we gonna die?"

"No." Levi paused, and then softened his tone. "No, not if I can help it. I don't know how to defeat them for good, but I do know how to make them someone else's problem. If my plan goes accordingly, they won't trouble our world again. They're revenants, but of a type previously unknown to me. When we're done, I can search for their physical forms—probably buried in a grave somewhere near the original Roanoke Colony. Usually, if you destroy a revenant's physical remains, you destroy its spiritual form, as well. I'm hoping that rule will apply to our adversaries."

"It damn well better."

Levi leaned against the wall. His shoulders sagged. He seemed tired. When he looked at Donny again, he seemed ten years older.

"Go upstairs," Levi said. "Join the others. But be ready. After you've completed your task, do not cross the lines of salt—for any reason—until you hear from me again. Now, I must pray for God's guidance and strength. When I'm done, I'll let them know where we are."

Donny nodded. He started to leave and then hesitated. Turning, he thrust out his hand. Levi shook it.

"Good luck," Donny whispered.

"May the Lord protect us all," Levi answered.

Then Donny went upstairs and waited for Levi to ring the dinner bell.

After Donny was gone, Levi quickly went to the pantry door. He placed his forehead and palms against it, closed his eyes and murmured a prayer in a language not spoken on Earth. Slowly, the light returned and began to creep out from beneath the door again. Then the light changed color, first turning red and then pale blue, before settling on a sickly grayish hue. When Levi straightened up again and pulled his hands away from the door, they were shaking. His forehead was bathed in sweat. He placed his hand on the doorknob. It was warm and wet. He turned it, opening the door just an inch. More light leaked through.

He pulled out his cigarette lighter and, one by one, lit the bowls of sage. The thick, pleasant aroma quickly filled the house. Levi breathed deep, drawing strength from it. His aches and pains vanished. His mind was soothed. He patted his vest pockets and discovered that at some point during the night's battles, he'd lost his knife. With no time to mourn the loss, he selected a steak knife from one of Esther's kitchen drawers and stood beneath the front door. Gritting his teeth, he turned his right-hand palm upward and sliced it open with the knife, moaning slightly from the pain and hoping the others wouldn't hear him. Then he made another cut, forming an X pattern in his flesh. Blood flowed over his hand and splattered onto the floor. It streamed down his wrist and crept beneath his shirtsleeve. Grimacing, Levi held up his red right hand

and smeared blood over the words written above the door. He did this three times, moving from left to right, as if he were painting. Then, he stood back and surveyed his handiwork. Satisfied that the words were obscured, Levi opened the front door.

"Get ready," he called to Donny as he hurried back to the kitchen. "They'll be coming now."

As if in confirmation, the creatures' cries echoed across the town. Levi sat cross-legged in front of the pantry door, lit by the glow coming from the other side, and squeezed his wrist, hoping to stanch the flow of blood.

He did not have to wait long. His foes arrived within minutes. They made no attempt to mask their approach. Their cries and threats preceded their arrival. Even so, he felt their presence long before they reached the house. The sensation filled him with loathing . . .

. . . and terror. A terror he hadn't felt in quite some time. He focused on his breathing and tried not to panic. He needed to keep his thoughts clear and his will strong. Was it his imagination, or was the scent of the sage fading?

"Your will be done, Lord."

Shadows moved in the open doorway. There was a sibilant hiss, and then all five entities appeared. They paused, standing at the threshold. One of them sniffed the air.

"Sage, and salt. And blood. We know these ingredients. What paltry trick do you cling to now, Levi, son of Amos?"

"No trickery," he called. "The way is open to you. Enter freely and of your own will. I give you my word that I will not harm you in this place."

The creatures hesitated for another moment. Levi worried that they might not take the bait. Then, one by one, they entered the home.

The tallest pointed. "The remainders are clustered upstairs. See to them, that our work here might be done."

Levi's pulse increased. "Why? Are you afraid to face me instead?"

"Do not try our patience, bearded one."

"I seek not to offend, but I must admit that I'm perplexed. The others cannot harm you, and yet you focus on them first. I would think that instead, you would wish to deal with me first. After all, I'm the real threat."

The five shadowed figures crept closer, nearing the stairs. Levi held his breath, hoping they wouldn't divert, and hoping Donny could hold his ground if they did.

"Your arrogance will be your undoing, little magus."

"And your self-assuredness will be yours. It always is for your kind. Greater is He that is in me, than he that is in the world."

"*He* has forsaken you. He has forsaken all of you."

"He has done no such thing."

That's it, Levi thought. *Keep coming. Just a few more steps . . .*

The creatures halted at the stairs. Two of them glanced up, sniffing the air. One licked his lips.

"My God is stronger than yours," Levi taunted. "You know this to be true. I serve the one true God."

"Your God has no power over us, and neither do you."

"If that's true, then face me, cowards."

That did it. Levi grinned.

Snarling, the revenants forgot about the humans upstairs and stalked toward him. Their eyes and teeth flashed in the darkness. The air grew colder and the gloom seemed to deepen. Levi shivered. Beyond them, he saw a figure sneak down the stairs, moving silently, and dart toward the front door.

Thank you, Lord. Just a moment longer.

The dark men entered the kitchen. Levi remained still, projecting calm. His legs were still crossed. He held out his hands, palms up.

"Now," he said, smiling up at them. "I guess you're wondering why I've called you here."

One of the figures raked its talons along the wall. "Enough of this. You've stalled long enough. Now you die."

"Go ahead, Levi," Donny shouted.

The revenants turned at the sound of his voice, just as Donny fled up the stairs. Two of them raced over to the stairwell, but halted when they reached the salt.

"What is this?"

"It's salt." Levi stood up again. He was still grinning. "You'll note that it now covers all entrances and exits from this place. I know it's not really a sphere, but according to the Law, it still counts as a circle."

The figure closest to Levi smiled. "Very good, little magus. This was unexpected."

"Thank you. I like to think on my feet."

"Of course, it is a futile gesture. There is one thing you didn't consider, Levi, son of Amos. There is one crucial flaw in this pitiful attempt to defeat us."

"Oh? And what's that?"

"You are trapped in the circle with us."

"No." Levi's smile vanished. "It's *you* who are trapped in here with *me*."

Levi sprang to his feet as they charged toward him. Everything now came down to timing and placement. He had to be exact, had to make it look natural, or all of his efforts would be for naught. He would die here, in this broken circle, and Meeble's minions would win.

He darted to the left and ran toward the slightly open door, seemingly attempting to evade his attackers and get behind them. The ruse worked. They slammed into him in front of the pantry. Their talons and teeth slashed at him, ripping and tearing. Levi howled in pain as his blood began to flow. The creatures howled with him, shouting angry curses in a language not their own. Levi let his knees go weak, allowing their combined weight and the force of their attack to drive him backward. He prayed they'd come with him, and his prayer was answered. They clung tightly, their claws sinking deeper into his flesh. Half-blind from pain, Levi crashed into the pantry door and tumbled through to the other side. The revenants fell with him. They toppled to the ground together, but his opponents were too enraged to notice that their surroundings had changed. Biting his lip to stifle his screams, Levi lashed out with his foot and kicked the door shut.

Esther's pantry vanished, taking the rest of the world with it.

Slowly, their attack ceased. One by one, they withdrew from him and stood, staring speechless at their new surroundings. Levi did the same. The overcast sky was filled with grayish yellow clouds of mist so impressive in size that they almost appeared to be floating landmasses. The soft ground was spongy and slick. White, fibrous strands of what looked like peach fuzz sprouted from the surface. Moisture seeped through Levi's clothing and when he pulled his hands away, his palms were wet. His skin felt slimy, as if he'd been grasping earthworms or slugs. The landscape was featureless, save for a variety of sickly gray and white toadstools, mushrooms and other fungi. Some were miniscule. Others were as tall as redwood trees. The air was thick with the smell of mildew. Far off in the distance, a black river of what looked like tar wound its way through the fungus. It was spanned by a cyclopean bridge made entirely of mold. Beyond that, on the horizon, great gray mountains towered into the poison sky. They were dreary looking and somehow obscene, and the sight of their peaks filled Levi with dread. A city composed of windowless black towers stood in their shadow. Atop the tallest mountain sat a giant geometric sculpture, a shining trapezoid that spilled light onto the valley below. Despite his immediate danger, Levi was awestruck by its size. He'd read of the monolith before, but to see it like this, to actually view the shining trapezoid . . . No written account did it justice.

The shadows stirred.

"What trickery is this, little magus?"

Groaning, Levi stumbled to his feet. Blood ran from both of his arms as well as his back, chest and face. He'd broken the index finger of his right hand, and he was pretty sure that his right wrist was sprained, too. The flesh was already beginning to swell, and the pain made him nauseous.

"No trickery. I promised you that I wouldn't harm you in Esther's place, and I have honored my word. I have brought you elsewhere."

"You speak in riddles."

"No, I don't. Welcome to your new home, gentlemen."

They turned on him, growling. Their elongated talons had shrunk back into their fingers, and their clothes and faces weren't so dark anymore.

"Don't bother trying to shape-shift," Levi continued. "You can't anymore. In fact, if I'm correct—and I suspect that I am—you'll find that you're all quite powerless here."

"Meeble's strength follows us wherever we go. It is within us."

"Back on Earth, perhaps, but not here. Not in this place. You see, this is not your master's domain."

Grunting, the tallest of the five made a dismissive gesture with his hand and pulled himself up to his full height. "After all your boasts, you have merely delayed the inevitable, Levi, son of Amos. You may be able to walk the paths of the Labyrinth, but bringing us here will not save you. What do my brothers and I care for worlds? We will lay waste to this one, just as we laid waste to your own. This world's populace shall know of our master's power, and we will feed here just as well."

"Go ahead, then. Leave your mark. Carve *Croatoan* in the trunk of one of those great mushrooms. Carve your master's name here, in the domain of Behemoth!"

They gaped at him. The fear on their faces was

palpable, and Levi couldn't help but laugh. After all of the terror they'd caused the people of Brinkley Springs, not to mention countless other human beings going all the way back to the original Roanoke settlement, it felt good to see them scared and to know that he was the source of their fear. He forced himself to ignore the twinge of pride.

"I see by your expressions that you understand now. That's correct. We stand beneath the noxious skies of Yuggoth, home of Behemoth, the Great Worm and one of the Thirteen, who is the equal of your master."

"You lie."

Levi shook his head. "You know that I don't. According to the Law, you are forbidden to do your work here, lest you risk a war between the Great Worm and your master—a conflict which would ultimately anger He Who Shall Not Be Named. I don't think Meeble would appreciate such insolence."

His opponents began to tremble. Whether from fear or rage, Levi couldn't be certain. Perhaps both. Either way, they were still dangerous, even without their powers.

"Open the door," the shortest one said. "Return us to our world and we will let you live. On this you have our word."

Levi shook his head. "Not a chance."

"Then you have doomed yourself, as well, little magus." The tallest of the five stepped closer. "If you know of Yuggoth, then you know what grows here. Even as we speak, you are breathing the poisoned spores into your lungs. You are inhaling Behemoth's seeds. They will take root in your body and begin to grow, ultimately transforming you—if the wounds we inflicted do not kill you first."

"I've had worse," Levi bluffed. In truth, his legs felt wobbly and he was growing weaker with every moment. He needed to stop the bleeding and attend to his injuries. His wrist continued to swell, and the skin around it felt hot to the touch and had turned an angry shade of red. His finger, bent and swollen, throbbed painfully with each beat of his heart. He took a deep breath. The air was sweltering and thick, and coated his tongue. Levi grimaced. It was like breathing hot soup. He smacked his lips and tasted mildew in the back of his throat.

"This will be the end of you, bearded one."

"Perhaps," Levi said, "but I'd rather succumb to the white fuzz than return you to my world. Better to turn into a mushroom than to allow you to continue your work."

As he talked, Levi pressed his left hand to the wound on his chest. It was bleeding profusely. He cupped his palm and his hand filled with warmth.

"Open the door," the shortest one repeated. This time, his voice had a pleading tone. "We promise to return to our place of rest and bother you and those under your protection no more. Again, you have our word."

"And what of next time?" Levi asked. "What happens when you come out of hibernation and murder another town? What about all the others you'll kill? No, I'll not have that on my conscience. There's enough blood on my hands."

"Dead men don't have consciences." The revenant who said this glanced at his brothers and laughed.

Blood dripped through Levi's fingers. "I'm not dead yet."

"Then let us rectify that," the tall one said. "Powerless or not, there are five of us and one of you. You are outnumbered and you are wounded."

They moved toward him in a half circle. The two on the ends tried to flank him on either side. Levi flung a fistful of his blood at the one on the left, spattering his face and clothing.

"By His blood I bind thee. By His blood I command thee. By His blood, which was shed for me, do I trod on thee."

Shrieking, the dark man recoiled, clawing at his face. Smoke rose from his clothing and skin. He collapsed to the ground and lay writhing and kicking as the smoke grew thicker.

"The power and the glory forever, amen."

The others hesitated, glancing down at their brother in confusion and panic. Levi cupped his hand to his breast and gathered more of his blood.

"Now there are four of you," he said. "Did I mention that without your abilities, my powwow works on you?"

They charged him all at once, rushing forward. Levi splashed a fistful of blood in the face of the closest attacker. The dark figure reeled backward. The other three slammed into Levi, pushing him to the ground. He struck the surface hard, yelping as his wounds were opened afresh. The ground itself yielded, seeming to suck him deeper. A flurry of blows rained down upon him. Their fists battered his face and chest. A punch to his stomach forced the air from his lungs. He gasped, breathing in more of the noxious, musty air and tasting mildew and blood. His stomach lurched. The pounding continued. Levi closed his bruised and swelling eyes and exhaled.

"He loses consciousness already, brothers."

"He does, indeed. Stay awake, little magus."

"We have only just started with you. We do not need our powers to rend the flesh from your bones or show you your insides. We can do it with our bare hands."

Levi ignored the rough, chattering voices and focused on himself. The pain faded until he no longer felt the blows and punches, even though they continued to fall upon him. He could no longer hear his attackers, no longer feel their crushing weight. Gone, too, was the cloying, potent stench of the planet's atmosphere and the wet, slimy touch of the ground. There was only Levi, floating above himself. He looked down at his body, watched with a sense of detachment as one of his attackers wrapped their hands around his throat and squeezed. Summoning all of his strength, Levi found his center and then returned to his body.

He forced what little air remained in his lungs through his nose and simultaneously pushed with his mind. His shoulders stiffened and his body trembled as he shoved harder, visualizing his will as a physical bludgeon. Then his eyes snapped open and all three of his attackers were shoved backward as if they'd been struck. They flew through the air like rag dolls, soaring away from him before ultimately slamming into the fibrous, fungal surface.

Levi struggled to sit up. Each movement was agony. One of his eyes had swollen completely shut and the other was only a slit. He strained, trying to find the spot where the doorway had been. If he couldn't find it, he'd be trapped here with them. His opponents would never let him live long enough to open a second passage. Wincing, he turned his head. The three attackers lay still, apparently stunned by the force of his psychic defense. The other two—the ones he'd splashed with blood—were now just smoking piles of ash. He wondered where their spirits had gone. Here, or back to Earth, where their original bodies still lay buried?

One of the three remaining revenants twitched. Levi tried to stand up, but found that he couldn't. The pain was too great. Resolving to try again, he bit his lip—and screamed aloud. It had been smashed and split by the beating he'd taken, but the pain helped him focus. It forced him on. Still, despite his best efforts, his body refused to obey his commands. Levi crawled forward on his hands, trailing his useless legs behind him. His feet carved shallow furrows in the ground, and his elbows made sucking sounds in the turf as he pulled himself along. Stagnant water pooled around him, welling up from below the surface. Levi was suddenly aware of being very thirsty, and for a brief moment, he considered drinking the loathsome liquid. Just a little bit, enough to quench his thirst.

"No . . ." He meant to shout it, but the utterance was barely a croak.

Whimpering, Levi focused on the terrain. He dragged himself through the ashes of his enemies, smearing them against his damp, bloody clothes, until he'd reached the spot where the door should be. The wind howled, racing across the gray-white plain. Levi raised one trembling hand and almost blacked out. His vision wavered. His ears roared. He forced himself to take another deep breath, inhaling more of the sickening air. It felt gritty, as if he'd breathed in sandpaper. The sensation passed, and his vision returned. Levi raised his hand again, stretching one quivering arm forward. When his broken finger brushed against the invisible door, he moaned. The crooked digit throbbed. His vision blurred again, and this time, it did not clear.

Running footsteps squelched behind him. Levi rolled over just as the tallest of the revenants flung itself at him. The attacker landed next to him, face-first in the terrain. When he lifted his head, his cheeks and chin were covered with white fungus. Snarling, he bared his teeth. Despite his pain and delirium, Levi noticed how yellow they were now. They looked old and brittle, not at all the shining white fangs that had glinted in the darkness of Brinkley Springs.

Levi made a fist, grabbing a handful of the damp soil, and flung it into the dark man's face. Then, using the last of his physical strength, he crawled forward and plunged both his middle finger and his broken index finger into the revenant's eyes. There was a brief moment of resistance, as if he were pressing against a balloon, and then it vanished. His fingers slid into the sockets with ease. Jellied pulp squirted out around his knuckles. The revenant screamed.

"That's it," Levi whispered. "Scream. It's better when you scream."

His opponent shuddered and then lay still. Levi pulled his fingers from the ruined sockets and glanced over at the other two. Both were beginning to stir. The roaring grew louder in his ears and his vision blurred a third time. He tried reaching for the door again but for some reason, his arms no lon-

ger wanted to work. Like his legs, they had ultimately betrayed him.

He collapsed onto the spongy ground and stared
through one slit at the empty space in front of him.

"Your will be done, Lord. On Yuggoth, as it is in
Heaven."

And then, a dark crack appeared in the air. Dim
candlelight flickered inside of it. Levi heard voices—
Randy's and Marsha's, followed a moment later by
Donny's.

"He said not to break the circle." Donny sounded
frantic.

"But he's gone," Randy said. "Let's look in the
pantry. Maybe he went back through that . . . other
place, again."

The crack grew wider. Moaning, Levi crawled toward it. Marsha and Randy stood in the doorway,
gasping in surprise at the vista spread out before
them.

"Don't breathe," Levi gasped. "Get back and don't
breathe it in."

He heaved himself through the open door and
tumbled onto Esther's kitchen floor. The linoleum
felt cool beneath his skin. Randy, Marsha and Donny
hovered over him, their expressions concerned and
alarmed.

"Jesus, Levi." Donny scanned his wounds. "You
look like you've been through a meat grinder."

"We've got to get him to a hospital," Marsha said.

"No." Levi shook his head weakly. "Must . . .
close . . . door. Get rid . . . of . . . circle."

"How?" Donny asked.

"The salt." Randy stood up and then glanced
down at Levi. "We've got to get rid of the salt, right?"

Levi nodded.

"How do you know that?" Marsha asked.

"I don't know. I just do. He was fooling with salt earlier. I reckon it makes sense."

The three of them brushed the lines of salt away from the doors and windows with their hands and feet. Slowly, the light beneath the pantry door faded. When they were finished, Donny returned. He knelt and pressed Levi's copy of *The Long Lost Friend* into his hands. Levi couldn't feel the book between his numb fingers, but knowing it was there made him feel better. He waited until Donny looked into his eyes again and then let his gaze fall upon the pantry door. Then he looked at Donny again.

"You want me to check?" the younger man asked.

"Yes . . ."

Slowly, Donny opened the door. He crouched as he did so, ready to leap out of the way should something charge through it. He relaxed when Esther's canned goods stood revealed.

Levi smiled. He took one last shuddering breath, and then the darkness consumed him.

CHAPTER TWELVE

The first things Levi became aware of when he regained consciousness were the warm feel of sunlight on his face and the smell of incense. There were soft pillows beneath his head, and if he wasn't mistaken, a feather comforter pulled over his body. He heard water dripping and then a moment later, a cold, wet cloth was placed on his forehead, chasing away the warmth from the sun. Levi opened his eyes. Myrtle stared down at him. Esther stood over her shoulder. He was lying in a bed. The room seemed strangely familiar. His finger was splinted with popsicle sticks and his wounds were bandaged with gauze.

"You're awake," Myrtle said. "Welcome back. How do you feel?"

"Much . . . much better, thank you. Where are we?"

"Your room," Myrtle said. "We moved you up here after . . . well, after everything happened. We didn't know what to do. The menfolk said that you'd told them we couldn't get out of town. So we brought you up here and I went home and got some of my things, and we've been caring for you as best we can."

"The soul cage is most likely gone," Levi said. "I would guess you're all free to leave town again."

"Is that what it was? That's what was keeping us here? A soul cage?"

He nodded.

Myrtle frowned. "I've read about them. I thought they were tiny things."

"Not this one. It took an incredible amount of power to construct, but it surely vanished when its creators left this level."

"Level?"

"Level of reality. Plane of existence. When they left this world."

"Will they be back?"

Levi paused before answering. He was keenly aware that both women were staring at him intensely.

"I don't think so. In truth, there is still much I don't know about them. But I don't think they can return, and after I've finished my business in Virginia Beach, I'll take measures that I think will ensure they never bother anyone again. Their mortal remains—the remnants of what they once were before their transformation—must be located somewhere on Roanoke. All I have to do is find them and destroy them."

"Do you think it's safe to wait that long?" Myrtle asked.

"What do you mean?"

"Well, your injuries. I would imagine it will be several days at the very least before you're up and about again."

"I appreciate your concern, and everything you've done for me, but really, I'm fine." After quickly verifying that he was dressed beneath the sheets, Levi pulled back the heavy feather comforter. Then he pulled up his shirt and peeled back the gauze, wincing as the medical tape pulled at his hair. The ragged slashes and tears that had crisscrossed his chest and abdomen only hours before were now closed. Only pink lines remained. He held up his splinted finger. While still puffy, it was no longer crooked. The bone had obviously been set.

"How . . . ?" Myrtle's hand fluttered to her throat.

"I'm a fast healer." He took her hand and smiled. "And I had you looking after me. I'm sure that helped, as well. You're quite a capable woman, Myrtle. God has given you the talent of healing."

He released her hand and Myrtle blushed. Beaming, she stood up and almost tripped over the chair. Esther turned around and Levi noticed she was hiding a grin behind her hand.

"Why don't you be a dear, Myrtle, and run downstairs and get Mr. Stoltzfus some water? I'm sure he's thirsty after his ordeal."

Myrtle nodded, still blushing. "Yes, of course."

She bustled out of the room and they heard her humming as she went down the stairs.

"You're quite the flirt, Mr. Stoltzfus. I reckon Myrtle is quite smitten with you."

Levi chuckled. "Thank you, Mrs. Laudry. Thank you for letting me use your home. I'm sorry for what I brought into it. I know that my ways are not your own, and I respect that. I'll be out of your hair within the hour."

"No. I'm the one who is sorry. I was wrong about you, Levi. You saved us. I may not agree with your methods, and I darn sure don't understand everything that happened here last night, but I do know one thing. God sent you here. God has his hand on you, and he placed you here in Brinkley Springs so that you could confront those demons."

"Yes, I believe that He did."

"This isn't the first time such a thing has happened, either, is it?"

"No."

Her expression turned sad. "That must be a very lonely existence."

"No lonelier than Christ felt when he prayed in the garden the night before his crucifixion. I do what I'm called to do, Esther. It's not like I have a choice."

"Well, I thank God for you, Mr. Stoltzfus."

"Thank you." He paused. "Are you okay?"

Esther dabbed at her eyes with her sleeve. When she spoke again, her voice was thick with emotion.

"I don't know. I lived here all my life, and now . . . it's all gone. Brinkley Springs was dying before they came. I knew that. Another ten or fifteen years and this would have been a ghost town. But still, I never imagined it would die like this. Murdered. All those people, folks I've known for years. Still, it would have been worse had you not been here."

Levi nodded, unsure of what to say. He doubted that any Bible verse or homily he could offer would comfort her.

"It really is amazing how quickly you healed."

"In truth, it wasn't my wounds that concerned me the most. It was the spores in my lungs."

"Spores?"

"Yes. To rid us of our enemies, I had to transport them elsewhere—to a place where the very air will kill you."

"Will you be okay?"

He nodded. "I will be. Had I not had the opportunity to meditate and clear my system, I might not be, though."

"Meditate? We thought you'd passed out from blood loss."

"And I had. Blood loss and shock. But even in that state, I was aware. I knew what I had to do. It's really nothing more than another form of prayer."

"But how did you—?"

The door opened. Myrtle entered the room, holding a bottle of spring water. Behind her were Donny, Marsha and Randy. All three stared at Levi in astonishment.

"There's no way you should be awake, let alone sitting up," Donny said. "But I reckon I'm not surprised."

He stuck out his hand and Levi shook it firmly.

"How is everyone?" Levi asked.

"About how you'd expect," Donny said. "Jean Sullivan's been crying a lot. Her son seems okay, though. Kids adapt quick, you know? Paul has been pretty quiet. I think he's still in shock. He's outside, surveying the damage."

"His dogs?"

Donny shook his head. "They didn't make it. That was the first place he went. He came back here, after. He didn't say much, other than that they were dead. I got the impression that whatever happened to them, it wasn't pretty."

"No," Levi said, "I don't imagine it was."

"We locked Gus in one of the bedrooms," Donny continued. "He's not violent or anything, but obviously, he's not right in the head. We didn't want him running off into the woods or anything."

"I checked on him a little bit ago," Marsha said. "He was drawing mazes on a notepad. But at least he was calm."

"And Mr. Perry?"

"He's taking a nap downstairs on Esther's sofa," Donny said. "I think this experience wore him out."

Levi nodded. "I think it wore us all out."

"I want to do what you do," Randy said, stepping forward. "I mean, the way you took care of those fuckers . . . I can do that, too, right?"

Levi glanced at Donny and Marsha, and then back to Randy.

"Is it true?" Randy persisted. "Can you teach me to do what you do?"

"No," Levi lied, thinking back to when he was Randy's age. "I can't teach you. I was wrong."

"But . . . but all that stuff you said about my aura and shit? I thought I was special."

"I was mistaken. I was under a lot of stress. The truth is, you're normal, Randy. You're not magic. You don't have the ability. You're just normal. And trust me, that's a very good thing to be. Don't despair over it."

Randy's expression turned to confusion and disappointment. Levi hated that he'd lied to the teen, and hated even worse the pain he saw in Randy's eyes. But that pain was much better than the pain a life like Levi's would bring him. He glanced at Marsha and Donny again. Both nodded at him in silent understanding.

"You're sure?" Randy asked. "You're sure that I'm not like you?"

Levi nodded. "I've never been more sure of anything in my life."

* * *

Dee whinnied happily as Levi fastened her harness.

"I'm glad to see you, too, girl. You missed all the fun."

The horse stomped her foot and snorted.

"Oh, don't start that. Trust me, you were much better off down by the riverside. You lucked out this time."

"She's beautiful."

Levi turned. Marsha and Donny were crossing Esther's yard. Marsha gazed at Dee lovingly.

"Can I pet her?"

"Of course," Levi said. "I think she'd like that."

Marsha stroked the horse's flank, and Dee swished her tail and nodded her head.

"No traffic yet," Donny said, looking down the street. "But they'll be coming through soon—folks from other towns, passing through here on their way to work, and long-haul truckers on their way north or south."

"Yes," Levi said. "Are the phones or electric working again?"

"The power is still out. So are the land lines. But cell-phone service is back up again. Spotty as ever, but it was like that before they came."

"Have any of you called the authorities yet?"

"No." Donny ran a hand across his crew cut. "To be honest, Levi, we're not sure just who the hell to call. I mean, who do you report something like this to? You got any ideas?"

Levi shrugged. "Start with the local authorities. It doesn't matter, really. Once word gets out—and it will get out—everyone will descend upon this place. The state police. The National Guard. The FBI. Black

Lodge. The cover-up will begin almost immediately. They'll blame the events here on terrorists or something similar. Perhaps a biological incident. They'll attempt to buy your silence and complicity. If they can't do that, then they'll discredit you."

Donny raised his eyebrows. "Black Lodge? Those guys really exist?"

Levi shrugged again. "So I'm told. I'm surprised you know of them."

"I heard some stuff when I was in the army."

"Well, just be careful. If you're still inclined to leave, Donny, I'd do it this morning, before word of what's happened here gets out. I imagine the next few weeks will be very trying for everyone involved."

Marsha stopped petting Dee and moved to Donny's side. He put his arm around her and hugged her tight.

"I'm not leaving, Levi. I've decided to stick around. The town needs a defender, now that you're moving on."

Levi smiled. "That's excellent, my friend. It sounds to me like you've come home for good."

Donny kissed Marsha's head. "Yes, as a matter of fact, I think I have."

Still smiling, Levi climbed up into the wagon and reached out a hand. Donny shook it. His grip was still firm and strong.

"I hope," he said, "that you can do the same one day, too, Levi. I hope you can go home for good."

"Thank you, Donny. That would be nice, but I'm afraid I walk a different path, and I must go where it takes me."

"Take care, Levi."

"You, too, my friends. Good luck to you both."

He took Dee's reins in his hands and flicked them. She began to trot, and the wagon rolled slowly behind her. The sun cleared the treetops, climbing into the sky. In the distance, Levi heard the sound of motors. He glanced back once as they rounded a corner. Marsha and Donny stood with their arms around each other, watching him leave. Levi raised his hand and waved. They returned the gesture. It occurred to him as he watched the young couple fade from view that maybe Brinkley Springs would live again. Maybe they were the seed that would spark new growth. Maybe the town would get a second chance at life.

His smile faded as he remembered Donny's final words.

I hope you can go home for good.

"I hope so, too," Levi whispered. "But I don't know that I'm ready yet."

Dee whinnied and tossed her head.

"Come on, girl." He flicked the reins again. "We've still got a long way to travel before we even consider going home."

AUTHOR'S NOTE

If this is your first introduction to the ex-Amish magus Levi Stoltzfus, you might also want to read my
novel *Ghost Walk* (as well as its prequel, *Dark Hollow*),
which marks Levi's first appearance. Both books
should be available in paperback at your local library or bookstore. If your local bookseller doesn't
have them in stock, ask them to order the books for
you, or order them instead from any online retailer.

Judging by what you tell me on my Web site and
Twitter and Facebook, Levi seems to be a fan favorite. He's a favorite of mine, as well. I enjoy writing
him. You might like to know that he will return for
at least two more books. One of those stories takes
place in the weeks following this novel and tells what
happens to him once he finally reaches his original
destination. The other novel will focus on his even-
tual return to the Amish community that cast him
out all those years ago, and will fill in most of his
backstory. I'll let you see them both when they're
finished.

I'd also like to take a moment here to give a shout-
out to Don D'Auria, my editor at Leisure Books.
This is my eleventh novel with Leisure, and Don has
been my guide and sounding board for every one of
them. Believe me when I say that none of this would

be possible without him. As I write this, Don and I are hard at work on books twelve through fifteen. It's a good relationship, and I'm looking forward to working with him on many more.

As always, thanks for buying this and for all of your continued support. I like hearing from you and finding out which of my books you liked (and which ones you didn't like). You keep reading them and I'll keep writing them.

Brian Keene
Somewhere in central Pennsylvania
November 2009

Turn the page for an advance look at Brian Keene's
next terrifying novel . . .

ENTOMBED

Coming in February 2011

CHAPTER ONE

I was sitting in the movie room, watching an episode of *Aqua Teen Hunger Force* for the twentieth time and talking to the head of Dwight D. Eisenhower, when the rest of the group decided that we should all start eating each other.

Pickings were slim for my viewing pleasure. The bunker's media collection consisted of a season of Reba McEntire's old sitcom, an episode of *The Wiggles*, a couple of Will Ferrell movies, the remastered and updated first *Star Wars* trilogy, a season of *Aqua Teen Hunger Force*, a season of *American Idol*, and a documentary about deer hunting. I avoided watching *Reba* because seeing Joanna Garcia, the actress who played Reba McEntire's daughter, made me horny, and that was a totally unhelpful feeling to have when one is sixty feet under the ground. Ditto *The Wiggles* (say what you will, but some of their dancers are totally fucking hot). I'd watched *Star Wars* a few times since we came down here, but it still pissed me off that in this updated version of the film, Han Solo no longer shot first. Will Ferrell Fuck him. I never liked Will Ferrell's movies—he was about as funny as cancer. Watching the deer hunting documentary just made me hungry—which was an even less helpful feeling down here than being horny. And I'd thought that *American Idol* sucked even before the world ended, and saw no reason to start watching it now. It didn't matter who won, since they were probably all dead now.

That left *Aqua Teen Hunger Force*, which was okay with me, although sometimes I wished that someone would have left some *Metalocalypse* DVDs down here, too.

I had the lights turned off. The media room was lit only by the glow from the huge flat-screen television that occupied most of the wall at the front of the room. I was sitting in the left-hand side of the front row, right next to Eisenhower's head. The chairs weren't very comfortable, and they squeaked every time I moved around. Before Hamelin's Revenge turned the world to shit, the chairs had only been used by visitors to the bunker—tourists who sat in them once a day to watch a seven-minute documentary on the facility's history. Eisenhower was a big part of that history, which was why his head was in the movie room, too.

Eisenhower didn't say much. He couldn't. He was a bronze bust. But that was okay with me. He didn't have to say anything. He was a good listener, and a good listener was what I needed—especially since most of the other people down here were slowly turning bat-shit crazy. There was more than one Eisenhower in the room. Framed pictures of him hung on the walls, along with photographs of the hotel sitting above the bunker, and a few of the facility when it was under construction—black and white images of the Army Corps of Engineers swarming over the site.

Swarming, just like the dead rats that swarmed

out of the sewers in New York City. That was how this whole thing started—Hamelin's Revenge. New York seems so far away, especially here in the mountains of West Virginia. But what started there swept across the rest of the planet in less than a month's time. It happened during the evening rush hour. The rats crawled out of the sewer and began attacking pedestrians. Being dead, they moved much slower than a living rat would, but that didn't matter. The city was so choked with traffic that their pickings were easy. The sidewalks and streets and bus stops and subway platforms were gridlocked, packed with commuters. People tried to get away but there was nowhere to go. The rats fed. Many people were bitten to death, the flesh stripped from their faces and hands, their stomachs chewed open so that their attackers could get to the good stuff inside. Many more victims were trampled to death as their fellow New Yorkers fled.

The breaking news dominated television and the internet that night. At first, MSNBC called it a riot, and both CNN and FOX speculated that it had been a possible terrorist attack. Soon, they confirmed that it had been rats—dead rats. As impossible as that sounded, eyewitness accounts confirmed that the rats were indeed dead when they began their attack. Pundits scoffed at this, and the authorities refused to comment, but soon enough, the live footage proved this to be true, as unlikely as it seemed. The coverage was fluid and the situation on the ground grew more chaotic with each passing hour. FOX had footage from inside a hospital. The emergency room was filled with wounded New Yorkers. Those who had suffered bites got sick very quickly. A short time later, they died. And after they died, they came back, just like the rats.

Before that first night was through, the media already had a name for it—Hamelin's Revenge, the return of the rats the pied piper was hired to get rid of. It didn't seem to matter that Hamelin was the name of the town, rather than the piper himself. I don't know. I used to wonder sometimes if the media had names and graphics on standby, just waiting to use them when all hell broke loose. It certainly seemed that way that night. There was Wolf Blitzer on TV, with a big graphic of a pied piper standing behind him and the words "Hamelin's Revenge" superimposed over the character. Dead people and dead rats attacked the living, and then those who'd been infected joined their ranks. The media called the dead cannibals, but then, during a 2 a.m. news conference, the White House Press Secretary used the word that was on everyone's mind.

Zombies.

By dawn the next morning, the National Guard had locked everything down. New York City was officially quarantined. They blockaded the bridges and tunnels. The Guardsmen were given the order to fire on anyone trying to escape the city, and some of them did. They gunned down civilians in cold blood. Then some of the other soldiers refused the order and turned on their comrades. And while dissent broke out in the ranks, Hamelin's Revenge broke out of the city. It showed up in Newark, then Trenton, and then Philadelphia. By the end of the second day, it had spread to Buffalo, Baltimore, Washington, D.C., and over the New York border into Canada. The president declared martial law. The army was mobilized. But by then, it was too late. You could shoot a zombie but you couldn't shoot the disease that caused it in the first place. All it took was one bite, one drop of blood, pus from an open sore—any exposure to infected bodily fluid—and you became one of them. People that died normal deaths—from illness or accidents or murder—stayed dead, but those who came into direct contact with the disease and managed to get infected—they became zombies. At first, the disease only affected humans, rats and mice. By the second week, however, it jumped species and started showing up in dogs, cats, cattle, bears, coyotes, goats, sheep, monkeys and other animals. Some creatures, like pigs and birds, seemed to be immune. Most weren't so lucky. And some species that had seemed immune at first later became infected, like squirrels and deer.

Once the disease began jumping from species to species, it became unstoppable. America, South America and Canada fell first, followed by Europe, Asia, Africa and finally Australia. After that, we lost what little television coverage remained. The last thing any of us saw, as far as I know, was footage of zombies shuffling through the streets of Mumbai. Of course, the zombies weren't the only threat. There were roving gangs of looters, criminals, extremists and military and law enforcement personnel who'd decided to watch out for themselves, rather than the rest of us. The new law was the law of the gun.

Washington, D.C., was evacuated early on. They sent President Tyler, the vice-president, the cabinet, the Pentagon bigwigs, and all of the House and Senate members and their staff and family to secure underground bunkers in Pennsylvania, Virginia,

Maryland and Colorado. Bunkers just like this one. I have to wonder if they're in any better shape than we are. Probably. I doubt our leaders are sitting around voting on whether or not to resort to cannibalism. At least, not yet.

I'm hungry.

This bunker was built as a relocation center back in the early sixties, when the Cold War was heating up. Eisenhower commissioned it, which is why a bronze bust of his head and all the photographs and pictures of him are down here with us. In the event of a nuclear attack on the United States, the bunker was supposed to house the members of the House and the Senate, along with their family members and a few staffers. It was big enough to hold just over a thousand people. To build it, they tunneled eight hundred feet into the mountain, and eighty feet underground. No, it wouldn't survive a direct strike from a nuclear warhead, but it was deep and secure enough to protect its inhabitants from firestorms and radioactive fallout. The site was easily accessible from Washington. It was less than an hour away by railroad or plane, and the interstate ran nearby, as well. Back when the government kept it stocked with supplies, people could have stayed here for up to one hundred and twenty days.

To prevent the local hillbillies from becoming suspicious during construction, a cover was devised for the operation. The public was told that a new luxury hotel was being built on top of the mountain, and that it would bring jobs and economic development to the area. And that's exactly what happened. A beautiful, ritzy resort hotel—the Pocahontas (named that because of its location in Pocahontas County)—

was erected, and it attracted the wealthy, powerful and elite from around the world. Generations of actors, politicians, oil barons, banking magnates and others were among the frequent guests. The hotel employed locals, providing a nice alternative for those who didn't want to slave away in a coal mine, cut timber, try their hand at farming, or just sit back and collect welfare (these are the four biggest occupations in West Virginia). Over the years, the town grew and expanded. So did the Pocahontas, adding new wings, a golf course, tennis and racquetball courts, stables and an equestrian trail, and even its own private runway for small planes. And in all that time, no one above ground, other than the hotel's administrators, ever suspected what lay beneath the mountain—until one Sunday morning a decade ago, when an investigative reporter for the *New York Times* broke the story on the front page. When that happened, the facility was rendered useless. The government immediately decommissioned the bunker and turned ownership of it over to the hotel. At one point, a data storage company wanted to lease it from the hotel's management, but the Pocahontas had other ideas. For the last ten years, its been open to visitors and guests of the Pocahontas—an added tourist attraction to an already luxuriant establishment. I should know. I've been one of the bunker's tour guides for the last three years. It was either that, or get a job at Wal-Mart, and I fucking hate Wal-Mart.

That was how I ended up down here with the others. By that point, the shit had already hit the fan in New York and Philly and elsewhere, but it hadn't become widespread. At least, not here. We'd had reports of a few zombies, but West Virginia is such a rural state, with so much wilderness between towns, that it didn't seem like an epidemic. It was like watching 9/11 or Hurricane Katrina—you knew it was happening and you felt connected to it, but at the same time, it seemed so far away. Bad things always happen to other people. Not to you. Not until they show up at your front door unannounced and come inside and stay for a while.

Martial law hadn't been declared in West Virginia yet, and the hotel was still making us show up for work, even though lodging reservations had dropped to zero. I was standing out back, sneaking a smoke with a few of the Mexican guys from the kitchen, when the dead arrived at the Pocahontas. We smelled them before we saw them, but we didn't know what the stench was or where it was coming from. It was hot outside, and there was only a slight breeze— strong enough only to move the air around rather than cool us off. We all caught a whiff at the same time. I frowned. It was like smelling the world's biggest pile of roadkill. One of the other guys said something in Spanish. I don't know what. Probably, "Goddamn, that stinks." The stench grew overpowering. And then . . . there they were—shuffling out of the woods and across the parking lot toward us.

I think their silence was the scariest part. The dead were quiet. No moans or gurgles or cries. I mean, it was obvious that they meant business. They bore down on the hotel with a single-minded determination, hobbling and pulling themselves forward despite the fact that some of them were missing limbs and major organs, or trailing intestines behind them like leashes. Most of the zombies were human, but there were dead animals, too. Rats, mostly, along with a few foxes and skunks and a black bear cub that was missing an eye and most of its lower jaw. That didn't stop it from coming, though. The dead are determined sons of bitches.

Two of our groundskeepers drove toward them in a golf cart. To this day, I don't know what those guys were thinking. It's not like they were armed or anything. I have no idea what they intended to do. Maybe run over the zombies? Whatever it was, they never got a chance. The dead might have been slow, but they could swarm you until there was nowhere left to run. That's what happened with the groundskeepers. They ran over a zombie groundhog with the golf cart, but the corpse got caught beneath their back wheel and slowed them down. Bits of matted fur and decayed flesh were smeared across the pavement. Then, the driver made a sharp turn. I guess he was trying to dislodge the dead critter. Problem was, golf carts aren't made for hairpin turns. He tipped the fucking thing over on its side, and before they could scramble free of the wreckage, the zombies were on them from all sides—penning them in. One man started screaming as the dead shuffled closer. The other one sank to his knees and began praying in Spanish and frantically crossing himself. It was a slow death for them both. The zombies crowded in, closer and closer, until both the golf cart and the victims were lost from sight.

That was all the rest of us needed to see. We turned and fled. Behind us came the most awful sounds— tearing and ripping and biting. We ran back into the hotel, only to learn that the shit had hit the fan inside the Pocahontas, as well. Zombies had come in through both the main entrance and the meditation garden. They were swarming through the lobby and around the elevators and beginning to make their way down the long concourse of ritzy stores and shops that occupy most of the hotel's first floor—jewelers, a humidor, candy stores, coffee shops, a bookstore, clothing stores and other businesses catering to the guests because none of the locals in town could ever afford to shop in them.

I ran into my buddy Mike, who worked in the hotel's banqueting department. Looking back on it now, it's his fault I'm in this goddamned situation. He reached out and grabbed my shoulders, stopping me in midrun. I tried pushing him away, but he squeezed harder. My hands curled into fists.

"Let go of me, Mike! You see what's happening?"

"The bunker," he yelled. "We've got to get everyone into the bunker, Pete."

And just like that, everything changed. It was like Mike had uttered some magic words. I was still scared, but my head was clearer. I was thinking about survival, rather than just running around in blind panic. My fear wasn't ruling me. I was ruling it. People ran by us. The hallway was filled with screams and shouts. I suddenly felt like an island.

"The bunker . . . hell, why didn't I think of that?"

"You've got a key, right?"

I nodded. As one of the tour guides, I had one of seven plastic key cards that would let us into the bunker. I was about to speak, when I noticed Mike's eyes grow wide. He bit his lip but I don't think he was aware that he was doing it. He stared at something over my shoulder. I turned around, wincing at the sudden stench. A group of zombies were shambling toward us.

"Shit."

"Tell everyone you can," Mike said. "I'll meet you down there."

"Where are you going?"

"The kitchen. There's no telling how long we'll be down there. We'll need food."

"Good idea. Be careful."

"You, too. Just make sure you keep that door open for me."

I promised him that I would, and then he ran down the hall, easily dodging the dead. His movements reminded me of a football player charging toward the goal. I turned the other way and headed for the bunker.

The next time I saw Mike, his throat had been torn out, his nose was hanging by a flap of skin, and one of his eyes was missing. That didn't stop him, though. He showed up at the bunker door, just like he'd said he would.

And then he tried to eat me.

There were two entrances to the bunker. The first one was via an outdoor tunnel on the other side of the mountain, some distance from the hotel. Normally, when we gave visitors a tour, we started from that entrance after taking them there via a short bus ride. The entrance had a ten foot high steel blast door with a big sign affixed to it that said DANGER: HIGH VOLTAGE. The sign had originally been put there to scare people away—random hikers or hunters who might have stumbled across it—but it was obsolete now. The Pocahontas kept the sign there as part of the ambience. Since the bunker was now nothing more than a museum, it added a touch of authenticity.

The other entrance was located inside the hotel itself, adjacent to our basement-level conference center. The conference center was a huge, open room where various organizations and groups held conventions, employee meetings, dinners and things like that. It was a very plain room. The carpet was thin and worn. The overhead lights were too bright. The walls were a drab off-white color. I once overheard a hotel guest refer to the décor as "wholly uninspiring." But one of those uninspiring walls concealed the bunker's second entrance. When the partition was slid back, it revealed a second steel blast door, bigger than the door guarding the outside tunnel entrance. It was twelve feet high and twelve feet wide and weighed over twenty-five tons. Despite its size, the blast door was easy to open. Any healthy person could have done it. There was a wheel you turned to open or close the door, and all you had to do was apply fifty pounds of pressure. On tours, we always exited the bunker through this door, and it always took our guests by surprise when they emerged back into the hotel.

A shriek brought me back to my surroundings. A woman's voice. I couldn't tell whose, shouting about something biting her face.

The zombies were flooding into the lobby and there was no time to wait for an elevator. I took the stairs two at a time and paused at the bottom of the stairwell. I put my ear to the door and listened, trying to determine if the conference center was safe or not, but I couldn't tell. The screams from upstairs were too loud. Taking a deep breath, I slowly nudged the door open and peeked into the room. Either Mike's warning had been heard, or others had the same idea as him, because there were a group of people cowering by the wall. Most of them were people I knew—employees of the hotel. A few looked like guests or visitors. One heavyset guy had a cable repairman's uniform on. My friend Drew was among them, and I felt better when I saw him. I stepped through the door and hurried over to them.

"Pete!" Drew rushed toward me. "Tell me you've got a key to get inside?"

Nodding, I pulled the key card from my back pocket. Drew sighed with obvious relief.

"Thank Christ. I thought we were trapped down here."

The group milled around me, blocking my access to the partition. Behind us, something thudded in the stairwell. They scrambled out of the way, and I hurried over to the wall and pushed the partition into its recess, revealing the blast door. The sounds in the stairwell grew louder. I flashed my key card. The lock disengaged, and I turned the wheel. The door rumbled open with a deep, ominous boom.

"Everybody inside!"

I didn't need to tell them twice. The group hurried into the bunker, jostling one another in the process. Drew was at the rear of the procession. He paused when he realized that I wasn't following.

"Aren't you coming?"

I shook my head. "I've got to wait for Mike. He went back to the kitchen to get us some supplies."

Drew glanced at the stairwell and elevator doors

and then back at me. His eyes were wide and his expression grim. "Do you think he can make it?"

"He's got to. Otherwise, we'll starve. There's no food in there. Just a vending machine."

From behind us, someone asked, "What's the hold up?"

Drew and I turned. It was the cable repairman. He stared at us in confusion. Fear had made his face taught and pale. He had a receding hairline and his forehead was slick with sweat. He smelled sour. This close, I could read the name sewn above the pocket of his uniform: CHUCK.

"We're waiting on somebody," I said.

Chuck blinked. "But those things . . ."

"Aren't down here yet. My friend Mike went to get food and supplies. Soon as he gets here, we'll close the door."

"Screw that," someone else called. I couldn't tell who. The group was all bunched together. "If you want to hang around and wait for your friend, go ahead. But close the damned door first."

"I'll be honest, Pete," Drew said. "I tend to agree."

"We're okay down here," I insisted. "The zombies are on the ground level."

Then the stairwell door banged open and a herd of corpses tumbled into the conference room, making a liar out of me.

RICHARD LAYMON

"If you've missed Laymon, you've missed a treat!"
—Stephen King

The Funland Amusement Park provides more fear than fun these days. A vicious pack known as the Trolls are preying on anyone foolish enough to be alone at night. Folks in the area blame them for the recent mysterious disappearances, and a gang of local teenagers has decided to fight back. But nothing is ever what it seems in an amusement park. Behind the garish paint and bright lights waits a horror far worse than anything found in the freak show. Step right up! The terror is about to begin!

Funland

"One of horror's rarest talents."
—*Publishers Weekly*

ISBN 13: 978-0-8439-6140-9

Valley of the Scarecrow

The legend of Joshua Miller has chilled residents of Miller's Grove for seven decades. The town's children all know about the man who sold his soul to the devil and his macabre death at the hands of outraged townspeople—bound to a cross in a desecrated church, sealed away and left to rot.

But he didn't rot. His skin withered and his body mummified until he resembled a twisted human scarecrow. And he didn't truly die. And now, after seventy years, blood will revive Joshua Miller. He will finally be free to exact his unholy revenge. With a burning hatred born in hell . . .

THE SCARECROW WILL WALK AT MIDNIGHT!

GORD ROLLO

"A talent of horrific proportions."
—The Horror Review

ISBN 13: 978-0-8439-6334-2

BRIAN
KEENE

They came to the lush, deserted island to compete on a popular reality TV show. Each one hoped to be the last to leave. Now they're just hoping to stay alive. It seems the island isn't deserted after all. Contestants and crew members are disappearing, but they aren't being eliminated by the game. They're being taken by the monstrous half-human creatures that live in the jungle. The men will be slaughtered. The women will be kept alive as captives. Night is falling, the creatures are coming, and rescue is so far away. . . .

CASTAWAYS

ISBN 13: 978-0-8439-6089-1

To order a book or to request a catalog call:
1-800-481-9191
This book is also available at your local bookstore, or you can check out our Web site **www.dorchesterpub.com** where you can look up your favorite authors, read excerpts, or glance at our discussion forum to see what people have to say about your favorite books.

INTERACT WITH DORCHESTER ONLINE!

Want to learn more about your favorite books and authors?
Want to talk with other readers that like to read the same books as you?
Want to see up-to-the-minute Dorchester news?

VISIT DORCHESTER AT:

DorchesterPub.com
Twitter.com/DorchesterPub
Facebook.com (Search Pages)

DISCUSS DORCHESTER'S NOVELS AT:

Dorchester Forums at DorchesterPub.com
GoodReads.com
LibraryThing.com
Myspace.com/books
Shelfari.com
WeRead.com

☐ **YES!**

Sign me up for the Leisure Horror Book Club and send my FREE BOOKS! If I choose to stay in the club, I will pay only $8.50* each month, a savings of $7.48!

NAME: _____

ADDRESS: _____

TELEPHONE: _____

EMAIL: _____

☐ I want to pay by credit card.

☐ **VISA**   ☐ **MasterCard.**   ☐ **DISCOVER**

ACCOUNT #: _____

EXPIRATION DATE: _____

SIGNATURE: _____

Mail this page along with $2.00 shipping and handling to:
Leisure Horror Book Club
PO Box 6640
Wayne, PA 19087

Or fax (must include credit card information) to:
610-995-9274

You can also sign up online at **www.dorchesterpub.com**.

*Plus $2.00 for shipping. Offer open to residents of the U.S. and Canada only. Canadian residents please call 1-800-481-9191 for pricing information. If under 18, a parent or guardian must sign. Terms, prices and conditions subject to change. Subscription subject to acceptance. Dorchester Publishing reserves the right to reject any order or cancel any subscription.

GET FREE BOOKS!

You can have the best fiction delivered to your door for less than what you'd pay in a bookstore or online. Sign up for one of our book clubs today, and we'll send you *FREE* BOOKS* just for trying it out... **with no obligation to buy, ever!**

As a member of the Leisure Horror Book Club, you'll receive books by authors such as

RICHARD LAYMON, JACK KETCHUM, JOHN SKIPP, BRIAN KEENE and many more.

As a book club member you also receive the following special benefits:
- **30% off all orders!**
- **Exclusive access to special discounts!**
- **Convenient home delivery and 10 days to return any books you don't want to keep.**

Visit www.dorchesterpub.com or call 1-800-481-9191

There is no minimum number of books to buy, and you may cancel membership at any time.
*Please include $2.00 for shipping and handling.